Praise for Must Love Breeches

"A fresh, charming new voice."

— Tessa Dare, New York Times bestselling author

"Historical romance meets sci-fi time travel, and what a fun intersection of genres it is! ... It's a delicious twist on historical drama and romance, and let me assure you, there is plenty of romance and sex."

— USA Today

"Time travel and romance taste great together in Quarles's Must Love series launch.... Filled with historical tidbits and larger-than-life characters, the sweet story is a delight..."

— Publisher's Weekly

"... clever, original, and so good that you want more as soon as you put it down. It's a delicious mash up with something for time travel romance lovers, Jane Austen de-vo-tees, and those who simply enjoy a fresh take on historical romance. Her unique premise combines the best elements of contemporary and historical romance, while incorporating all of the fish-out-of-water elements a time travel romance."

— a Night Owl Reviews Top Pick

"Time travel is a tricky genre to play in and 'Must Love Breeches' broaches the subject well, delving into the past with ease, and returning to the story's present with deft ability."

— InD'Tale Magazine

"The moment I started reading this book I immediately thought of Outlander by Diana Gabaldon and Confessions of a Jane Austen Addict by Laurie Vierra Rigler. The concept of time travelling to one of my favourite time periods. I immediately fell in love with the concept and the plot! This book was amazing! A definite top ten contender and I can't wait to re-read it as I breathlessly read as fast as I could to learn what would happen next."

— Kiltsandswords

"Ms. Quarles has a tremendous talent for writing. This time travel historical romance makes for a captivating read. It left me wishing the book went on forever. The dia-logue, all the charming wit, and amazing sex scenes make the story a page turner. Her name should be beside Karen Marie Moning and Diana Gabaldon."

— Miranda with LovesHistorical

ALSO BY ANGELA QUARLES

Beer and Groping in Las Vegas
Steam Me Up, Rawley

Must Love series
Must Love Breeches
Must Love Chainmail

MUST LOVE

Kilts

A TIME TRAVEL ROMANCE

MUST LOVE SERIES BOOK THREE

ANGELA QUARLES

Unsealed
ROOM PRESS
Mobile, Alabama

MUST LOVE KILTS
Copyright © 2016 Angela Trigg
Cover design by Kim Killion
Developmental editing by Jessa Slade
Line editing by Erynn Newman
Copyediting by Julie Glover

Unsealed Room Press
Mobile, Alabama

ISBN: 1535200529
ISBN-13: 978-1535200523

To the hot men in kilts and the lasses who love them

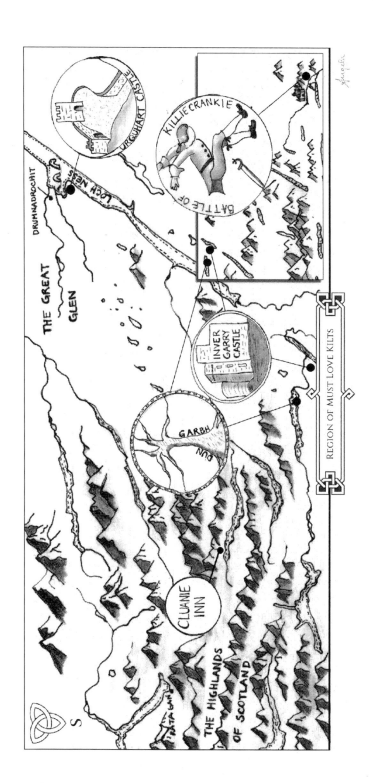

Prologue

Cluanie Inn, Highlands of Scotland, July, Traci's present day

"SHIT. SHIT. SHIT." Traci Campbell yanked open a dresser drawer at the Cluanie Inn. Mid-morning sun streaked through the corner windows. What would normally be gentle illumination was an annoying glare arrowing straight through to her pounding headache. The guy outside at the gas pump honking his horn was not helping.

One eye scrunched closed against the light spear, the other barely cracked open, she dumped the drawer's contents onto the carpet and shoved her clothes into her already overstuffed backpack.

Adrenaline spiked with frantic worry still coursed through her veins, messing with her Scotch-soaked brain and coating her tongue with a bitter, metallic tang. Plus, God, she sported the mama and papa of all hangovers.

"What else do I need? What about money?"

Of all the times to mess up from a night of drinking, this screwed the pooch, stomped on it, and left it whimpering in a pile of goo. She dragged the back of her hand across her nose and sniffled.

What had she been thinking?

Oh, yeah. She hadn't.

Ha, ha, what else was new, right?

She slung the backpack onto the four-poster bed—mussed from a night of drinking, laughing, and singing songs with Fiona. God, Fiona really sucked at singing. The pissed-off guest in Number 3 had abbreviated that bit of fun—the pounding on the wall a solid clue to her sister's lack of talent.

An empty bottle of Glenfiddich mocked her from the nightstand, accompanied by two empty glasses. *Oh God, Fiona. Please be okay.*

"What else? What else? What else?"

She cradled her head, which mimicked an overblown, painful balloon. Pretty please, couldn't she just snuggle the poor thing in that cool, so-soft pillow right there, sleep, wake up, and have everything right in the world? Or, like the computer games she helped design, restart at an earlier save?

She plopped onto the bed and pulled out her phone, the bed's jouncing messing with her head. *Fuck.* She did the one-eyed wince, scrolled through her contacts, and hovered over the only one who could possibly help—Katy. Her muscles jumped with the need to act—but, God, no. *Stop. Assess.*

Traci pulled in a trembling breath. *Well, here goes nothing.*

She tapped the call button, her thumb shaking.

The electronic ring tone seemed overly loud, as if saying, "Are you sure you want to call? You still have time to hang up."

The sound of a slight inhale told her Katy answered and not her husband. For him, a definite deliberation always came across the line, a pause, and his rumbling, medieval-Norman French accent.

"Traci! Robert and I were just talking about you!" Her good friend's soothing voice failed to relieve her anxiety. "How's the vacation going? Still planning to swing back through Wales on your way back to London?"

Traci picked at a wrinkle on the barberry-colored wool petticoat of her seventeenth-century dress. "Er, fine." Ha. "And…well, listen, I need to ask you something. If someone wanted to go back in time, what would be your advice?"

Silence.

Traci drew the phone away and checked the call status. "Katy?"

"I'm here. Why do you ask?"

"Just curious." Traci stretched across the rumpled bed and grabbed the silver calling card case that granted wishes via funky magical powers. Katy and Traci had speculated that the case transported you wherever—and *whenever*—your ideal mate existed. It had worked for Katy, who had married her medieval knight right before Christmas two years ago, and it had worked for Katy's friend Isabelle, who'd stayed back in time with her hunky viscount.

A drawn-out sigh came across the phone. "You know I love your spontaneity, but this isn't something you should undertake lightly. Before doing this, stop and think for a minute. I gave that case to you believing you'd be responsible."

Traci's throat closed up, and it took her a second to reply. "Too late," she rasped.

2

"I'm serious. Traveling back in time can be scary and dangerous, and you need to prepare. I mean it. I know I overdo it with the planning, but listen, okay? You'll need the right clothes, the right kind of money—"

"I don't have a choice," she choked out. Her fingers tightened around the phone.

Another Katy-sigh came through the line. "Yes, you do."

"No. I really don't. I left...scratch that...I *lost* my sister back there."

Chapter One

∽

Take a little dram of passion,
In a lusty bowl of wine.
"The Man of Fashion," *Jacobite Reliques*

Ten hours earlier

*T*RACI CLASPED A hand over Fiona's open mouth and pushed her down onto the brochure-strewn bed, snickering. "No. No more singing. The guest in Number 3 says so."

Fiona squirmed away, grabbed the bottle of Glenfiddich on the nightstand, and topped them off. "To Scotland then."

Traci clinked glasses, humoring her sister. "To Scotland."

While all the clan-this-clan-that sightseeing had been driving her bonkers, it was achieving her main goal—getting to know her sister better.

They'd arrived yesterday in this remote corner of the Highlands with two purposes—for Traci to climb the local peaks and add to her tally (bagging a Munro as climbers called it) and to island hop, ending on the Isle of Skye for the Highland Games. Exhibit A for how much she wanted to bond with her sister—she'd sworn off attending the Games when she'd left home for college.

Fiona lifted the bottle and squinted at the bottom, leaning a bit to the side. She put a hand down to steady herself. "We're all out. Maybe there's some we can buy from the bar downstairs."

"We've probably had enough. That was a full bottle, you know."

Fiona burped and did an oops-face.

Ha. Ha. Nothing like alcohol to grease that bond-forming. "I can see you learned to drink like a pro in college." Not. This trip was actually Fiona's graduation present from their Scot-obsessed parents. And because Traci had moved to London shortly after her own graduation

4

three years ago, she really hadn't seen Fiona since their mid-teens.

"Well then, to hot Scottish men in kilts." Fiona raised her glass again.

"Yeah, we haven't seen any." She sipped the Scotch and threw an arm around her baby sister. The affection came easier now that their relationship's rough, tentative edges had smoothed from bouncing around and partying in their room.

Fiona hopped away and leaned back against the pillow on the head-board. "There was that one in Perth, but he wasn't hot. If we'd been born back in the day, we would've seen plenty."

Traci snorted. "That's a myth." Scot-obsessed and unshakeable in the belief that all men in kilts were hunky and hot back in the day—that was her sister.

"How can you know?" Fiona sat forward.

"I don't. But there couldn't be more hot men then than there are now. You need to let go of your unrealistic fantasies about men."

"Why?"

"It's unhealthy. I should take you back and show you." The sooner Fiona had her eyes open, the sooner she could face life—and men—on her own terms. Because fantasies could only lead to heartache.

Luckily, she had Big Sis to hold those eyes open.

Fiona regarded the silver calling card case perched on the nightstand, and her eyes shone with a determined, alcohol-fueled glint. "Yes, you should show me!"

Before Traci could react, Fiona grabbed the case.

Shit. "We can't go back!"

Why the hell had she told her sister about the case? Oh, yeah, the bonding thing—it was a hungry beast for sharing. So she'd blabbed. About how it had taken her friend Katy back to medieval Wales. And taken another woman back—Isabelle, a friend of Katy's—to pre-Victorian London.

Fiona got that look she remembered from childhood. This wasn't going to end well. "Why not? I bet you a hundred bucks there were more hot men in kilts in earlier days."

The energy-panic of being swept up in her sister's bets constricted her chest. "We don't have supplies! Plus, it's not safe." And boy had Katy drilled it into her to not use the case without being properly prepared.

Fiona leaped off the bed and yanked open the armoire. "We have our outfits for the Highland Games next week. Our late-seventeenth-century personas. We can wear these and pop to that time just long enough"—she spun around and tossed over Traci's dress—"for me to win that bet!"

☙

"Shh. Shhhh," Traci spluttered. Yep, she might be a teensy bit tipsy. She stumbled up the rocky, dirt path to the inn's entrance. Shit, it was dark. The moon, a pale sliver, joined the two torches sputtering in the ground near the door to provide the only illumination.

"Holy crap. I can't believe that worked," Fiona whispered. "We're actually back in time?" She clutched her stomach.

A few minutes ago, they'd rubbed the case and made their wish. The weird tug-squeeze-swirl *had* been a little unnerving. Looming before them in the murky dark, with a blanket of stars capping the valley between the mountains, stood the same inn, but in 1689.

"Yes. Told you I could."

Wow. Look at those stars…

Traci drifted to a stop, gazing up, but when her sister didn't respond, she cast a glance downward.

All the color in Fiona's face dropped right out. "I didn't really believe you. I think I was just drunk enough to pretend." Torch light flickered across her face as she lifted her chin and straightened. "We're doing this. I can't believe it. Let's go in."

Why, why, *why* had she let her sister rope her into this? But when Fiona had uttered the three-letter word *bet*, the outcome had been inevitable.

Good God.

Traci tugged her sister's arm and pulled her up short. "Remember. We're only peeking inside to settle the bet, and then we're leaving."

"Yeah, yeah. But do you know what this *means?*" Her eyes begged for understanding. "What events we can see? Wait till Mom and Dad hear about this."

"We will *not* be telling them." She yanked on the iron-banded wooden door, which opened with a low creak. Couldn't she share something with her sister that didn't also involve their parents?

They slipped through the opening, and a wall of heat, spiced with soured whisky and yeast and stale sweat, rolled over them. Scots in multi-colored kilts and blue bonnets clogged the common room of the inn, drinking their whisky and shouting and singing.

6

Aaand…that was more than enough taste of Ye Olde Scotland, thank you very much. But one salient detail overshadowed all: no *hunky* men in kilts. Not. A. One.

Hello, hundred bucks!

Dark wooden beams criss-crossed a low ceiling, the walls yellow-stained plaster. A peat fire burned in the rough-stone fireplace. "Oh, Fiona, this would be a perfect setting."

"For romance?"

"No. My design team needs one for a side-quest location in the new game."

"You are *such* a hopeless geek."

Her sister pushed past, then morphed into wall art. "But where are the hot guys?"

"There aren't any. And now *you*"—she nudged her sister—"owe me a hundred bucks."

Fiona slumped her shoulders. Oh, that face. Traci stifled a snort.

Fiona pushed away from the wall and flicked her blonde braid over her shoulder. "Not yet, I don't. This village is probably an anomaly. I bet the women in this time call it Nastyville or something." Her eyes flashed with a hint of defiance. "But the night's still young!"

"Nuh-uh. We're going back. I won."

"No way. I'm staying." She rubbed her upper arms. "There's more here for me. I can *feel* it."

Uneasiness swirled through Traci's gut. The words *I'm staying,* had been laced with weight, as if she meant *permanently*.

"Oh, all right." She was *so* going to regret this. "Let's just sit at that table near the shadows. We can people watch for a few more minutes." Traci edged farther into the room. Silence descended. Chairs scraped back, and several men stood. But all of them stared.

Er…

Fiona shrugged, so Traci took another step and Fiona interlaced their arms.

The closest Highlander rumbled in Gaelic, his face bunched into a scowl. Fiona opened and closed her mouth, cleared her throat, and replied in stilted Gaelic. Unlike her sister, Traci had never bothered to learn.

Traci leaned down and whispered, "What's going on?"

"They're wondering why we're unescorted."

What the hell? She took in the wary gazes. "Why does that matter?"

"Women—respectable women—apparently don't do this."

"Will they let us stay?" Even the scruffy dog by the fireplace gave them the side-eye.

"I don't know." Fiona crossed her arms, her gaze skittish. "I told them we were looking for our cattle-herding brother."

"Well, that settles it. Let's go back." Traci stepped back. "And then you'll fork over that hundred bucks, because I'm telling you…" Traci leaned closer. "Hunky men in kilts are a myth."

Traci backed up and—*oomph*—bumped against a solid, warm wall. She startled, stepped on her hem, and lurched sideways. Strong hands gripped her waist and pulled her upright. Strong hands doing as simple a thing as holding her waist, but God, the grip felt dangerously possessive. The stranger's body heat warmed her back with awareness.

"Whoa, there, lass. I have ye."

The voice—deep, accented, and laden with the right serving of sinful fun—made the hairs on Traci's arms stand up and go, "Hey there, handsome." No. She didn't have *time* for this.

Fiona's mouth hung open a smidge, and Traci mouthed, "Hot?"

"Oh, yes," her sister whispered.

Great. Just great. Heat flashed up her spine from where his hands *still* clasped her waist. And were they moving slightly, as if taking the measure of her curves?

Curves she'd rather not have someone know their extensiveness. Big-boned, her mother had called her, which Traci knew was polite speak for "hefty for a tall girl."

She smoothed a shaky hand down her suddenly too-tight bodice, fluffed out the skirts of her *earasaid*, and turned, breaking the man's firm grip. And stepped back. And looked up. And up. And that said loads because she topped five-eleven in flats.

The definitely manly specimen before her crossed his arms, which—dammit—did some interesting things with his obviously powerful biceps under his funny short jacket, crossed by a leather strap over one shoulder and a plaid draped saucily over the other. Could a plaid be draped saucily? Well, for sure this guy's was. A white handkerchief encircled his neck with two jaunty knots, and a blue, flattish hat sat slightly askew on his dark-brown hair. A strange combo of power and playfulness radiated from him. Which was the real him?

He caught Traci's gaze and held it, his light-blue eyes the most arresting shade she'd ever seen. Power. It was power.

But then he winked and bowed his head, his hair cascading forward. Jeez, his hair was saucy too. And he smiled so broadly and so sincerely, it lit up his eyes, creasing the skin around them as well as his cheeks, transforming his entire face as if everything in the world delighted him, and he mirrored the delight back in his all-encompassing grin.

Her breath left her in an undignified puff. Oh yeah. Her sister had the right of it. Hot. In a kilt. And he knew it. Her untrustworthy heart gave an extra thud in case she hadn't gotten the memo that he had the goddamn key to turn her crank. She thumbed the ring on her right hand, twisting it round and round.

Yep, time to skedaddle.

He raked his eyes down her body and back up, and the heat of his gaze swept across her skin. "My profound apologies for interrupting what sounds like an interesting discussion. What are ye believing is a myth then? If it's the wee fox that patrols the nearby glen and turns into a buxom lass on foggy nights, I saw her with me own eyes."

෪

AYE, THIS IS the one.

Never mind he said that about every lass he met. The night was young, the lass was lovely, and he was of a mind to have a bit of fun. Iain had long since learned his heart was a stupid bastard, always falling hopelessly in love.

He'd fall in love with this one too. Pour his heart out. And be left, as always, empty-handed.

Aye, but it was fun while it lasted, was it not? This latest his heart had decided to martyr itself upon was uncommonly tall, drawing his eye as he'd entered the public rooms at the inn. That and the sumptuous curves outlined by the odd dress she sported. He let his gaze roam, from the heart-shaped face framed by dark red hair to her long and graceful neck, shapely bosom, and the lovely hips he'd lately had excuse to clasp. And, by God and all the holy saints, he'd taken that excuse, even though she hadn't truly needed his support.

He flexed his hands, which already missed the warmth of her curves.

Anticipation sluiced through him, and heat flared in his lower back, tightening his cods.

Her use of English instead of *Gàidhlig* only increased her mystery. Said lass regarded him, aye, but not with lust. Nay. Apparently, judging by her expression, he'd grown three heads since he'd been admiring her pleasing form.

Hmm. Not how it usually went.

Her cheeks turned an endearing shade of pink, like the underside of a poppy he'd seen drawn in a botany book at university.

"The myth…er, the myth about…" Her accent was oddly flat, unlike any he'd heard, even from the English who'd managed to penetrate this far into the Highlands.

The accent might be flat, but the tone was enticing, like a promise. Of course. Because why wouldn't it be? He sighed. *Here we go, heart.*

The lass eyed her companion, who remained silent, then returned her gaze to Iain's, her cinnamon-brown eyes alight now with a new determination.

"The Loch Ness monster. That myth."

"Aye, well, that one's real enough too." He waved over his cousin Duncan, who'd reacted to his suggestion of a drink as if he'd been tasked to watch sheep being sheared. The others in his patrol of the MacDonell's territory would follow shortly, but they could fend for themselves. This would be exactly the spirit-lifting his cousin needed.

He spoke in *Gàidhlig* to the nearest men. "These ladies are indeed with escorts, but I thank you for your concern."

In a lower voice, he said to the ladies in English, "May we interest you two lasses in a wee dram, in the promise of tales to enliven this drab evening, and compare notes on what's real and what's myth?"

"I don't think that—"

"Yes! Thank you," blurted the other lass, whose eyes immediately rounded. Then she clapped a hand to her mouth. Oddly, her fingernails were painted purple.

His heart's fancy shook her head and tugged on her friend's sleeve. "We were just leaving," she murmured and avoided his gaze.

Nay. Not so soon.

The friend pulled back, her expression mulish. "Oh no, we're not. I've won our bet now, and we're staying." To him and Duncan, she flashed a triumphant smile, her gaze lingering appreciatively on his cousin, who blushed clear up to St. Peter's gates. Interesting.

That's the spirit, lass. "Here, listen to your companion." Iain swung around the nearest empty table and seated himself on the bench. He motioned to wee Maggie, who wasn't so wee anymore. "Over here, would ye please?"

She bustled over after setting down a tray of drinks several tables over. "And what will ye be having, Iain?"

"Four whiskies to warm our hearts and our cheeks, I thank you."

To his extreme gratification, the ladies settled opposite, with Duncan beside him. A warm hardness nudged his leg, and his heart kicked up a notch. Had the lass come around?

A groan floated up from under the table, and a heavy weight plopped onto his feet. Och, nay. Just flea-bitten Fearghus, the mutt Maggie kept for protection.

He peeked under the table, scratched the fur ball's ear, and was rewarded with two thumps of his tail on the wooden floorboards. Iain unearthed a bannock from his sporran and tossed it to the bugger. Thankfully, the other men at the inn turned back to their own companions, and cheerful banter soon filled the room. Nearby revelers began singing, "*Bithidh an Deoch-sa an Làimh mo Rùin*, This Drink will be in the Hand of my Love." Well, wasn't *that* a hopeful sign.

"Now, lasses, I'm Iain, and this here's Duncan. What brought ye to our fine establishment?"

His new love examined him most unenamoredly, indecision clear on her features. She exchanged a weighted look with her friend.

The friend, bless her, extended a hand across the table, straight toward Duncan, her grin wide. "I'm Fiona." Duncan flushed a deep red. "And this is…" She stumbled when Duncan awkwardly took her hand, raised it to his lips, and kissed it. Her eyes rounded again. She swallowed. "And this is my sister, Traci. We're just here for a little bit of adventure," she finished on a whisper.

Adventure. Iain liked the sound of that. Acutely aware of Traci watching him while he kept his gaze on the sister, he said, "Well, then you've come to the right place."

∾

TRACI TOOK ANOTHER sip of Scotch. Boy, was this stuff stronger than she was used to. But her whole body—heck, the whole room—was humming with happiness. She'd been reluctant to stay, but alcohol had already colored her judgment, and Fiona had been a freaking bulldozer on a mission. Now here they were, sitting at a table drinking whisky with two seventeenth-century Highlanders.

One of whom—Iain—was a delicious presence beside her. He pressed closer, his heat and scrumptious scent enveloping her—leather, clean wool, and a musky-something that was already driving her nuts. And he was waiting, with eyebrow raised and one lock of dark hair caressing his forehead, for a response to…

She laughed, and even *she* could feel how free it made her feel. "I have *no* clue what you just said." Seriously, his English was a lilting, rolling puzzle at times. Oh, and what cute ears—they were almost pointed, like an elf's. Maybe his head would move again, and she could get another glimpse.

She kept watch.

Aaand leaned over too much and bumped her cheek into his shoulder. They both laughed as he gripped her shoulders and set her upright. Damn, this whisky was strong. She rubbed her cheek. Somehow, she was now on the same side of the table.

He spoke slower. "I said, the stars have always enthralled me."

Oh yeah, she'd remarked on the brightness of the stars outside. It was becoming harder to focus.

Iain set down his whisky. "The philosophy club I attended while at university in Edinburgh discussed an Italian named Galileo Galilei who believed stars are a great distance away and that perhaps the sun shares much of the same properties."

"Galileo, the father of modern science!"

Iain chuckled, the sound coming from deep within. "That's quite an accolade, being the father of knowledge, but aye, he was an enlightened man."

Traci opened her mouth and snapped it shut. She was forgetting *when* she was, she'd been having such a fun time.

"Some of the regents at university didna wish to discuss his views, of course, but there were some scholars who had read his papers and held forth at the clubs." He propped an elbow on the table and rested his head against it, listing forward. "But I'm not understanding this stardust notion."

"Well, if the sun is a star, and stars have life—birth and death—then there are pieces of stardust that make up our world." She plunked her elbow onto the table as well and rested her head. God, that had sounded much clearer in her thoughts. Plus, having to monitor what scientific ideas she mentioned made her head spin. Or was that the alcohol? "So…" She trailed off, because how the hell could she talk about the conservation of mass, which probably wasn't proved yet?

"So if the Greeks were right, 'nothing comes from nothing,' then…" He clasped her hand and brushed his thumb over her palm in light, enticing circles. She shivered. "Then your wee hand could be made from stardust."

He understood! Three years ago in her senior level astronomy class, her mind had been all shit-this-is-so-cool, like only a college kid can get.

Warmth bloomed across her skin as he still held her hand. Seriously, handholding was getting her all hot and bothered? But she was. The space between them had less air. Not in a can't-catch-her-breath way, but in how there was less of a wall between them. As if he easily fit in her space. For sure, the smile she sported was a dopey grin.

He smiled, his head tilting, and his hooded gaze dropped to her lips. Oh! There was his ear making an appearance. Such an adorable ear.

And was that her hand skimming a finger along his ear? Whoa, the room tilted a little too much there—

—She laughed at Fiona's quip. All four of them huddled around the table, another round of drinks in the space between.

Iain tossed another lump of some kind of hard bread to the dog—Fearghus—under the table. "Aye, but ye don't know the full of it. I'd never seen my uncle so flummoxed."

Joy danced through her like champagne bubbles, and she wanted to keep sipping forever. Being here with Iain felt so natural, somehow—

—She was standing, her hand clasped in Iain's while everyone around them was singing or shouting in Gaelic, egging them on. Her dopey grin was out again. The door banged open, and two rough Highlanders strode in and scowled at the enthusiastic crowd, which quieted a notch.

"Dinnae mind ol' Ross there. His scowl is worse than his tongue." Iain leaned down and winked.

All the same, she was glad she had Iain and Duncan as protectors—

—"Oops." She giggled and grasped Iain's arm as they stumbled up the steps—

—Oh, yes—

Chapter Two

❧

O far far frae hame full soon will I be,
It's far far frae hame, in a strange country
"Our Ain Country," *Jacobite Reliques*

After dawn, the same inn, 1689

BANG!
Traci bolted upright, clammy confusion thickening her pulse. *Where the—?* This wasn't her bed. She pressed her hands into the thick covers and blinked. Vacation. Oh, yeah. But this wasn't their bed at the Cluanie Inn either. Pounding footsteps and strident voices charged past her door.

Oh, shit.

Her stomach heaved, and she frantically scanned the room, which was bare except for the bed, a rickety chair, a table, and a dresser. *The window.* She clamped a hand over her mouth, scrambled to the open casement window, and threw up a whole river of stomach-processed Scotch.

She gripped the window ledge with shaky hands and pressed her forehead to the cool sill, breaths erratic. *Oh God.* Her clammy skin flashed cold, and the world's sharpest, orneriest, oh-shit-that-hurts pain speared her head, radiating from the crown.

Her stomach empty of ill-advised alcohol, Traci eased down onto her butt on the floor and transferred her forehead to the plaster wall under the window. She needed a Bloody Mary IV, stat.

Where was she? *Okay, think.* Glaring fact number one: she'd had one hell of a bender. Her thoughts croaked backward, lurching around, trying to piece last night together.

Oh, yeah. The bet. With her sister.

Her heart faltered.

Oh crap. Oh crap. Oh crap.

Please don't tell me I was such an idiot as to get rip-roaring drunk while in a different era!

Her memories fractured after they'd zapped back in time and started drinking at the inn. Two handsome faces populated most of them. A name—Iain.

Her eyes bugged wide as another *very* telling fact registered. She glanced down. Jesus Christ, she was as naked as a damn jay bird. Her stomach threatened another revolt, and she pawed her way to the sill and threw up again until she was dry heaving.

Shit. She wiped her mouth, leaned on one elbow, bent partway around, weight on the sill, and eyed the tousled bed.

Empty.

But... More images surfaced. Her in the bed. With that guy. Iain. The impression that they'd had sex. Damn good sex. Iain laughing over something she'd said. Some snuggling.

She groaned. There might have even been a bout of blanket-fort making with his kilt, which, jeez, she'd had no idea the gobs of fabric it made up.

No surprise to find him gone, though. She'd just shove that niggle of disappointment aside. She raised her chin. This was why she preferred to sleep with flirts like him in her own time. Because they both knew, going in, that it was just sex.

She cradled her head in her hands and leaned on the sill, relishing the slight, but cool breeze from the window. Okay, so she *had* been stupid enough to get drunk, zap back to the seventeenth century, get *more* drunk, and sleep with a guy. That bet... She'd wring her sister's neck.

She lifted her head. *Fiona.*

Shit. Where had *she* gone last night? Traci couldn't remember. *Shit. Shit. Shit.*

Her gaze darted around the room. There—her clothes. On shaky legs, she shuffled to the crumpled pile on the floor and with verrrry slow movements, donned each piece of clothing. Anything faster or more jarring was just not an option with the pain pounding in her head. By the end, one question was solved that she'd been afraid to know the answer to—at the bottom of the stack lay her pouch.

Jarring be damned, she yanked open the stringed top and shoved her hand inside. Oh-thank-God—the calling card case was still there. She closed the pouch and tied it to the belt of her outfit.

A pitcher on the dresser next to a bowl caught her eye. She stepped to the battered piece of furniture, poured the water into the bowl, splashed her face, and rinsed her mouth.

Okay. She could now upgrade her health stats to 2/100. She focused on the door. Somewhere in this inn was her sister. *Well, she better be.*

Stomach still behaving? Check. New mission: retrieve Fiona.

She pressed one hand to her stomach and another to her still clammy forehead and approached the door, her body curled in on itself as if it were ninety years old instead of twenty-five. She put her ear to the wood and listened; she *really* didn't want to bump into anyone. Except Fiona.

With half of her mind focused on monitoring her questionable stomach, she slipped out and crept down the low-ceilinged hall. Ahead lay a gap in the floor with steps leading down, but her foot froze mid-air. Footsteps. Several of them.

She spun around and stepped inside the first unlocked door. A dark shape was hunched under a mound of covers. A voice croaked from its depths, a sleepy mumbled string of Gaelic.

Her muscles tightened, but the figure didn't move. Outside the door, the footsteps passed by, and a door slammed open and shut. She bit her lip, eased the door open, and checked the passage. Clear.

She hustled down the steps, her head protesting with each jerky step. "A Bloody Mary with all the spicy fixings. Item One on the agenda when I get back," she whispered.

At the bottom of the stairs, she eased into the main room. Duncan—was that his name?—was huddled over a table, eating. Alone. She pivoted and headed toward the back. Asking about Fiona would be her last resort, since that risked encountering Iain. First, out back, where she had a vague recollection of a privy. Maybe Fiona had come down with Duncan and…

A harsh voice at the landing above hollered in Gaelic. Her head whipped up, and her steps quickened because, while she couldn't understand his words, he was pointing at her and beckoning to his cronies with his other hand. They bounded down the steps, two at a time. Fear jolted through, creating a nasty mix with her hangover. Their stern faces and their alien tongue fused with another memory—these same men entering the inn last night and a subtle tension coloring the crowd's mood. They'd glared at her and Fiona then too.

And now these men were after her for some reason?

Duncan. She hesitated, turned to dart back into the main room, but the lead man had one step left before he reached the bottom and blocked the way.

Shit.

Okay. She could fix this. Traci fumbled into her drawstring pouch and bolted for the back door. Perhaps, like in her computer games, she could return to an earlier saved version. Return to before she met Iain and Duncan, grab her sister, and come back. She slammed through the door and fell back against it. Breaths coming in sucked-in-gasps now—because what the hell?—she gripped the silver case and made her wish just as the first body slammed into the wood.

Bam.

The force jolted her forward, but she pushed back, surprise working in her favor. The world spun, and that now-familiar atom-swirling feeling swept through her. *Shit.* Not helping her hangover.

But then the swirling just…stopped. The door banged at her back, the impact vibrating through her bones. Heart now pounding as if she'd quadrupled her jump-rope routine, she tried again. And again.

Oh crap.

So. No manipulating whatever-the-heck kind of magic this was to be in a time stream twice. Got it.

Forgive me, Fiona. She made a different wish—the door crashed open and threw her forward. As before, the world tilted, and the fuzzy feeling sluiced through her body. The whatever-vortex spit her out the other side, and she fell onto her hands and knees.

Oh. God. She pulled a slow breath through her nose as her stomach went all queasy.

She lifted her still-pounding head and glanced over her shoulder. She buckled to the ground, relief rendering her muscles into goo. She'd made it back to her own time. A blacktop road now threaded past the inn and opposite, on a small rise, flapped the six flags welcoming tourists to Cluanie Inn from various nations. But her relief was short-lived. Now what? On its heels came a stomach-curdling thought—in her hungover state, she'd panicked. And abandoned her sister.

&

"Okay, this has to work."

17

Several hours after the frantic phone call with Katy, Traci stood in a ravine across the road from Cluanie Inn. She tightened her grip on her cloth sack—Katy had nixed the backpack. Too conspicuous.

Oh, she'd royally screwed up. Again.

She had to make things right. Again.

She had to find—and rescue—her sister. Again.

She tied the sack onto the pony she'd purchased—another Katy suggestion—and eyed the docile mare, which was unlike any horse she'd seen. It was a shaggy Highland pony. Broad-shouldered and sturdy.

"Please go easy on me." She listed forward, pressed her forehead to the pony's fluffy neck, and pulled in a deep breath, the earthy scent of pony and leather oddly calming. "Okay, you with me? Let's do this."

The mare blinked, her ears kinda loose.

That'll have to do. It better—the last time she'd ridden one of these things was at horse camp one high school summer. "You're now Glenfiddich, because I couldn't parse what he said your name was. Sorry."

Traci had argued with Katy about her need for the pony. Because she was just popping back, grabbing her sister, and returning, but Katy kept harping on one thing: *you need to be prepared.* So, Traci had bought her and the antique side-saddle from the riding stables in Ratagan, thirteen miles northwest along the shores of Loch Duich. She'd paid a pretty penny to the owner, who was reluctant to part with one of his stock. He'd even grumbled about her last name. "Never trust a Campbell."

Traci led Glenfiddich to one of the many boulders peppering the landscape and swung up into the saddle, securing her leg around the first pommel like she'd seen pictured on the web. It might be *called* a pony, but it was nearly as tall as a horse. God, this was like a real-life computer game—saddling up and heading to her first quest location. Except this was way too real. She shivered as chills prickled along her skin.

She clasped the calling card case and glanced around. All clear. She gripped the pony's mane in case she needed actual contact—not just through the saddle—and made her wish.

Nausea gripped her insides, and the pony stumbled. Blood pounded in her ears, and she leaned over, squeezed her eyes shut, and murmured words to stay-calm-be-a-good-girl to her new pony.

Her ears popped, and she pried open an eye.

Whew.

She and Glenfiddich had made it. She thumped the pony's side and led it up the incline, the oddness of riding side-saddle just one more thing keeping her off-balance that day. The stable owner had assured her the pony was trained for a side-saddle, so there was that. At the rise, she pushed out a relieved breath.

Gone was the paved road winding past Cluanie Inn. In its place was a well-trod path. She peered at the sky. The sun was a little toward the west. That would match with her present time—2:30 PM. Katy and Isabelle had figured out one rule: once a new person used the case, time passed at the same rate in both places. Which explained why Traci hadn't been able to go back to before all this mess had started.

Now to find Fiona. Who had better have stayed put. Traci shoved aside any other alternative, because, well, those just *weren't* possibilities. Though Katy had considered them, hence all the supplies she carried, and Glenfiddich.

Traci gently steered Glenfiddich toward the inn. Early afternoon light speared down through the heavy clouds overhead, and despite being in the same place, the time period was immediately apparent by something as simple as sound. Specifically, its lack.

Her pony's hooves clomped down the emerald green hill as she trotted toward the open glen and the inn nestled within. Spanning the horizon were the green slopes of the South Glen Shiel Ridge, splashed with swaths of purple heather. Sweat slicked her palm at the enormity of her task.

That bet—oh, boy—had it gotten out of hand. When would she learn? Always, she screwed up where her family was concerned. And always, she screwed up when alcohol was involved. And a hot guy.

Her whole body flushed as images of Iain and all that they'd gotten up to flooded her brain.

Jesus Christ. Could she stop thinking about him for *one* second?

She'd make this right. She had to.

Up ahead, a lone groom tended several ponies in the stable yard, and Traci adjusted her course.

The stable boy caught sight of her and loped out to help her get down. Unfortunately, he didn't speak English, so with hand signals and patience, she got him to hold her pony temporarily while she went inside.

What was "thank you" in the Scottish Gaelic Fiona had taught her? Ah, yes. "*Tapadh leibh*," she said hesitantly.

She pushed open the door and stepped into the inn. The now-familiar smell of the room evoked more memories from last night. She found Maggie cleaning a table. Fearghus the dog was walking in a tight circle before the hearth fire and flopped down with a beleaguered grunt. Otherwise, the room was empty of guests.

"Hi there, Maggie. Do you have a moment?" They'd lucked out with their choice of inn—Maggie was a Lowlander and spoke English.

"Aye. What are ye after, then?"

"Last night my sister Fiona and I…we shared some…drinks with Iain and Duncan. But at some point, my sister disappeared. Is she still here?"

"You lost your sister?" Her voice held a trace of disbelief as well as a healthy dose of scoffing.

Heat crept up the back of Traci's neck, and she crossed her arms. "Well, things got *involved* last night, and when I woke up, I…I couldn't find her."

"Well, she left with the MacCowans, didn't she?"

Good God. Had her sister just up and left? With a group of men? Was she that kilt-addled? Yes. She was. Mom and Dad hadn't had to drag *her* every October to the Highland Games in Stone Mountain, Georgia.

"Who are the MacCowans?" She was missing part of the picture, and Maggie's thick accent didn't help.

Maggie straightened from rubbing the table with a rag and planted her fists on her hips. "Why, Duncan and Iain and their men. At least I think it was them. Can't expect me to keep track of everyone, can ye?"

"Did she leave willingly?" What the hell was she going to do now?

"She seemed willing enough, if ye ask me."

"Where would they have gone?"

"I imagine they headed back to Dungarbh keep."

Gah. Did she have to milk every single answer out of this woman? She pasted on a smile. "And where would that be?"

Maggie pursed her lips, but complied. Ride two days southeast along Loch Cluanie, then along the river down to Loch Loyne, and south to Loch Garry. Traci repeated the directions. Thank God, Katy had insisted on the pony.

"Are you sure it was Iain and Duncan? What clan tartan were they wearing?"

Maggie swiped her broom at her. "Are ye daft, woman? Now I've told ye all I ken, so be off with ye if you're not paying for anything. Some of us have to work."

Traci stormed out of the inn and retrieved her pony. "You're lucky I already have the time off, Fiona," she muttered. They'd been in the first week of her three-week vacation. Would serve her sister right if she left her here. It probably fulfilled all her friggin' fantasies.

She pulled up short. But what if Fiona hadn't gone willingly? Or what if she'd changed her mind?

The stable lad held out her reins, and she hoisted herself onto the saddle and aimed her pony east. "Jesus Christ, Fiona, what have you gotten into?"

Her throat tightened, and she latched onto the outrage now searing through her—anything to shove aside the fear and guilt and regret that had been building all day. If she'd been a better sister—if they'd been closer—Fiona would've known that Traci wouldn't abandon her. Or maybe Fiona was worried about what had happened to *her*?

She kicked Glenfiddich into a canter. She really *did* feel as if she were in a real-life quest game. Maybe soon she could vent her frustration with an epic battle.

Ha. Yeah, right. Those skills didn't translate here.

But as she rode, her mismanaged actions this morning replayed over and over. If she'd stayed, if she'd somehow sidestepped those men and shouted the inn down until she found Fiona…

She reached the peak of the first hill and reined in her pony. Almost the full length of Loch Cluanie stretched out below, disappearing among a range of mountains on the horizon. On either side of the blue loch stretched more green mountain ranges. Before coming here, she'd known Scotland was mountainous but had pictured it like either the Rockies or the Blue Ridge Mountains—a swath of land butting up against mountain ranges. But the Highlands were *all* mountains, or foothills and bumpy bits leading up to a mountain. As if the land were a huge green and purple paper bag that a giant had scrunched up, with the low bits filled by the bluest lakes.

Time travel achievement unlocked. Now if she could only level up her scouting abilities.

But all that rolling and craggy emptiness sent a slither down her spine.

Somewhere out there was her sister. Somewhere out there, she might be scared and in trouble.

And it was all Traci's fault.

Chapter Three

❧

The Campbell and the Graham are equally to blame,
Seduc'd by strong infatuation.
"The Awkward Squad," *Jacobite Reliques*

" *I*'M TELLING YE, Duncan, I heard a noise down by the burn when I went to wash myself. Someone's about, and I don't fancy learning when it's too late that it's some trespasser on our lands." Iain pulled on his lèine and belted his féileadh tighter around his waist.

He didn't need any *more* surprises this day. A day which had inexplicably left him feeling restless. He *never* felt restless. In truth, his blood fair rushed at the prospect of a good fight. Traci occupied too much space in his thoughts today, and he was sick of it—sick of himself and his mooning.

Duncan was roasting a hare over their camp fire, and he pulled it from the flames and speared the stick into the ground. "Mind the fire, lads. We'll be away but a moment."

The others in their patrol grunted, turning back to cooking their food, sharpening their *sgianan dubha*, or scratching their wee balls.

"All right, then, cousin of mine. Let's see what this noise is." Duncan clapped a hand on Iain's shoulder, jostling him forward. His mother's nephew, Duncan had spent his fosterage with Iain's family and stayed. He'd also been in love with Iain's older sister and was distraught when she'd been given to the MacLeods to strengthen an alliance two years past.

They strapped on their broadswords and ensured their pistols were loaded with dry shot. They'd had trouble recently with reivers from the MacKenzie clan. But as they slipped into the darker depths of the glen, his mind did the usual foolishness when his heart had been snared. There, the bark of the tree, highlighted by a glint of the moon, was like Traci's hair when he'd brushed his fingers through to reveal the darker

22

tresses beneath. And there, the pale rock's color was the shade of the spot underneath her ear…

Ach, concentrate, man. Concentrate.

After Traci's disappearance, Iain had rejoined his men, crushed, again, that another dalliance had ended so swiftly. Without even a leave-taking. All were convinced the lasses were traitorous Campbells, sent by the clan that had been behind every depredation his clan had suffered since before his grandfather's day. Their power had grown too great in the Highlands.

He thinned his lips. He'd thought that after what they'd shared—and what they'd promised each other—she'd last longer than his usual interludes. He shoved thoughts of the lass of the curling red locks from his head. And his heart.

At the stream, they searched but found no malingerer, or even a trace of one.

"Over here," Duncan called.

Iain trudged to Duncan's side, who crouched by a wind-stunted rowan tree. "Someone passed by recently." He pointed up the slope. "And headed that way."

Anticipation quickened Iain's steps. He hoped it *was* a party of MacKenzies; his muscles fairly itched for a good fight. Aye, that would chase the lass's memory from his mind.

Silently, they picked their way up the ravine until they reached the summit. They crouched and surveyed the near darkness below, illuminated only by the half-moon above.

Iain nudged Duncan and pointed. "There."

A wisp of smoke trailed up from the top of a patch of trees, its light-gray plumes barely discernible against the darker green foliage.

At Duncan's nod, they worked their way down and crept to the spot they'd seen. As they neared, the way ahead grew lighter from the fire, the orange glow casting shifting shadows along the overarching branches.

The light outlined a lone figure, leaning to the side and seemingly asleep with his head propped up in his hand. No weapon was strapped to his side, nor was there one within reach.

Wariness tightened Iain's muscles, and a shiver of awareness streaked from the back of his neck down his spine. This was too easy. He waited for the time it took for the fire to pop once, twice. He eased his pistol from its spot at his back. As silently as he could, he pulled back the hammer.

With his free hand, Iain signaled to Duncan, who nodded and crept around to the other side of the clump of trees.

Iain waited for Duncan's signal and studied the scene, though he did not stare directly at the light—he had no wish to impair his night vision. He strained to hear others lurking in ambush, but all was quiet except for the occasional pop from the intruder's fire.

Even without directly looking at the figure, something seemed familiar. The slope of the neck, the shape of the hand resting on a bent knee…

Before Duncan could signal he was in place, Iain stood, a wide grin on his face. A new anticipation tightened his muscles, and his restlessness suddenly had a focus. He took back his wish to not have another surprise this day. This was indeed a surprise, but it was a welcome one. He'd blundered this morn—their patrol leader had *not* been pleased—but here was his chance to redeem himself.

He whistled an all's-well to Duncan, uncocked and holstered his pistol, and strode into the firelight, uncaring at the noise he made.

The figure by the fire startled, straightened, and shot her gaze to his, her eyes wide. She scooted back and dragged an ungainly lump of a bag into her lap like a shield.

Iain crossed his arms and leaned back slightly on his heels. "Well, hello, my lovely wife."

Chapter Four

Mony a traitor 'mang the isles
Brak the band o' nature's law ;
Mony a traitor, wi' his wiles,
Sought to wear his life awa.
"Will He No Come Back Again," *Jacobite Reliques*

$\mathcal{W}$IFE?

When Traci's heart returned from being flung up into the treetops, she took a deep, calming breath. Or tried to. It was shaky as all hell. And her heart was still quibbling about returning to her chest.

The firelight limned the strong, tall—*holy God, he's hunky*—lines of the last person she thought she'd see again. And that she'd really hoped not to. Despite the fact her sister was with his party.

Her sister.

At that sobering thought, she scrambled to her feet and braced herself, gripping the neck of her cloth bag tightly. And jumped when a branch snapped behind her, making her heart go all bat-shit crazy again. She whirled around. *Jeez.* She was going to have a friggin' heart attack.

Duncan strode into the fire's orange glow and struck an identical pose to Iain's—arms crossed, muscles bunching under his linen shirt, kilt falling in loose folds against his muscled legs.

"Where's my sister? Where's Fiona?" She faced the man she'd shared just a leeee-tel bit too much with last night. Her body flushed with heat remembering his seductive words, his skilled hands, his heavy-lidded gaze. Yeah, more charged memories returned. "And what do you mean 'wife'?"

Iain chuckled, and his head tilted forward, his gaze seemingly trying to latch onto hers over the popping, sparking fire between them. "Dinnae pretend ye forgot. My feelings are trampled, no doubt."

She narrowed her eyes. "I think I'd remember a wedding ceremony." And where the hell was her sister? She squinted past the too-hunky man, but all was darkness.

"We handfasted, lass. Don't ye remember?"

"Handfasted?" she squeaked, and her gaze snapped back to his. In the fuzzy memories of the night before, one sorted itself in her mind's eye—a cloth wrapped around their clasped hands and her repeating some words in Gaelic, Fiona's and Duncan's grinning faces egging them on. "Was that what that was?"

A sick feeling curdled in her stomach as she vaguely remembered laughing and joking with Iain about giving their attraction a go, or some such crap. Obviously Scotch made her act like a romantic idiot.

Glenfiddich, you are officially on my shit list.

Iain clasped his hand to his heart and staggered back a step, the ham. "Aye, you've wounded me. I think me pride has suffered a mortal blow."

"Your pride will survive, I think," she drawled.

"Not with you about, I fear. 'Tis at least a wee bit bruised. Will ye kiss it to make it better?"

"I can't kiss your pride."

Duncan stepped around her, laughing and looking at her over his shoulder as he passed. "Ah, but, lassie, you dinnae ken what he calls his pride and joy."

Unbidden, her gaze shot to Iain's kilt and what lay hidden below.

Iain jutted his hips forward and bounced once on his toes. "I see ye remember now." His voice was pitched a touch lower, and the rumbling, intimate tone wound through her, sparking more memories and twining them tight into her.

Heat flared up her neck to her cheeks. "Enough. Where's my sister?"

Iain and Duncan exchanged a look. "We don't have your sister."

An icy chill flashed through her veins. "But Maggie said she left with you this morning."

"Then Maggie was mistaken," Duncan said, his voice firm.

"Why would she lie? She said Fiona left with the MacCowans. Where are the rest of your men?" When they remained silent, irritation edged into the flash of fear. "Take me to your camp. Now."

"Bossy thing, aren't you?" Duncan looked her up and down.

"Aye, that she is." Iain winked at her. "Very bossy."

Another memory surfaced, of her ordering Iain onto his back when they'd fallen into their bed. Her lady parts clenched.

She shoved her stupid libido aside and crossed her arms.

Iain sighed. "We'll take you to our camp. Had no other idea in mind. Besides being my wife, 'tis not safe for you to be out here alone." He approached her, and a heated awareness grew inside her with each step. She thumbed her ring, taking comfort in its familiar presence.

"And," he continued. "I'd like to know why you disappeared on me this morn."

God, the morning's events were so grainy. "Me? You were the one gone, not me."

"I left for a wee bit to use the privy, and when I returned, I found the woman who'd pledged to spend a year with me gone from our bed. Looked all over the inn for you, but no one had seen ye leave. 'Twas like you'd disappeared into thin air."

Iain reached her side and kicked dirt onto her pitiful fire. "C'mon, lassie. Let me take you to our camp, and we can discuss this further." The edge of his plaid draping across his hip brushed her arm, and she shivered. She stood rooted to the ground as the air crackled with the magnetic pull of this maddening but handsome man. Having him so close, his heat buffeting her, his strength looming over her, brought back all the memories from last night in a rush, brought back all the ill-advised reasons that had urged her into sharing a night with him.

And dammit if her body wasn't going *yay, let's do it again.*

Long ago, she'd learned that she had the worst judgment when it came to men. Specifically ones who were too hot for their own damn good. She'd taken to embracing those bad decisions—having fun with them, but not expecting anything more. Otherwise—hello, heartache. But this time, she'd embraced a bad decision a tad too hard.

She was married? To a hot, playboy Scot in 1689?

Epic. Even for her.

❧

As TRACI HIKED between the two hulking giants beside her, she tried to remain calm. Her sister would be at that camp—these two had no chance to warn the others to hide her—and she'd grab Fiona, make her wish, and disappear. And she gave zero shits if the Highlanders witnessed them disappearing.

They could just chalk it up to magic, or faeries, or aliens, for all she cared.

Glenfiddich nudged her neck from behind, her soft sigh near her ear her only comfort.

They forded the stream where she'd taken a drink earlier that evening and penetrated deeper into the dark rolling glen, the moon's feeble glow barely illuminating their path. A chill evening wind whipped around their bodies, tugging at her skirts.

And then, good God, it hit her.

She was walking with a pony, in a dark glen, with two Highland warriors.

And she wasn't the least bit afraid.

She felt safe with them, which didn't make any sense. She instantly became wary, because her romantic instincts were shit.

Now each darkening ravine they passed through, each casual brush of Iain's body against hers made her draw inward, muscles tightening. By the time they reached the outskirts of their camp, she was exhausted by the tension. Tension wound so taut within her, she'd swear the next crunch of heather underfoot would make her splinter into a million fractured pieces.

Yeah, she needed to get to her sister and kiss this damn time period bye-bye before she got herself into any more trouble.

Iain and Duncan strode into the camp, but Traci hung back, ready to flee if either of them made a grab for her.

Confident that she was following right behind them, Duncan and Iain greeted their men. She scanned the flickering light, heart lodged in her throat.

Where are you, Fiona?

She circled the group, keeping Glenfiddich close beside her. She edged up to a lone tree, taking comfort in its solid presence at her back and her pony on one side. Her gaze skipped along each figure around the camp fire.

None were Fiona.

What the hell? Where was she?

Had Maggie lied?

Iain spun around until he found her. "Ah. There's my wee wife. What're ye doing huddled by that tree? Come into the fire's warmth. No one here will harm ye."

Wee wife? Was he making fun of her? She'd only been "wee" when she shot out of her mother's womb. She'd not let his taunts affect her.

Traci studied each man—about a dozen—and they stared back with a mixture of curiosity and suspicion. She crept forward, her bag gripped in her fist. It packed a wallop if they got any ideas. Or she'd jump on her pony and flee.

"Where's Fiona?" Her heart pounded at voicing the question, because she'd now get the confirmation she could already guess at: her sister wasn't here.

Duncan swept a hand around the camp fire. "As you can see, we have her not."

"But why would Maggie lie? I need to find my sister."

Iain crossed his arms. "Perhaps we can aid you in your quest. She could not have ventured far."

She swallowed hard. "But she didn't 'venture' off. Someone took her. Maggie said the MacCowans. She could be in danger."

"There's no one in these parts but our sept and that of our clan, MacDonell of Glengarry. If she's near, we will hear of it."

She faced Duncan. "What about you and Fiona? What happened last night?"

Duncan's jaw tightened. "We drank for a while longer, but she insisted on having her own room for the night. I stayed in the common room. I saw neither of you again after we parted last night."

There was something more there; she could tell in the set of his face. "What aren't you telling me?"

What looked like hurt, quickly concealed, crossed his face. "Nothing other than the particulars of the discussion that transpired between us. Which is private. If your sister shares it with you, that's her decision."

Frustration strained her voice. "When I woke up, I…I panicked. A group of men was after me, so I, er, escaped without Fiona. I wonder if *they* took her?"

Iain stepped toward her, a frown marring his smooth, high forehead. "Who were these men? What did they look like?"

She gave a description as best she could. Duncan glanced at Iain. "Sounds like Ross."

"Who's Ross?"

"Ross MacCowan is one of our leading tacksmen and currently the leader of our patrol. But he wouldn't have taken your sister."

"Then why did it look like he was after me? Is he here?"

Duncan and Iain shared another look. Iain waved a dismissive hand. "Probably only to question you as a stranger in these parts, that's all. 'Tis his duty. He split off with a smaller group to investigate some trouble with one of our tenants."

Had Maggie been mistaken? They seemed sincere.

Iain continued, "Come. Our patrol is over, and we're making for our keep. Accompany us, and we can assemble a search party."

It felt as if all the rocks in the vicinity were now pressing into her chest. This couldn't be happening. The old memory of the last time she'd made a bet with her sister—and had to find her when she'd gone missing—added to the dread and disbelief. She'd been eleven, and her sister eight, and their stupid game had not only sent her parents into a panic, but all participants at the Highland Games that year.

Traci had been awash in guilt and shame and determination to make things right for her sister and her family. And then insidiously, when she'd found a sobbing Fiona and brought her back in triumph to her parents at their tent, she'd been awash in jealousy at how her parents had fussed and cooed. While the adult in her *now* knew her parents hadn't loved Fiona more, at the time she'd been tangled up and helpless, looking on the reunion scene from the outside. Another example of how she didn't fit in with her family.

She shoved the old memories aside and studied Iain and Duncan, then the rest of the party. But especially Iain. One of her personal rules? Never interact with insatiable flirts after they slept together. It kept things neat. And by things, she meant her emotions and her boundaries and her expectations.

She paced away from him, and back. Could her need to find her sister really depend on a hot playboy in a kilt? One she'd gone so far as to stupidly handfast with? Really, universe?

She took a shaky breath. "If I go with you, you promise you'll help me?"

Iain nodded. "Consider it a sacred vow. If your sister is on our lands still, we will find her."

What choice did she have? She didn't know the land or its people. At all. Her shoulders slumped. "All right. But what about tonight?"

Iain looked her over, satisfaction and wariness flashing through his eyes. "Tonight, we rest."

She surveyed the bare dirt, grass, and rocks and dropped her bag to the ground. Keeping one eye on the curious stares of the men, she pulled out her thick blanket. She'd planned on sleeping on the ground tonight anyway, so she might as well claim a spot. But she wouldn't sleep a wink.

Iain kicked a guy who lay near the fire. "Move your arse, Lochloinn. Allow the lass a spot near the fire. And take care of her pony, would ye?"

She edged closer, eyeing each man.

"Here, let me help you." Iain clasped part of her blanket and stepped close, his rugged male scent washing over her, making her skin prickle with recognition. She'd bet her sister would be all gushy about that smell, want to bottle it, and call it something like Eau de Hunky Highlander. Her throat tightened, and she backed away, needing to put space between their too-close bodies. The *only* way this could work—partnering with him—was to keep her distance.

"I'm not sleeping with you here," she said in an undertone so only he could hear. She'd flirted and fooled around with him, because he was the type it was easy to do that with, where no expectations for more existed. But it was good to be clear.

His chuckle was low, sounding like sin running through her blood. "Aye, that I ken. Plenty of time for that later."

She regarded him from the corner of her eye, and he winked. Yep, a flirt.

But, dang, was he tall. She'd never felt dainty in her life, but she did next to him. He had to be at least six four. And while his brute strength and nearness should have set off alarm bells, they were ridiculously silent.

She tugged the blanket from him, and he let it go with a chuckle and another outrageous wink. Ignoring his draw, she arranged her spot near the fire and curled up on the hard ground, its coldness seeping into her.

She strained to listen to the movements around her, especially when Iain went from man to man and held a quick, but low, conversation with each. Finally, when no one bothered her, she relaxed. And exactly because her romantic instincts were shitty, she slipped the knife from her boot and gripped it tight under her blanket. A presence shuffled behind her—a *swish* of cloth against cloth, a masculine grunt—and a strange heavy awareness along her back told her it was Iain. And that same awareness told her he was being just loud enough to tell her his location. Directly behind her. She kept her back to him, though she could feel his stare like a physical touch.

Then, body no longer twitching at every little noise, her mind whirred off to the main problem at hand: her sister.

Fiona, where the hell are you?

ℭↄ

IAIN VISUALLY TRACED the dips and curves of his wife's body curled up by the fire, her posture and attitude all fierce independence. And a wee bit prickly.

Prickly he could deal with.

But this independence?

Ach, nay, it did not bode well. Not at all.

How in all the bumps on old Nessie's back was he to keep her from discovering their plans? Everything—*everything*—hinged on secrecy.

Once again, a spontaneous action of his had endangered his clan. The hairs on his arm rose. Had she been placed in their path at that inn to dupe him or another clan member into marriage? When Ross had discovered his foolishness in handfasting a Campbell spy, he'd given him but one task—distracting the lass. He ground his teeth and jerked his plaid across his shoulder.

Letting her disappear on him hadn't exactly highlighted his competence either.

And he didn't believe for one moment that her sister had "disappeared."

Aye. Mighty suspicious, to have two obviously highborn Campbell women playing at commoners at that inn as his clan prepared to depose King William and restore the rightful King James to his throne. Treason in the eyes of the English. And he'd fallen right into their hands, as gullible as a newborn babe. He'd *handfasted* with her. With a *Campbell*. Clearly, he had a knack for the peat-headed decisions. Could he be any more of a bumbler?

He could only hope bringing her back to the keep didn't compound his errors.

All in his party were agreed, though: best to keep this one close, even if 'twas her aim to be led to their keep. She'd learn nothing but carefully planted misinformation. The pledge to search for the sister had been an easy one to make, for she must be found before she ferreted out their treasonous plans.

He pinched the bridge of his nose. Did the lass have to be so damn lovely? Every glimpse of a rounded shoulder or a bent elbow, no matter that her skin was obscured by cloth, conjured the erotic images of their night together.

He flopped onto his back, relishing the bite of the rough, cold ground. He forced his head to follow, to deny himself the sight of her shoulders covered in her flowing hair, the dip of her waist, the flare of her hip.

He tightened his plaid around his body. If only he could as easily force his inconvenient cockstand to subside.

Why did she have to be a Campbell? And possibly a spy? This was most decidedly *not* Campbell territory. For such a pro-government clan member to be deep in MacDonell territory could have only one purpose—reporting treasonous activity. 'Twas just his luck.

Because no matter how much his body and his heart were already curled up and staring doe-eyed at his wife, she could *not* be his. So what was he to do with her? No matter what, he must make things right with his clan.

God's blood, perhaps Ross had the right of it. What had he said when he'd stopped by the inn in time to hear her name during the handfasting? In truth, Iain had been shocked at hearing her clan name, but he'd been too deep in his cups and too enamored.

Ross had pulled him aside when he'd left their room to take a leak. "What's done is done. We all know what you do best, cousin. Apply your amorous talents toward the spy. Get her secrets and prevent her from learning ours." Iain gave a dry laugh—a mission that had lasted all of the space it took him to return to their room and find her gone.

Aye, he could play the happy-go-lucky bridegroom with a woman who'd duped him and distract her until they reached their keep and he turned her over to his uncle, the clan's chieftain. Didn't mean he'd like the pretense.

Chapter Five

༆

The piper came to our town
And he played bonnielie
He play'd a spring the laird to please
A spring brent new from 'yont the seas
And then he gae his bags a wheeze
And played anither key
"The Piper o' Dundee," *Jacobite Reliques*

*T*RACI SWAYED IN her saddle and gripped the pommel. She pushed her feet harder against the stirrups—Lord, her butt couldn't take any more abuse. Her pony splashed through the shallow, slow-flowing river, wetting the hems of her skirts, adding to the early morning chill on her skin. Once clear of the river, Glenfiddich picked her way up the rock-strewn path that Iain and his men told her led to their keep.

Every step of her pony thudded in her consciousness, for every step stretched, thinner and thinner, the invisible link to her sister. She worked to ignore the sensation, because for once, Traci was doing the *smart* thing. Her knowledge of the region in her own time was for crap, so her stunningly logical mind—ha!—had figured her knowledge would be for crap in the seventeenth century too.

But, yeah. It would do her sister absolutely no good to go running off in her usual slapdash manner.

Traci must face this challenge the *right* way, and the right way meant having help and a plan. Her sister's life and well-being depended on it. Her sister's words from the other night came back to her, taking on a different shade of meaning: *No way. I want to stay. There's more here for me, I can feel it.*

Traci rolled her lips inward. Even if Fiona was just exploring, indulging in her love of all things Scottish and hunky, Traci had to be smart about it.

Iain had promised the help. If that ended up not happening, *then* she'd strike out on her own. And damn the consequences.

Meanwhile, she'd do the other smart thing—stop Iain with this "wife" thing. She wasn't here to flirt—okay, she'd ended up flirting on their ill-conceived night out clubbing in seventeenth-century Scotland, but *now* was not the time or the place. Nothing good would—*could*— come from that. Ever. Not only did she not want to live in 1689—*hello, no running water!*—but Iain was not the settling-down type.

As if her thoughts conjured him, Iain pulled up alongside, his knee brushing hers, and she tensed. Glenfiddich shied to the side, and she softly cooed to her and patted her muscled neck.

"So, wife." His stupid-sexy voice plucked the strings drawing her to him. "You ready to take your rightful place? By my side and in my bed?"

Direct, wasn't he? She glared at him and opened her mouth to say that, no, she'd not be doing that, it had all been a mistake, yadda, yadda, yadda, when mirth sparkled in his eyes that he made no effort to hide.

She changed tack. "Why, yes I am. Especially since I'm not convinced I properly sampled the wares." She injected a bit of seductive teasing into her tone and eyed him up and down.

Shock widened his eyes. He reared back, and a rich, melodic laugh echoed down the path and jangled her senses. His pony danced away. "Aye, you sampled, lass. More than sampled. But if ye wish to make *extra* certain, I'd be happy to oblige." He dipped his head in a bow, his gaze holding hers. "Only say the word, and I'll be by your side. Or across it. Or on it. Whichever way you desire."

On the last word, his voice dropped in pitch, and its rumbling, seductive tone instantly put her back in that bed with him. Her body flashed with heat. *It* remembered him well.

She ruthlessly shoved her response down. "Talk. Talk. I think that's all you're good for. I know your type." And she did. Some of her situational frustration slipped away as she fell into the familiar and harmless banter she always enjoyed with guys like him.

"Type? I dinnae ken."

She waved a hand in the air. "A flirt. You're all about the chase. The bigger the challenge, the sweeter the victory. And then it's on to the next challenge."

HEAT FLARED UP the back of Iain's neck and a lead weight of resentment settled in his gut at Traci's assessment of him.

He laughed, of course, because it was the expected response. A response honed by the wishes of his mother to keep her and everyone else happy and entertained.

Aye, he was a flirt. Traci wasn't the first to level that charge. But her words, said so lightly and matter-of-factly, cut through sharper and more deadly to his self-assurance for having come from her. He jerked his head to the side and gripped the reins tighter. Why? Why had he expected to be *seen* more clearly by *her*? Because they'd handfasted? Shared a night of passion together?

It *was* what he did best. He *was* good at it. He *did* enjoy flirtation.

As a youth, he'd fallen in love with one fair lass after another. Each one he believed in his heart to be the lass for him. How could a mere lad resist a softly curved cheek? The glow of silky hair in the sun? Their sweet breath and their sweet smell?

Flirtation was how he got them to talk to him, pay attention to him, like him. But it ended up being *all* they'd seen.

And—the inevitability settled in with his resentment—it was all she saw now. What did he lack?

He deployed his smile. "Of course, my wife. But I easily conquered you, did I not?" He inwardly winced as the words dropped between them, and pain flashed through her eyes, quickly masked. He'd only meant to continue their banter, to show she'd not scored a direct blow.

He reached across that space and covered her clenched fist with his much larger hand. It might not soothe her, but touching her again for the first time since they'd been separated certainly soothed something in *him*. "But the victory was just as sweet. Mistake that not."

She tossed her braid over her shoulder, her dark red hair the color of well-aged claret. His fingers twitched on her hand, and he pulled away before he could impulsively reach up and undo that braid. See how her luscious hair looked—free and unbound—in the light of day, the sun playing with its colors.

She fixed him with a saucy stare, and his loins tightened uncomfortably under his plaid and sporran.

"How do you know it was you conquering me and not the other way around?"

Yes. Good question. And a potent reminder. Again, he'd let himself fall under her sway. 'Twas daring for her to express such a notion out loud, but then, she was a daring lass. He took in her form, sitting rather ill-at-ease on her pony. Definitely not a horsewoman. He berated himself. *She is a spy.* But the notion was a slippery one to hold onto as he contemplated her prickly, teasing, delectable person.

She duped you. Remember that, you dearg amadan.

He nodded. "You have me there, my wife."

He edged his mount away. If she thought him a flirt, fine. His clan had assigned him that role, and he'd play it. His clan didn't need to bear the brunt of his latest blunder. They wanted her kept out of the way—distracted.

But by all the fickle fae creatures in the land, it chafed that she viewed him exactly as did everyone else.

His lips tightened, and he glanced ahead. Curse his fool heart. Or should he say, inept heart?

But, aye, he'd play the flirt.

For his clan.

ᜠ

THE BRIGHT SUN overhead warmed Traci's skin and finally dispelled the morning chill. She followed behind Iain, and they crested a stony ridge. She gasped, and Glenfiddich stopped and reared her head up and down.

Iain pulled in his reins, his pony dancing beneath him, tail high, blocking her path. "Ah. Here we are, my wife. Welcome to Dungarbh."

Below stretched the bluest lake she'd ever seen, the sky reflected in perfect detail on its surface. Loch Garry, Iain had said. They'd approached from the south side and now faced northwest, the lake spanning east to west. The nearest shore stuck out a bit, with a stone causeway extending to a cluster of stone buildings and docks. A small distance away, three islands clustered together in the center of the lake. From those rocky islands rose a fully intact castle. Banners snapped in the breeze along the battlements, and small fishing boats dotted the otherwise blank and smooth surface of the lake.

Tiny hairs rose all along her skin. Goose bumps followed. God. This was Scotland. An ephemeral *something* tugged at her heart, her soul, and for a moment she could kind-of-sort-of grasp why her sister and her family made such a big friggin' deal about their Scottish heritage.

No lie—bagpipes seemed to echo off the mountains surrounding them like a craggy rim of a bowl, the spirits of ancestors seemed to swirl around her, caressing her, welcoming her, and the wild and free air seemed to beckon to some long-forgotten, long-neglected part of her soul. She could almost hear, feel, taste it—a tantalizing siren song luring her, making her heart, her whole being, swell with emotion.

Holy crap. She shook herself. *Ridiculous.*

Had she switched bodies with Fiona?

It was her *sister* who loved Scotland, not her. It was her *family* who loved Scotland, not her.

She tightened her lips. All the times she'd been made to practice some dance or craft or song for the Highland Games crowded her memories. Memories that stretched back the entire length of her childhood. God, by the time she skedaddled off to college, she thought she'd scream if she witnessed one more guy strutting around in red-chapped, knobby knees and a kilt. College had been freedom. Freedom to explore her *own* interests, which her family had never taken seriously and so had never let her explore.

Because each friggin' October they went to the Highland Games in Stone Mountain, Georgia, and each friggin' October she had to parade around with the rest of their family, pretending at all this Scottish heritage crap. Her family had come over so long ago—before the American Revolution for God's sake—so how exactly were they Scottish again?

They weren't. They were *American.*

But you couldn't tell that to her parents. Oh no. And she'd tried. And tried.

They were obsessed with the "family" symbolized in their clan, but what was the point of that, if they neglected to embrace their immediate family?

She narrowed her eyes and swept across the scenery once more. Ugh. Stupid scenery. Stupid imaginary bagpipes. Just hearing the instrument's skirling reminded her thank-you-very-much of the biggest example in her life of how she didn't fit in with her family, or anywhere really.

A pony beside her snuffled, and a kilt-draped, muscly dude nudged past and picked his way down the ridge. Others followed, passing on either side of her and Iain, their saddles creaking, their voices muffled.

Iain raised a brow and nodded toward the path. She'd swear to God his eyes were twinkling.

"I'm coming, I'm coming," she muttered.

She kicked Glenfiddich, who obediently angled down the path. She leaned back to keep her balance and soaked in the scenery jolting before her from her pony's gait.

Damn it, it *was* beautiful.

But she'd resist its lure.

Soon they reached the shore and trotted across a stone causeway about a hundred feet long. It ended at a small island surrounded by a wooden palisade. Behind it, in the distance, the castle loomed larger and larger until it filled the horizon. Several children erupted from the open gate at the end of the causeway and pounded across, a pack of dogs swirling and yipping around their ankles. The excited kids launched themselves at some of the men surrounding her. Shouts of joy filled the air.

And then, because-of-course, some dude popped up on the palisade and played the friggin' bagpipes.

Could they be any more Scottish?

She laughed at herself. Well, they *were* Scottish. What had she expected?

She shielded her eyes to get a better look at the piper, and her gaze snagged instead on the man standing alone several feet from the musician. His arms were crossed, and it was hard to tell from this distance, but she'd swear he was glowering. Glowering straight at—

No. Not her. She followed his trajectory: Iain. Who was oblivious to the intense focus, laughing and ruffling the heads of several children.

Chapter Six

cx⁀

Ken ye wha supped Bessy's haggies?
Ken ye wha dinner'd on our Bessy's haggies?
"Bessy's Haggies," *Jacobite Reliques*

*I*AIN RODE THROUGH the open gate and kept an eye on Traci, who took in the courtyard and the stone castle farther out in the loch. He'd always been rather proud of their complex. The small island where they stood sheltered their livestock when needed and contained large stables. Along the northern shore skirted the wooden docks and the homes of the families that managed the ferry and stables. Enemies would have to cross the narrow causeway, and then they were still met with several hundred feet of loch before they reached the main complex of stone buildings accessible only by ferry or boat.

But how did she view it? Were the thatch-roofed buildings and wooden palisades primitive to her? Campbells boasted finer establishments, he was certain.

Her perusal was keener than usual, as if she cataloged defensive placements and numbers of men on watch, and his uneasiness grew. Such intense interest certainly lent credence to his clan's worries that she was a spy of the mighty Earl of Argyll, head of the Campbell clan.

Her hands, which up till now had loosely held the reins, were tense. One hand still lightly gripped the leather, but the other was fisted in her lap, and she kept opening and closing it, as if she caught herself being tense and stretched her fingers out in an attempt to relax. Over and over. Open. Close. Open.

He dismounted and handed the reins to a waiting stable lad.

If she were a spy, she wasn't very subtle. Likely, the earl, in his arrogance, assumed Iain's clan would not suspect a lady spy. But his clansmen weren't soft skulls, like the English the earl usually reckoned with. Irritation swept through him—how had he been taken in by her?

He had to have been truly the numbskull his uncle constantly accused him of being to have not seen the signs.

He stepped over to Traci, who remained atop her pony and surveyed the area and his clan, a slight furrow marring her lovely brow. He slapped a hand onto her luscious thigh.

Traci whipped around in her odd saddle, and her gaze dropped to his hand. Her eyes narrowed.

"May I assist you down, my wife?" he asked in English. All within earshot who understood gasped, and he grinned widely.

She jerked, and her attention skipped around the growing crowd, panic sparking in the depths of her eyes.

'Twas clear she'd stay atop her pony until King James reclaimed his throne if Iain didn't do something to alter her position. 'Twas also clear what was required of him to that end. He sighed. What a hardship.

He grasped her by the waist, and, as if involuntarily, her hands dropped to his shoulders to steady herself. He eased her off the horse and made extra certain she slid down the entire length of his body. Slowly. Vindictively.

His family wouldn't be shocked. Nay, they'd be shocked if he didn't do such a bold action with a lass who was his wife.

As her shapely thighs brushed down his, and her fair bosom dragged across his chest, his senses sparked to life. The folds of her dress rode up partway, placing some artificial distance between them, but he wouldn't complain—he had his hands around her wee waist, her breasts mashed against him, and her sweet breath coming just a bit faster against his neck, heating his blood. His gaze locked with hers. Christ, but she was lovely. Wisps of red hair had escaped her braid and fluttered across her creamy cheek.

Ach. Now, he was as hard as the Stone of Scone. Why had he thought this a good idea again?

But as he continued to stare into the depths of her brown eyes, a realization struck him. A trace of fear shimmered there, as if she were afraid to turn around and face his clan. As if she'd latched onto him, her only lifeline.

An odd feeling pinched his heart at that notion. To be someone's sole anchor—it made him ache to wrap her within his embrace and tuck her head under his chin.

Was the lass treading in deeper waters than she'd reckoned on?

Well, he'd play his role—the foolish lover. She played off that with ease. And if she was in over her head with Argyll's schemes, he'd be her lifeline in the deep, treacherous waters.

He gently eased away and cradled her chin, bestowing a wink to give her focus. A swallow bobbed down the white column of her throat, and the sight brought a rush of new memories. Memories which stirred his blood, aye, but also brought a conviction that she had not manipulated him into the handfasting. It had been spontaneous, sincere, strangely fragile.

His aunt and uncle pushed through the last of the crowd and stopped before them. They must have been alerted to their arrival, for they usually remained on the main island of their keep.

Iain cleared his throat, draped an arm over his wife's shoulders, and tugged her tight against his side, disconcerted by her continuing silence and acquiescence. Though he'd known her but a short while, he knew this was not her usual state. "Everyone, this is my wife, Traci Campbell, handfasted two nights past," he said in English. "Traci, this is my uncle, the chieftain, and his wife Marjorie."

"You married?" his uncle asked in Gaelic, his voice laced with a hard edge. "And a Campbell, no less? Are you truly that daft then?"

The back of his neck heated and tightened, but he said lightly, "I'm not sure I knew she was a Campbell at the time." He regarded Traci's stunned face and winked. "But, aye."

"Which Campbells are you connected with, dear?" his aunt asked in English, stepping closer. She smiled kindly at Traci, bless her. Even though he knew he had to be careful and keep Traci at a distance, it felt right to put her at ease.

Traci cleared her throat. "The Campbells of…Stone Mountain."

Everyone who spoke English exchanged glances, their faces puzzled. His uncle cocked his head and scowled. He crossed his arms. "I've never heard of that branch. And your accent is odd. Do you not speak Gaelic?"

She straightened slightly against his side. "No. Ah, my sister and I were raised by my mother's family down in…Cornwall. We only just arrived in Scotland."

"And hitched yourself for a year and a day to the lad with the most roving eye in all of Scotland." His uncle shook his head, his eyes pitying. "Good luck to ye, lass."

Traci stiffened beside Iain, and he was certain he had tensed as well, though he was practiced at not showing how their opinions bothered him. His family had never understood him. Though perhaps he'd not tried too hard to help them.

Let them think what they will. If he was to play the fool with her, if this was the only task they could trust him with, he'd do it, and do it well. He'd not let his mistake harm his clan. Again. Pain lanced through him, taking him by surprise. Long ago, he'd come to terms with his father's death—and his role in it. And long ago, he'd learned that he was not someone to entrust with his clan's safety. So why did that knowledge feel now like a fresh wound?

"Ye must be half-starved, Iain," his aunt said, her grin wide. "We didn't expect you for another day, but we can have the cook get something prepared for the lot of ye 'ere long."

He turned to the path that led to the docks and the ferry. "Aye, that would be most welcome."

๛

"We can't share a room." Traci put her hands on her hips at the entrance of a room at the end of one massive wing located on the third island.

Iain brushed by, dousing her with his stupid manly scent, and eyed her as he passed. "We can, and we will. We're married now. 'Twould look odd otherwise."

He strode across the room, his gait loose-legged and confident, and knelt before the fireplace as if that settled matters. He stacked blocks of peat and lit a fire.

The pungent, earthy smell of peat filled the room, and she stepped farther inside. "You can't be serious. And I'm not convinced we're married. We didn't have a priest."

He stood and brushed off his hands, his heated gaze raking her body. "You know about handfasting, do you not? No witnesses required. No officiant. As long as the couple agrees to commit, they are bound for a year and a day. At that time, if we don't suit, we may part ways."

Wow. It sounded so…pagan. Who'd have thought?

Still.

"Listen." She fought the urge to cross her arms. "Now that we're alone, we need to get a few things straight. First, I'm not going to be around that long. I have to find my sister and return to our…home.

Second. This thing between us?" She waved her hand in the space between them. "It's not happening. The sex was great"—*what I can remember*—"but it was a one-time thing. It would be best, for you and for me, if we keep that in mind. So…no sex."

His eyes widened, and his brows lifted at her bluntness, but she'd learned long ago that bluntness was best where emotions were at stake. While rude, it was clear. She didn't want to hurt him, or herself. He'd thank her later.

Besides. She knew his type. Being attached to one woman was not his style. Normally, his type was perfect for her needs—that night at the inn being a neon-blinking example. But with the stakes so high, it was time she was responsible for once. If she indulged, she'd get emotionally entangled. It had happened before. Hence, her rule. What fool let that happen with someone like him? She was only here because they'd promised to help find Fiona.

As was her habit when she felt herself slipping where guys were concerned, she fiddled with the ruby ring she'd purchased at an antique store shortly after the second of two back-to-back wake-up calls she'd received her senior year in college. The intricate filigree was seductive in its swirls, around three dark red rubies. She bought it to remind herself that trouble for her heart came in flirtatious packages.

"No sex?" He crossed his arms, and damn him if he didn't purposely flex his biceps under his shirt. "Well…if ye think ye can resist, who am I to argue?"

She tossed her bag onto the floor and shook her head. Yep, she had him pegged. "I can resist all right. Don't you worry, buster. So. Why don't we take turns with the bed?"

"You want to have relations with the bed?"

"I don't…" She clamped her mouth shut when his eyebrow notched up a hair, and his eyes held an extra gleam. "Ha. Ha. Funny." Even when he made bad jokes, he was charming, the bastard.

He shrugged. But his lips twitched. "I'll see if I can get an extra pallet up here, though the servants might wonder. Perhaps I can tell them it's to avoid wakin' the others with a squeaky bed."

She narrowed her eyes. "Just get the pallet."

He gave an elaborate bow, complete with a hand flourish. "Aye, my lady. As you wish."

He raked his gaze down her body and back up again and sauntered out the door whistling.

Well, someone *thinks he's funny.*

And, no, that heated perusal had *not* tested her resolve.

But as she suspected, he wasn't too upset by her request. Now all she had to do was make sure he kept his end of their other bargain—recruit a search party for her sister.

❧

TRACI SWALLOWED HARD as she stared around the cozy hall. Overhead, arched stout wooden beams held up huge chunks of…granite? But, unlike castles in her own time, this one appeared new—the wood fresh, the mortar still whole between the stones. Newly woven hangings decorated the walls, their colors sharp.

Neither did the hall echo as much as she thought it would. Must be the wall hangings and how the place was filled with people and objects. The room was located on the second island. From what she'd seen so far, the three-island castle was a wonderfully complex series of connecting bridges and buildings. The first island was a courtyard surrounded by high stone walls and a double tower gate. This led over a wooden bridge to the second island, whose stone keep rose straight from the island's rocky cliff sides. The third island, which housed all the private apartments, could only be reached from a wooden bridge at the top of the keep and likewise rose straight from the cliff sides.

Now she sat with Iain at one end of a wooden slab of a table at the front of the hall, the chieftain and his wife in the center.

The latter weren't eating—not an official mealtime, Iain had whispered—but the rest of their traveling party crowded around the chieftain at the table, eating their fill and answering the chieftain's many questions about the state of the lands they'd patrolled.

At least that's what Iain had also whispered to her, since they all spoke in tongue-twisting Gaelic. So far, no one paid her any attention, which was fine by her. The less she interacted, the better. She could just see herself getting ensnared by some lie she'd have to tell, or accidentally showing her ignorance of the time and culture. A history buff, she was *not*.

The phrase "stranger in a strange land" looped through her mind as everyone talked and laughed around the table in their strange clothes

45

with their strange customs. And their even stranger language. A weird sense of unreality seeped into her to see such animated conversation and laughter and sharing and not understand *any* of it. She felt separate from her surroundings, like Oliver Twist staring into the window of a restaurant, into a world he could have no part of.

An undercurrent pulsed along the voices—that much she could pick up—and it seemed to center around the chieftain and Iain. Though Iain seemed unaware. Several times she caught the chieftain staring at him with narrowed eyes whenever Iain was focused elsewhere. Just like he'd done from the battlements on their arrival.

"They speak now of the night at the inn." Iain's warm breath brushed her ear, and his low voice rumbled through her. Would he quit that? She edged away from his seductive self and noticed the glances thrown her way—some curious, some suspicious. What could they possibly suspect her of?

She did *not* like the sudden attention.

And then the full force of the chieftain's penetrating intelligence centered on her, and she squirmed in her seat. "So you were at this inn of an evening, with your sister? And you say she disappeared?" His English was very good, and his voice rang with authority.

Shit. She straightened. "I *know* she did. We had just arrived, when…" Fierce heat rushed up her spine and flared across her face. "We met Iain and Duncan, and we…" God, she really just couldn't come out and admit what happened that night to this formidable chieftain.

Iain draped his arm around her and tugged her close. Her heart sped up. "You know how such matters proceed, my uncle. We struck up an understanding, handfasted that evening, and spent the night together in the time-honored tradition of the newly committed."

Good God. She could barbecue a whole rack of ribs, her face was flaming so hard. And what was with her embarrassment? She was *not* a blusher. Not anymore. No man would make her into a blubbering fool again.

Especially not flirts like Iain.

She raised her chin a notch and stared boldly at the chieftain, daring him to say anything to shame her. But to her surprise, he reared back his head and laughed. "Indeed. Say no more, nephew. It's surprising, it is, to see you settle for one lass."

Inexplicably, Iain stiffened beside her, though he laughed easily along with his uncle.

The chieftain drained his wine cup and wiped his mouth with the back of his hand. "But this doesn't explain the sister's disappearance. How did that transpire?"

"When I woke up the next morning, I…I couldn't find her. I asked around and was told she'd been carried off by a group of men." She left out what she'd done in the interim and cut to the more pertinent tidbit. "I set out to search for her and ran into Iain and his men."

The chieftain scratched his chin. "Do you have any notion of who took her?"

Was it her imagination, or did some of the men exchange wary glances? "I don't. Maggie, who runs the inn, thought Iain and his men had taken her, but she wasn't clear. I asked her what tartan they were wearing, but she ignored me."

The chieftain frowned. "Why would that matter?"

She cocked her head. "If they were wearing one particular plaid, then I'd know which clan took her."

He looked vaguely amused. "Would you now? And how is that?"

"I…because…don't you guys have a clan tartan and you only wear that tartan? For instance, the Campbell tartan is a dark and light blue, crossed with dark and light olive green, and—"

"Lass, I know not what parts of Scotland you've visited, but you're obviously misinformed. No clan has a set pattern that's readily identifiable as theirs."

They don't? What the hell?

She closed her mouth, unwilling to risk more ignorant comments about this time popping out. This was *exactly* why she hadn't wanted to attract attention.

"But it's not hard to fathom," the chieftain continued, "the mighty Campbell clan presuming to claim one for their exclusive use. Their poor weavers—they must be bored to tears, weaving the same pattern over and over." He grumbled some other words under his breath, but only those nearest him heard. They chuckled, avoiding her gaze.

She fought to make her natural sass remain an inner sass for now. Like it or not, she depended on him and the others and couldn't risk pissing him off. Her sister was relying on her. She repeated that over and over to her sassy side.

One of the warriors leaned over and whispered to the chieftain, his eyes darting to hers as he did so. The chieftain nodded and replied in a low tone.

While they talked, worry and fear gnawed at her enforced calm. So many things could go wrong. She had no allies, she didn't know the countryside or customs, and she suspected the law lay in the hands of the odd mix of sternness, suspiciousness, and easygoingness that was the chieftain.

As if sensing her discomfort, Iain, whose arm was still draped around her shoulders, brushed his hand down her arm and squeezed. *You have me*, the squeeze seemed to say. But did she? Who was he really? No one here seemed to take him seriously, if their reception at the gate was any indication. Could he really be depended on?

No. She had only herself.

But a long buried and lonely part of her yearned to inch closer into the warm shelter of his arm and body. A body that was—for once—taller than hers. To take advantage of his natural flirtiness and feel his comforting heat beside her. How ridiculous was that?

The chieftain stood abruptly, his chair scraping against the stone floor. Several of the men nearby reared back, respect clear in their faces.

Yes. They would defer to whatever this man decreed. A shiver ran through her body. *Shit*. She was *so* out of her depth here.

The chieftain motioned to the two of them. "We shall speak privately," he barked in English. "Follow me."

She glanced at Iain, who appeared just as confused by this statement. But he stood, and she did the same. What sort of reckoning was she going to face now?

Chapter Seven

Let foe come on foe, as wave comes on wave,
We'll give them a welcome, we'll give them a grave
Beneath the red heather and thistle so green.
"The Thistle of Scotland," *Jacobite Reliques*

"**W**HY DON'T YOU tell me what really happened at that inn, my dear." The chieftain had ushered them into what she assumed was his study, located in a corner tower staircase one floor above the main hall. She was gawking at the swords and pikes mounted on the dark-paneled walls, when his question and suspicious tone caused her heart to hitch for a beat.

She whirled around. "What do you mean?"

He eyed her warily as he strolled by her to his desk. He was shorter than her, but his shoulders were massive. "You're holding back. I wish for the truth, please. I'm sure I need not impress upon you that the clan's welfare rests upon my shoulders." He darted an odd glance at Iain.

How the heck did she have anything to do with the welfare of his clan?

"What we told you is true." She'd purposely added the *we* to bring Iain into the narrative and give him partial responsibility. Probably not fair, but what did it matter at this point? "We handfasted and spent the night together. When I woke up, I couldn't find Iain or my sister."

The chieftain's penetrating gaze snapped to Iain's. "And where were you?"

Iain coughed. "I was visiting the privy and got caught up talking to Ross and the other men in our party on the way."

The chieftain turned to her. "Why were you there with this supposed sister?"

What the hell? "She's not a supposed anything. She *is* my sister."

"And what were two obviously highborn ladies, sporting the name o' Campbell, doing at a lowly drover's inn wearing clothes that belied your status?"

Her heart beat a bit faster at that, as the only explanation she had was one she couldn't reveal. "We're, uh, new to the area and thought we were dressing appropriately."

He crossed his arms. *Damn.* He wasn't taller than her, but right now it felt as if he somehow stared down at her. "So you admit to dressing in an attempt to blend in with the locals?"

"Er. Yes?" Why did she feel as if that were the wrong answer?

"Where are you from?"

Since she doubted they'd believe she'd taken the perilous journey from America, alone with her sister, she'd opted for Cornwall. It was as distant as she could be from here and still be on this island, and she doubted they had ventured there.

"Truro, Cornwall."

"Then why did your sister explain your presence by saying you were looking for a cattle-herding brother?"

Alarm constricted her chest—she vaguely remembered Fiona giving that excuse. Dammit. "Er... That was just..."

"An excuse?" He folded his hands. "You can see why I'm having trouble with your tale—you have missing siblings everywhere." He tapped his thumb over his other. "Now you're not even from the region. I'll play along. What brings you to Scotland?"

"Vacation." She'd better stick as close to the truth as she could before she tripped herself up even more.

His thumb stopped tapping. "Vacation? I am unfamiliar with this English word."

"We were visiting here for fun." How would they phrase it? "During our leisure time."

His eyes narrowed. "Interesting. And was this at the behest of kin? A family member perhaps. Like the Earl of Argyll?"

It was clear he was trying to catch her at something, but she had no clue what. She *did* remember from her family's obsession about all things Clan Campbell that the Earl—later *Duke*—of Argyll was the head of the main branch of the clan.

"No...I don't even know the Earl."

"You're not related to him then, are you?"

"Distantly, maybe." And boy, was that distant.

His eyes narrowed again, and she glanced at Iain for support. Why, she didn't know. Though his brows pinched together, he didn't stick up for her. And why would he anyway? He had no clue about her or what had happened. His loyalty was to his clan and his chieftain.

All they'd done was flirt and have sex. And get handfasted.

But Iain pushed away from the wall where he'd been leaning, his face transforming into an uncharacteristic scowl. She'd known him for only a day, and already she knew that wasn't a normal look for him. "Why don't we stop speaking in riddles? It's giving me a headache. Aye, it looks suspicious that two Campbell lasses appear in our lands out of nowhere, but I just can't see them as spies." He waved his hand at her.

She reared back and stared at them both. *Spies?* That's what the chieftain suspected?

The chieftain watched her closely, seeming to note her surprise. "Hmm," was all he said though. He faced Iain. "That's why I'm chieftain, and you're not, boy."

Iain flinched but held his ground. "All the same. What could she be spying about?"

A new light of respect glinted in the chieftain's eyes, and he flattened his hands on the table. "What you say is true. It would be a fruitless endeavor even if they were spies." He smiled wide at her. "For we have nothing to hide." He spread his hands. "You must understand—as chieftain, I must be extra cautious."

She nodded, as he seemed to expect some kind of response. But, really, what the hell was going on? A strange vibe permeated the dark interior.

She drew her back straighter. "Now that we have that out of the way"—she hoped—"Iain said you'd help me search for my sister? I don't know the area and could use whatever help you can spare."

The chieftain darted a quick glance at Iain. "Of course, my dear. You're family now, and by extension, so is your sister. We shall organize a party at once and send them out at first light. Provide us with a description of her."

She shook her head. "I'd like to go with them."

"I dinnae think that's wise."

"Because I'm a woman?"

The chieftain seemed taken aback, but he recovered quickly. "Our clan does not underestimate the abilities of our women. You will learn that soon enough. Nay. 'Tis only that the men will move faster and less conspicuously without you as a member of the party. There will be places they may be forced to go that would not suit you."

She gritted her teeth. "I don't mind. This is my sister."

Iain stepped close and placed a hand on her shoulder. Heat radiated from the point of contact, and Traci hardened her resolve, itching to shrug off his too-comforting hand. "But I mind, my wife. Trust me. Trust our chieftain. If your sister is out there and in trouble, our clan will find her and bring her to you."

Not going after her sister herself went against every instinct she had, but as she stared into Iain's eyes, which were momentarily serious, she sensed his sincerity. She glanced at the chieftain, who nodded.

She stepped away from Iain, letting his hand drop, and wandered over to the lone window in the dark-paneled room, its surface made of the diamond-paned sections of glass she always associated with Shakespeare's time. She peered through the wavy surface to the loch beyond, bent and warped from the imperfections of the glass. She shifted slightly to the side, and the blue waters of the loch rippled with the movement. The impression of Iain's hand on her shoulder—its weight and heat—remained, competing for space in her thoughts.

What to do? She trailed a finger along the mottled surface of the window pane, its cool, textured surface helping to center her. What would Katy do? For sure, she'd think everything through, five gazillion times.

Traci doubted she'd last that long but, dammit, she did need to think it through more than she normally would. Traci's quick assessments and decisions were what made her good at her job, and—ha—good at her role-playing games, but as she well knew, this was no RPG. She had no do-overs. She couldn't muck things up like yesterday, reacting too quickly and assuming she could zap back to earlier and fix everything.

Her sister depended on her, but was she the most qualified to find her? Traci had no skills and certainly was no horsewoman—she *would* slow them down. They'd also have to accommodate her with simple things, such as going to the bathroom.

She blew out a breath. They'd move faster on their own. Feminine pride wanted to be stubborn and insist on going with them, but her throat choked at what was at stake: Fiona. And her sister didn't need her to be all Female Power. She just needed her to make the decision that would find her by the quickest and safest route.

Guilt and worry threaded through her, but she pivoted and swallowed her pride. "Fine. I agree." She took a deep breath. "And thank you for your help. I'm extremely grateful."

The chieftain bowed. "I'm glad you agree." Was that bow made and his words said with a note of irony? Who cared if it was? They were going to find Fiona and bring her back. And then she could skedaddle back to the modern era with her baby sister.

She stepped toward the desk. "Give me a moment to write a letter, so she knows it's safe to go with them."

Behind her, the door burst open, and Traci jumped. A towering Highlander pushed aside the guard who'd opened the door. Grime smeared his face, and his chest was still heaving from exertion.

The newcomer spared her no notice and strode into the room. He spoke urgent words in Gaelic and tossed an object onto the chieftain's desk, landing with a heavy thud.

Traci stepped closer, while Iain cursed.

On the table lay a burnt piece of wood covered in blood.

⌘

IAIN STARED AT the Crann Tara—the summoning stick, or fiery cross as the Sasannaich called it—its message clear to any Highlander: join us, or else.

His uncle held up a hand, stopping the messenger from saying anything further. He speared Iain with a harsh glare and barked in Gaelic, "Get her out of here. This is not for her ears."

"What's going on?" Traci's worried voice cut through the room's tension as everyone's focus landed on her.

He grinned widely. "Nothing, my wife. Clan business only. We're done here." He held out his arm to her. "Shall we?"

Her brow furrowed, but she stepped across the room and took his arm.

As they crossed the threshold into the hallway, the import of the messenger's delivery was like a physical pressure on his back. He had no need to hear the messenger's report to know what purpose the cross fulfilled: Dundee demanded the clans to rally support for the rightful king. Talk and speculation were over. It was time for action.

Chapter Eight

My laddie can fight, my laddie can sing,
He's fierce as the north wind, and soft as the spring…
"My Laddie," *Jacobite Reliques*

*T*HAT NIGHT, TRACI lay curled up in the huge, dark-timbered, four-poster bed, hearing every scurrying noise in the rambling stone edifice that Iain's clan called home. Let's be real, it was a friggin' castle. And it was just so damned…quiet. Outside and in. As if the quiet were a heavy weight, so that every whisper of a noise became a giant ripple through that weight, kicking her heart, her nerves.

Who knew that even a curtain moving in some unseen breeze made a noise? Well, it did. A kind of *swish-thurr*. And there were curtains on all four sides of her bed. A weird mixture of safety and fear infused her, being enclosed like that. As if she were wrapped in her own cocoon made up of just her bed, its covers, and pillows. But, on the other hand, she couldn't see what was on the other side of those heavy curtains. What if that *scrrritching* was a seventeenth-century rat coming to gnaw on her shoes? Or to steal up into her bed and gnaw on her bare toes?

She pulled her feet deeper under the covers. Man, if it was a rat, she'd friggin' lose it. She shivered. She'd hated rats ever since she'd been introduced to her creepy cousin's pet rat Ivan. Ivan the Terrible, she called it, because her cousin had trained it to sneak up on her whenever she was alone and press its disgusting, whiskery nose on her bare feet. Her cousin apparently lived for her shrieks.

A much louder sound than some would-be rat ricocheted through the room, and she stiffened, her heart pounding. A drawn-out creak followed.

The door. It was the door opening. *Iain. It has to be.*

She'd gone to bed much earlier—on purpose—to avoid the awkward moment when they had to go to sleep separately. But then she'd lain awake for several hours, trying to absorb all that had happened, her

54

mind unable to shut up.

A soft glow of light bloomed from the direction of the door, muted by the thickness of the bed curtains. A rustle and a thump. A muffled curse. The light bobbed and shifted from the left to the right side but didn't come closer to the bed.

It *was* Iain, right?

She eased back her covers, careful not to make a noise. She bit her lip and rolled up onto her side, placing her head near the gap in the curtain to her right. She reached forward and edged the fabric back, just a fraction.

She sucked in a breath but clamped her lips shut.

Oh. It was Iain all right. He stood, three-quarters of him facing her, highlighted by the orange glow of the lingering peat fire, his candle perched on the mantel. That light, mixed with the moon's feeble glow from the lone window, cast his form in shifting shadows. But, oh boy. It was enough to *see*.

See as he unclasped his kilt where it draped over a strong shoulder. See as the fabric rustled downward to pool in drapes along his back side. See as he grasped his linen shirt and dragged it up by slow degrees, revealing his powerful torso in the dim light. His muscles bunched and flexed as the fabric swished over his head.

Oh, what a lovely chest. So she *had* remembered that correctly.

And then… And then his long, strong fingers settled onto the belt holding his sporran and plaid, the light sprinkling of black hairs across his powerful chest narrowing down to a point where his hands had paused. His chin raised, and his eyes lifted to her position, but with her nestled in the dark depths of the bed, he couldn't possibly see her. All the same, she felt the heat of his stare, and she squirmed.

The light played across the planes of his strong hands and forearms, allowing her to note the miniscule shifting of muscles signaling his next move. His shapely fingers moved with practiced ease, and he unclasped the belt. The kilt dropped.

❧

IAIN DUCKED HIS head toward the fireplace to hide his grin. The little minx was watching him. He was sure of it.

When he'd slipped into their room, some fae sense told him she was awake. And if not, he'd discreetly hit a small chair on the way, its muffled scrape loud enough to catch her attention if she were a light sleeper but low enough to sound accidental. She thought she could resist him? He'd play her game and see who won.

Her eyes had been on him as soon as he reached the fire, caressing his skin and warming his blood as much as the fire. The air between them hummed with expectation and untold possibilities. But he exercised probably the most control he ever had in his whole, sorry life not to look in her direction. Instead, he'd angled toward her and undressed. Slowly.

His control was sorely tested, though, when her tiny, suppressed gasp emerged from the depths of the four-poster bed.

He'd tried to undress slow enough to tease, but not so slow that it was obvious. It could've been a tired sort of slowness, he reasoned. For once, he was keenly aware of the feel of fabric brushing across his skin as he lifted his shirt, knowing she watched every move. Keenly aware of the feel of his hair falling back into place against his neck after disposing of his shirt. His skin felt tight. Edgy.

Lord help him, but he couldn't resist one peek before he dropped his *féileadh*. He couldn't see her, couldn't see past the bed hangings, but oh, he knew. Knew she was there. Watching. Did her eyes wander all over his body in a feverish attempt to encompass all of him as fast as she could, or did they linger on one spot, and then move on? If so, *which* spot? His skin tightened all over, and his heart beat a touch faster, imagining where his troublemaker's eyes were at the moment.

He stretched his arms upward, flexed his biceps, and yawned, his jaw cracking from the force of it. Aye, but he was tired in truth. He flexed his arms back, enjoying the pull on his sore muscles, and stretched to one side and the other. He threw in a small flex of his arse muscles. Ach, now he was just showing off.

But knowing she watched had his cock stiffening in the warm air near the fire, his balls a little heavier in anticipation. Heat curled in his lower back, licking its tongues of flames on his burgeoning lust.

She could resist him? He dug his fingers into his hair and kneaded his scalp. Let her resist him and see how far *that* would go. His fingers stopped as he caught up to his thoughts—this was only a role. He could *not* have her for true. She was a spy.

But what if she weren't? He could make this handfasting last past its allotted time. He was more than a companion for bed sport. He was more than a useless appendage to the clan. He'd prove it.

Voicing their suspicions in front of her to the chieftain had been a calculated risk. Her shock seemed genuine enough, and even if she were a spy, making her aware of their knowledge and feigned complacency could throw her machinations.

Doubt about winning her for true seeped into his mind, cloaking the small kernel within him that, against all reason and proof, was convinced of his worthiness. Now, standing naked before her, he no longer felt randy or cocksure. He felt exposed. For it was not in attracting the lasses that he failed—they were plentiful and eager. It was in the keeping.

An aching loneliness and a touch of bitterness rushed past his exposed vulnerability and settled in his gut. His erection drooped. But instead of feeling defeated, a new determination filled him at the challenge.

Once 'twas clear she was no Campbell spy, he'd prove his worth. Perhaps this time he'd change his approach. A slow siege instead of jumping to the pleasures to be had. Why not? Through the ten years he'd been falling in love, his usual approach had proven its ineffectiveness. True, he and his minx of a wife had already jumped to those pleasures, and he ached to again experience her lusty demands in bed, but perhaps they should begin anew.

He'd woo her, he would.

This approach would still allow him to fill the role the clan wished of him—keep her distracted while they planned their insurrection—but he'd get a head start on his plans to win her for true.

With that resolution, despite knowing her eyes remained on him, he gathered up his *fèileadh mòr*, shook it out, and spread it across the straw and heather pallet he'd arranged on the floor. He lay down so his back was to her—only scant feet behind him—and fell into a fitful sleep.

☙

IAIN PARRIED GAVIN'S strike with his targe and pushed him off-balance with a decisive kick to his hip. Gavin stumbled back and grinned.

"Again," Iain shouted, and they fell on each other with a clash of steel. He welcomed the abuse his muscles were taking on the sparring field. Anything to push aside his urge to seek out Traci. He'd vowed to hold back, and he wasn't sure he could last a day. He was that pathetic.

He roared, parried, thrust, and drove himself and his men to their physical limits. It was here, when he worked out with Duncan, Gavin, and a few others of his age that he felt most in control. Most in harmony.

"Enough," Gavin panted and drove his sword into the ground. "I yield."

Iain looked to Duncan, but he remained lounged against a tree. "Nay. You've worked me over enough this day."

Lochloinn shook his head at Iain's silent plea. "We're no match for you on a normal day, but today it's pointless."

They sprawled on the ground, their pants the only sound for a short while as they passed a flask of whisky.

Iain wiped his mouth. "Duncan, what do you know of Aenghus's widow?"

"Only that she's having a hard time feeding her little ones now her husband's gone."

Iain drew his *sgian-dubh* and flipped it into the air, catching it by its tip. "So I've heard as well. Why has not my uncle seen to assisting her?"

Gavin and Duncan grumbled. Lochloinn answered. "He claims our harvest this year was too meager."

Iain frowned. Even so… It was a chieftain's duty to share what little he had with his people. Their repast earlier today had not been one of a chieftain doing poorly.

e⁄ɔ

IN THE CASTLE'S courtyard, located on Island One, as she called it, Traci played with some of the children—a game very similar to ring toss—and took stock of her situation. Two days had passed since her arrival. Two days of doubt and anxiety and shit-did-I-do-the-right-thing.

True to the chieftain's word, he'd sent out a search party for her sister early yesterday morning. As they gathered before the gate, she'd avidly watched from her bedroom's window. Seeing them check their saddles, attach their belongings, and kiss loved ones goodbye, the energy of a fresh adventure was almost palpable, even from the height of her window. Almost, *almost* she stepped away to rush down and ask to join them, but she'd resisted. She'd do the mature thing and let them do what they did best. It left her directionless here, but that couldn't be helped. What was boredom and frustration next to her sister's welfare? When they rode through, she'd climbed up onto the battlements and watched them disappear into the green and rocky distance to the west, her hands gripped tight on the stone in front of her.

They had to find Fiona. They *had* to.

She'd poured her frustration into her morning workout routines. With a found piece of rope, she jumped rope and worked through the rest of her calisthenics routine. In the past, it had been the only thing keeping her from plumping up, but now it calmed her. The growth spurt she'd had in college had helped her shed the last of her baby fat, but she always felt as if she was shoveling sand out of a hole as far as her weight was concerned. Especially since she refused to eat only rabbit food.

Thankfully, Iain had kept his word and slept on the pallet the last two nights. She'd been surprised he hadn't been sent with the search party—Fiona knew him—but the uncle insisted he was needed here. She suspected it was to keep an eye on her, though she only saw Iain at meal times.

But it had been enough to revise her earlier assessment—it was only the uncle who didn't take Iain seriously. All the others—from his fellow warriors to the servants—treated him with respect.

The only time she'd been alone with him was last night when she again pretended to be asleep and watched him undress by the meager light. Lord, was he a yummy sight. From her spot behind the curtains, her face just behind the gap, she drank in the erotic display when he undressed and settled into his bed.

Side-by-side with the illicit thrill, however, was a deep, aching pull all along her skin. A pull that demanded she slip out of the bed and approach him, then tug him, falling and laughing, into the cocoon of her big, made-for-sexing, four-poster bed.

But she'd resisted this too. It made absolutely no sense getting involved with his type, even if he were in her own time. Nothing but trouble and heartache. His type was safe to flirt and have fun with but no more. Though it'd been a long, long time since she'd had to deal with one still knocking around in her life after they'd had sex. Each night, she fingered her ruby ring to remind herself what had happened the last time she'd succumbed to a flirt.

She tossed another metal ring to a ginger-haired boy with the cutest, roundest cheeks, whose turn was next. The children were easier to interact with; they had no expectations for her behavior. The others? Traci looked at the surrounding activity. Everyone seemed infused with purpose as they went about their tasks and chores, an invisible space enveloping her that they didn't cross. The feeling of being separate, in her own bubble, wasn't helped by the fact that she couldn't understand a word anyone was saying.

Another worry plagued her now. She'd woken up this morning remembering Katy's caution that if she stayed too long in the past, she might get visited by a Mr. Podbury. Katy had explained that he was a man who'd been studying time travel when Isabelle met him in 1834, and who must have succeeded, for he'd shown up in 1294 when he tried to take the case away from Katy.

The ginger-haired boy caught her toss and shrieked with unabashed laughter. His sound of happiness was dwarfed, however, by a commotion at the gate. Shouts erupted from the barbican, accompanied by the grinding gears of the ferry gate opening.

The kids dropped their toys in place with an endearing trust that they'd remain exactly where they'd left them and rushed toward the commotion. She gathered her skirts and followed at a slower pace.

Had they found Fiona already? Her heart, as well as her feet, picked up its pace, her skirts swishing between her legs. She pushed through the flow of clan members heading in the same direction, for once feeling in sync with those around her. But wasn't it too soon for them to have found her sister?

Oh God, maybe this whole nightmare trip—well, nightmare except for Iain—would soon be over. She'd hug Fiona, take her to her room in the castle, and with the silver case, zap them back to their own time. Where they belonged.

The possibility quickened her steps. At last, she broke through to the front and then stepped back to make way for the men of the returning party. Fingers crossed, she eagerly scanned the members.

Disappointment seized her heart—Fiona wasn't with them. She peered closer. These weren't the same men who'd left yesterday. In fact, they were smaller in number, with a man she'd swear looked like the one they called Ross. The one who'd chased her at the inn.

She couldn't run up and ask them what was going on, but she knew someone she could ask: Iain.

⚭

IAIN THOUGHT NOTHING of the returning party until the chieftain requested his attendance in his strong room. What could he possibly want? That party had split off from theirs at the inn to check on a tenant to the north. Besides, the chieftain was interrupting Iain's seduction plans. He'd kept away for over two nights and a day, which was as long as he could stretch his resolve for the slow wooing. For while he'd kept himself removed from her, he'd kept an eye on her—watching her movements, whom she interacted with. And was convinced she was no spy. He'd been about to interrupt her game of quoits when this summons had waylaid him.

Now he crossed to the strong room, wariness weighting his steps. Rarely was he brought in on clan discussions and decisions.

Unbidden, memories assaulted him of walking the same path as a wee lad to meet his father for one reckoning or another. His father had been a stern but fair chieftain. His uncle, however, was stern and erratic. Mistrustful. Nothing like his brother. Aye, his father had been fair—to others—but Iain had found him impossible to please, no matter how much he'd tried. His knees had been as weak as a newborn calf's on each and every walk to that strong room.

He always wondered why he'd given a damn. Perhaps because his father's approval was so unattainable—the exact opposite of his mother. His mother fed off of his antics, his gaiety, as if she needed it to keep her spirits lifted. Until there came a time when even he could no longer keep her happy. She now lived a retired life in a nunnery on the French coast.

Guilt swamped him. Iain's wish to please and impress his father had led to the man's death. No excuse existed for that, and there was no going back.

He shoved aside that old, but no less painful, memory and pushed open the strong room's door.

"You wished to see me, uncle?" He sauntered into the middle of the room and stood, hands behind his back, bravado squaring his shoulders.

"Yes. Have a seat." His uncle turned from the peat fire and settled behind the desk. Iain took the closest chair and fought the urge to shift in his seat while his uncle speared him with his sharp gaze.

The chieftain sighed. "I must acquaint you with the latest happenings. We appreciate you keeping your wife distracted so we may forward our plans to aid Dundee. As you were uncommonly quick to point out, having her here—and keeping her ignorant—would allay any suspicions the Earl of Argyll might entertain. Besides, it would go against the bounds of hospitality to ask her to leave."

Iain nodded. "Of course."

"But we require your assistance with a new matter."

Triumph and vindication coursed through Iain at this new level of trust with clan matters. He merely nodded, gripped the chair arms, and kept his features neutral in case the request—and trust—was laughably minor.

"Ross's party carried unwelcome news, which casts this whole business in a direction I like not." He sighed. "I regret we did not tell you sooner, but we're responsible for the disappearance of your wife's sister."

Shock froze him initially, but outrage lashed him immediately afterward. Again, he fought to keep his outward appearance calm. Only his foot jerked forward. "And how is that, sir?"

"Ross wanted those Campbell girls off our lands. He meant to take your wife too, but she disappeared before you could return to the room and distract her. At any rate, his party proceeded to Invergarry castle to put her in the MacDonell chief's safekeeping. She's there now."

They hadn't even confided in him? They'd asked him only to play the fool for his wife? He would feel bitter about it if it weren't so typical. They didn't trust him unless they had to, and it seemed that was as it always would be.

"So we may retrieve her. I shall inform Traci."

"Not so quick, my boy. Always so rash. Think this through. The MacDonell wants answers. Their appearance, at this moment when the summoning stick is spreading across the Highlands, is too coincidental."

"It could be innocent, as she claims."

His uncle slammed his hand onto the table. "I say it's suspicious, boy."

Iain ground his back teeth and pulled in a measured breath through his nose. "I'm not clear on what you wish of me." He was pleased to hear his voice held none of the pain he felt at their betrayal.

His uncle and chieftain leaned farther forward, bringing his mighty personality to bear across the table. The air fairly crackled with his erratic authority. "I wish for you to use your considerable…persuasive powers to discover the truth. Discover their true purpose on MacDonell lands."

Shock coursed through him, and a chill raced down his spine. "You wish me to torture my own wife?" This time his voice came out strained.

His uncle glared at him. "Nay, you idiot. Use your famous charm. Legend has it women routinely melt around you. The spitting image of your father in looks and charm, you are. Use what you're good for, and get the truth. The summoning stick was clear—all clans need to join with Dundee at Struan. We're to be there by the twenty-ninth of July to secure Blair Castle against those loyal to King William. We cannot afford any word of this reaching government forces. Which means, no Campbells."

Iain gritted his teeth, but he stood and nodded. Resentment was a familiar but bitter taste in his mouth. "Aye, I will do as you bid, uncle."

"Exercise some discretion, will you, and keep her ignorant of your aim. Her presence is an inconvenience, since we need to send men to Dundee's rendezvous in Struan. Yesterday's search party went straight to Struan, with her none the wiser to our true motives, but I no longer have that excuse."

Inwardly he rocked at this latest revelation. Christ on the cross, it wasn't a mere revelation—'twas a betrayal. He'd *assured* his wife—in several conversations, no less—that his clan had been doing their best to find her sister. His clan had made a *liar* of him. The muscles all along his shoulders and neck tightened.

Outwardly, he granted his chieftain only a bow and the words, "I'm sorry you no longer have that excuse."

His uncle narrowed his eyes, but then waved to the door. "Off with you. Find out what she's hiding."

Iain strode to the door, though anger made his legs jerky. He'd wished to seek his wife to lay down a foundation for a future. But now he had to seek her out, yet again, to play the fool and get secrets from her?

Curse his uncle.

Chapter Nine

With soft down of thistles I'll make him a bed,
With lilies and roses I'll pillow his head,
And with my tun'd harp I will lead
To sweet and soft slumbers my laddie.
"My laddie," *Jacobite Reliques*

NOT MUCH LATER, Iain found Traci in the courtyard playing with the wee ones as was her wont during the day. Use his bloody charm?

Nay. He'd be direct, as the son of a chieftain should be. Directness was the virtue and the failing of his own father. Until now, Iain had never paid heed to the contrast between the ruling style of his father and that of his uncle. His uncle was only direct when it suited.

Though would the directness put Traci off him? He was tired of this aimless, lonely existence. The ache and conviction grew more acute whenever he caught sight of her playing with the bairns in the courtyard. He wished for wee ones of his own to care for and protect and a wife with whom to share them.

He thinned his lips. Blast it. Charm. His uncle was right. It was the surest way to gain the information he sought. While it galled, he'd do his duty. He'd not turn aside one of the few, paltry times the clan entrusted him with a task.

Some bluebells twisted through the dirt near the courtyard wall, and he snatched a fistful. He swept them behind his back and approached his wife. Young Griogair held one of her fingers and looked upon her with open admiration. Iain could fully sympathize with the lad. Would a boy of theirs have her shade of hair?

She bent over, whispering encouragement to the lad if his face was any indication, and the position outlined her delicious rump.

Ah, God. He *was* a useless sod. At the mere site of a luscious, feminine behind, his thoughts darted immediately to the carnal—to his hands gripping her hips, her bent over… Could he not stay focused for five minutes on clan business?

Stiffening his resolve, and attempting to *un*stiffen a particular piece of his anatomy, he stepped up behind her as she rose to her full height. He swept her hair from one shoulder to the other, presented his flowers in front of her, and whispered in her ear, "Care for a wee walk?"

He was gladdened to hear his voice sounded natural and not rife with the tension which tightened his limbs, but his whole body screamed at the unnaturalness. This was *not* right.

That same shimmer of awareness vibrated through him whenever he was inches from her, and he witnessed her involuntary tremble. It was as if the attraction, which vibrated between them while apart, gathered up tighter and tighter as they neared until it pushed against him when he was this close.

Her hand covered his, soft skin against rough skin, and she grabbed the cluster of flowers. She stepped away and faced him.

His heart clutched anew as he beheld her in the daylight. Her height brought her to his chin—no need to stoop at a neck-breaking angle to kiss this woman. Her light blue dress adorned her curves, and his hands fair itched to trace the dips and hollows of her luscious flesh.

He pasted on the smile he knew from experience made the lasses lean involuntarily closer. And…*there*—she started to list forward, but then she stood straighter, catching herself. *Smart lass. You shouldn't trust me.*

"Shall we?" He held out his arm, and she looked upon it in confusion. Then she shook herself and awkwardly placed her hand on his arm. Was she not used to being escorted about by a gentleman? He clasped her hand and tucked it into position, pressing her tight. That it brought her body snug against his side was an added bonus. God, just her scent—an enticing combination of lemon, lavender, and an earthy tang unique to her—was going to drive him barmy.

Since it was an unusually clear and warm day, he ferried her across the short stretch of water, and they strolled down the causeway and along the shore of Loch Garry, dodging around the grazing cattle.

Oddly, she stared at the cows as if unused to such a sight. A burgh lass then?

He cleared his throat. "How are you adjusting to life here, wife?"

"Well enough, I guess. Though I miss Fiona." She kicked a tuft of grass as they walked. "Who were those men? Did they have any news about my sister?"

He couldn't bring himself to lie to her, so he sought a diversion.

"You wound me. I seek to accompany you on a lovely stroll to wash away the cares of the day, and you choose such a sobering topic."

"Well, it is the topic uppermost on my mind."

He stopped and pulled her around to face him. "Uppermost? Are ye certain?" He stroked his finger down her cheek, and her breath hitched in a gratifying manner. Aye, she could deny the attraction, but it was there. He brushed his finger along her jaw and grazed the pad of his thumb across her plump lower lip. She stubbornly aimed her gaze away, so he bent his knees slightly and shifted to follow. Her warm brown eyes latched onto his, and their breaths came shorter. Slowly he straightened, keeping her gaze on him, and continued to stroke her kissable lips. And speaking of kissing…

He lowered his head, his heart beating madly, and watched every shift and movement for any sign she didn't welcome his kiss. But, dear God, he saw none.

Triumph and dread roared through his body in equal measure, for he ached to touch his lips to hers, to feel their softness, to taste her sweetness, but he worried it was too soon. Always he rushed his fences, and lately he wondered if that was the reason for his reputation.

His lips came within a hair's width of hers, and he felt as if he were crossing an unseen barrier. Again, his body screamed to breach that barrier, while his mind screamed it was too early.

Her lovely eyes fluttered closed.

Blast it. He pulled in a breath and brushed his lips once, twice against hers. A tentative overture, but unspeakably more intimate than he'd ever imagined. He eased his palm up her neck and clasped the back of her head. Her silky hair brushed his knuckles, and he pressed his mouth more firmly to hers.

She moaned and edged closer. On a slight hitch of her breath, she parted her lips. Never one to deny an invitation so generously given, he stroked his tongue past her delectable lips to taste her, to rediscover the exact recipe of her sweetness. Her tongue touched his, and blood rushed through his ears. So sweet. So, so sweet.

Yes. This. Her.

His hand tightened against her head, and he angled her closer. All thoughts of his blasted uncle and his blasted demands fled in the face of a new demand. He groaned, clasped her waist with his other hand, yanked her flush with his hips. Need ravaged through him, firing his blood. Dear God, he couldn't get enough of her.

Flashes of their heated encounter at the inn crashed through him as her scent and taste filled and consumed him. He welcomed the flood of sensual images, for he'd been unable to recall all of it from being too far gone in his cups.

But her scent, her taste unlocked *everything*, and he remembered this, how they fit together. Perfectly. In sync. Each stroke of his tongue more urgent than the last. She matched him, stroke for stroke, and delight and lust spun tighter when her hand scratched into his hair. She held his own head just as tightly as he held hers, as if she too couldn't get enough.

Yes.

He inched his hand from her hip and up her lush curves until the notch between his thumb and finger bumped into the underside of her luscious breast. The heat and weight of her rested just above his fingers— he yearned to turn his wrist and follow her plumpness, have the whole, delicious weight of it solid in his hand—but he sensed this would be another barrier to cross. He should stay and dwell in this moment and plumb its depths.

Amazing. Discovering these defined moments now in his life. If he crossed it, and she allowed it, they'd be down in the heather until he was stroking in and out of her in a fevered rush, taking his pleasure, giving her pleasure, searing past all the barriers, all the moments.

He yanked on all the threads of his control. Perhaps he could still not only do as his uncle bade, but also win his lady. He slowly parted their lips and rested his forehead against hers. Her fingers curled against his scalp, stinging him as a few hairs twisted in her grasp. Their breaths filled his ears, and her eyes were screwed shut.

But need, lust, demand rushed through his blood like an insistent force and pulsed in the air surrounding them, thickening the space between their bodies.

He closed his hands tightly at her sides, shut his eyes, and drew in a long, shuddering breath. His hands crept down to the small of her back and nudged her against his hardened cock.

The mission. The mission, you numbskull.

He jerked his hands back to her waist and curled them back into tight fists.

"So, my wife. What's your true aim?" He winced. That was not subtle. But he'd never claimed to be an expert at this subterfuge business. And by all that was holy, she scrambled his brains to porridge.

She pulled in a harsh breath and backed away, taking her heat with her. His body felt empty without her pressed along his front. The awareness that had swelled between them sputtered.

"What do you mean?" Her voice contained not a hint of passion, but rather suspicion and mortification. The last wisps of erotic possibilities puffed away at her tone.

Ah, well, there was nothing for it. "Merely that my uncle wishes to know your true reason for being on our lands."

She fisted her hands at her sides, a crimson blush flushing her neck and cheeks, his pathetic flowers drooping at her hip. "That's the reason for…for *this?*" She waved between them. "This is still about that spy nonsense? You believe him? And you were trying to seduce the answer from me?"

Ach, he'd muddled this for sure.

He stepped toward her, and she stepped away, her gaze wary. A furious blush rose in her cheeks.

His ineptitude made him restless. "Come, let us head back to the keep."

"No. I want to get to the bottom of this." Hurt laced her voice. "Did you bring me out here on purpose to soften me up for questions?" She straightened the arm holding the flowers, which brushed against her leg, and looked at him, her expression unreadable.

"Nay! I mean, aye. Not really."

She pursed her lips and crossed her arms, the blooms taking a further beating. "Which is it? You're not making sense."

"Aye, I was tasked with questioning you."

She flinched as if he'd struck her a physical blow. Damn if her reaction didn't cause him to feel as if he'd been struck as well. "And you figured it would be easier to kiss me first, I take it." Fury blazed from her eyes. "Typical."

Frustration and inadequacy to the task at hand further heightened his restlessness. He ached to soothe her hurt. The hurt he'd inflicted.

"Nay. If you'd allow me to finish…" He stepped forward again, and he took it as a sign of progress that she didn't retreat this time. "That kiss…" He swallowed. "That kiss was real. To me it was. It might have happened sooner than I'd planned—"

"Wait. What? What do you mean? You have things planned out, do you? Unbelievable." She turned to the side.

"You're twisting my words."

"They're your words, Iain." She speared him with her fierce gaze from over her shoulder. The way she angled her chin down matched the tilt of her eyes and brows, making her appear to be a fierce but lovely hawk.

"You're willfully misconstruing their meaning. There's nothing sinister happening with me. I'm a simple man, and the truth is, I find you very attractive. With the emphasis on 'very.' What happened was a result of that attraction. Which, I believe, is mutual." He raked his gaze down and up her length. "Try to deny it."

When she remained silent, triumph surged through him before he soberly remembered that was not where he usually failed. It was in convincing a lass he had substance, and right now he was failing at that. Miserably.

Instead of responding to his question, she raised her chin. "What does your uncle want to know? And I think now you'll explain whether this…" She waved between them. "…and the questions about me have anything to do with the party of men that just arrived."

"Their arrival did prompt the renewed interest from my uncle, who simply can't believe you and your sister are on our lands for innocent reasons. And I have to admit, 'tis rather strange. Especially since you are not commoners and so require chaperones."

"How do you know we're not commoners?"

"Your hands are smooth—unfamiliar with the hard labor that make the youngest hands turn old before their time. Your speech, while oddly accented, is educated. Also, 'tis obvious you are more familiar with the city than the country, and it's been my experience that lasses who are raised and work for a living in the city are shorter and more sickly looking. You have the health and height of someone who has eaten well for the entirety of your life."

She looked a bit taken aback by that assessment. And when he'd said "eaten well," she'd drawn herself taller and sucked in her stomach, as if self-conscious.

"I'm not fat."

Now it was his turn to be taken aback. "Did I say you were? Nay. You are quite shapely in all the right places." He raked his gaze down her form again until she stomped her foot.

She snapped her fingers in front of him. "Eyes up here, Romeo."

"Iain. And where were we?"

"My sister?" She said each word distinctly, as if she were losing patience with him. Ach, maybe she was.

"Ah, yes. So, you see, I've been tasked to find out why you're *truly* here."

She looked up to the sky as if praying for patience. "I already told you. We're here enjoying our leisure time."

"With no chaperone or escort?"

"Yes," she ground out.

He took a deep breath. He hated to do this, but this *was* why his chieftain had tasked him with this chore. "I'm sorry, my wife, but I don't believe you. Besides the improbability of what you say, you're keeping something back. I can sense it."

She whirled around and stepped away a few paces, arms still crossed. She rubbed a spot in the ground with the toe of her shoe, her back stiff with tension. That action alone confirmed his guess—she *was* keeping something from them. From him.

His instincts had been right. A weighty decision held her in its clasp. Whether to trust him, he felt certain.

A strange elation lifted him at the thought of her, of anyone, trusting him with something obviously serious, if her demeanor were any indication.

She spun around, determination written across her face, the wind teasing one dark red strand from her braid and fluttering it against her pale neck. Right where he'd like to nuzzle. Lucky hair.

"Okay. I'll tell you." Her voice was equal parts fierce and vulnerable. "But you have to promise me you won't tell anyone else. Not even your chieftain."

He almost opened his mouth to agree, so excited was he by her trust, but he caught himself in time. "I can't promise this. What if it places my clan in danger? My duty is to them."

She cocked her head and looked him up and down. "What about to your wife?"

Oh, she played dirty, his wife. "Are we married in truth in your heart?"

She hesitated but finally shook her head.

Pain lanced through him, though her denial wasn't a surprise.

"Then you'll understand that until such is the case, my duty is to my clan first, and then to you. But know that I will protect you and will keep your secret, as long as it does not place them in danger."

Her gaze focused on the horizon, and she chewed her lower lip. She looked down, her shoulders slumping. "I suppose that's all I can expect. I don't think my secret puts them in danger, so you should be able to keep it."

"That sounds fair."

She stepped toward him and worried her lip some more. She looked to the side and then down to the ground.

"What is it?"

"I'm getting to it," she said, her voice containing a bit of an edge. "It's just that it's really big, and it also puts *my* life in danger if you don't believe me."

She was serious, and he ached to be that man who could be looked to for important matters. He placed his hands on her shoulders. "Look at me." He stroked his thumb under her chin and directed her face upward to his. "I'll not put your life in danger, even if I don't believe you."

She swallowed so hard he heard it. She nodded and took a deep breath. "Okay. Oh boy." She stepped away, letting his hands fall. "See, the reason we just appeared and have no better explanation is that we're from…" She took another deep breath and stiffened, as if strengthening her defense, her resolve. "We're from the future," she finished in a rush of breath.

Chapter Ten

Let Sol curb his coursers, and stretch out the day,
That time may not hinder carousing and play...
"My Laddie," *Jacobite Reliques*

O H GOD. OH God. Oh God.

Traci's heart pounded as if it had only seconds to beat and was trying to squeeze out every last bit of life while it could. Jesus Christ, she'd just up and blurted that out, hadn't she? Just...just plopped her trust into his hands. But so much of what she needed to accomplish depended on his cooperation. And to be thought a spy? Not helping.

Iain's eyes widened, and he cocked his head. "I'm...I'm not sure I ken. What do you mean, you're from the future?"

Fear bloomed, and goose bumps pebbled across her skin. No going back. "I'm not from Cornwall, like I said earlier. I'm not even from this time. This is the year 1689, correct?"

He nodded slowly, his eyes narrowing.

"Well, I'm from about three hundred years in the future. My sister and I are. We, er, we used this magical device to wish ourselves to this time for a bet, and, well...now she's missing, and I need to find her so we can return to our own time where we belong."

He frowned, took a step back, and crossed his arms. "Let me see if I understand. You somehow magically came back in time to ours? From three hundred years in the future?"

"Thereabouts, yes."

"Using magic?"

"Yes."

His lips thinned, and he swept his gaze down her body and back up. "Are ye a witch?"

She stepped back. "No! Neither of us are. And that's precisely what I'm afraid of. I can't risk people accusing us of witchcraft."

He cocked an eyebrow. "Do you have a bit of the *sithiche* in you then?" His voice sounded genuinely curious.

"Shee-what?"

"Faeries, I think you English call them. They've been known to muddle with our folk."

"Our folk?"

"Aye, humans."

He was completely serious, and it almost made her laugh, seeing this tall, muscular warrior of a Highlander discussing faeries with such a straight face. "Er, I don't think so. Though we don't know how the artifact got its properties."

"So you came through one of the standing stones," he whispered. "There have been tales, but I'd never met such a traveler." He looked at her with awe clear on his face.

Wow. This was going better than she thought. "You mean like Stonehenge?"

"I know not of that one, but there are many stone circles that still dot our land."

Now she did laugh, the relief was so acute. "No. We didn't use one of the stone circles. It's a little silver calling card case. I can show you. I have it stashed away with my things in my—our—room. I also brought proof, in case you don't believe me." That was one of the things she'd made sure to secure before she left her time. Just in case.

He strode away from her and then whirled back to stare. "It's hard to credit, to be sure, but it makes a certain sense. Is that where you got the idea that each clan had a specific tartan? Do we do that in the future?"

"Yes. Each one claims a certain pattern."

"Amazing. That *would* make it easier to distinguish in battle."

"How do you do that now?"

"Each clan has a specific plant. We pin a sprig of it to our bonnets before battle."

Yikes. That seemed a bit tough. Would certainly take an extra moment to discern an enemy.

She shook her head. "We're getting off track. I can show you proof of my story."

He waved his hand. "No need. Though I would dearly love to satisfy my curiosity, I believe you."

"You do?" Relief ran through her so quickly, her knees loosened a bit. "Thank God."

"Though we should refrain from telling my clan. I'll do my best to convince them you're not a spy."

"Thank you." She took a deep breath. "What about my sister?"

"Aye, fuck." He marched away, his strides short and deliberate as if he were angry. His clan's castle filled the horizon behind him.

Dread curdled in her stomach. There was something he knew. Knew about Fiona. And something told her it wasn't good.

☙

IAIN CROSSED HIS arms and peered at the battlements that protected the castle. His home. The home of his clan, his only family.

And debated what to tell this woman.

Aye, he believed her. Tales were not few of time-walkers, though they went through the stones. But this required a more weighty consideration than he normally gave.

If she were lying, if she were a Williamite spy, his careless decision to trust her would put his whole clan in danger.

Perhaps he *should* see this proof of hers. Too much was at stake, and he couldn't allow another decision of his to endanger his clan.

He should do the rational thing and demand to see this proof, no matter how much doing so might hurt her pride. Playing the fool, as long as it didn't hurt anyone but himself, was fine. But actually *being* a fool and risking his family? His clan?

Nay. He'd deprived them of his father, their chieftain, by his tom-foolery. He'd not do that again, if he could help it.

And he would *not* dwell on her assertion she was planning to return to her time.

But, *torr caca*. Would taking away his belief in her ruin his chances to win her heart? He'd appear fickle. Frustration lanced through him, and he glared at the beloved contours of his family's stronghold.

No matter.

He whirled around and stalked back toward her. Again, he placed his hands on her shoulders and caught her gaze.

"I find I *do* require this proof of yours." He tapped his heart. "I feel it here that you tell me the truth. Please believe me." His voice cracked a wee bit on the last three words. He swallowed and held her gaze, wordlessly willing her to hear him out. "However, it's too important for me to trust my feelings in this. Especially with you concerned. Forgive the crudeness, but how do I know it's not my cock ruling my head? Nay. For once, I need to do this right. Do you understand? And can you forgive me?"

Her eyes grew rounder, and she swallowed. "Of course. Believe me, when it comes to wanting to make the right decision, and worrying about trusting your gut, I totally get it."

"Get it?"

She placed her wee hand over his, which still rested against his heart. "Er, I completely understand."

Relief washed through him. "That eases my mind. Truly." Seeking to lighten the mood, he asked, "So you make poor decisions too?"

She pulled away with a soft chuckle and looked skyward. "Oh, jeez, do I ever. Coming here was probably my biggest. It's my fault we even came here. My sister is missing because of me. But, yeah. Especially with my family, I just can never seem to do things right in their eyes." She returned her gaze to his. "No, that's not quite right. It's not that my decisions are usually piss-poor, it's just that…the decisions I make for myself are not the ones they want me to make. To *them*, I make piss-poor decisions. Anyway, the proof is in our room."

He held out his arm and tucked her hand in its crook. A new awareness suffused him as she nestled against his side—one of kinship in understanding. He chuckled. "It seems we share something in common in a way, for I'm the family bumbler."

Her hand tightened on his arm, and she looked at him in surprise, which gladdened his heart. "How so?"

"Let's just say that, like you, I can't seem to make a correct decision where they're concerned. I don't even bother trying anymore, and they let me have the freedom which comes from no responsibility, as long as I stay out of clan business."

Though he spoke his words with a light tone, resentment weighed heavy in his heart. He'd been a mere lad when his father had been killed. Killed when Iain hadn't taken their reiving party serious enough—treated it as a lark—and got his father, the chieftain, killed.

The last words his father said as the blood drained from his body still echoed through Iain's heart, his mind: *Can't you take anything serious, lad?*

By now they'd reached the gate at the end of the causeway, and they remained silent lest anyone overhear their speech. It wouldn't do to have anyone hear of her origins until—*if*—it was necessary.

They edged around several pigs rooting in a patch of mud, and all the while he kept a tight hold on her arm, their strides matching as they crossed the courtyard.

It hit him then. He was escorting a lady who had traveled back in time. His wife!

Another possibility followed as quickly—could she know the outcome of their planned rebellion? Could her knowledge aid his clan? If she could save them from grief, from coming to any harm, he'd risk much for her.

Suddenly, he couldn't wait till they were alone in their room. And not for the usual reason.

Mayhap she held the key for restoring—who the hell was he kidding—*placing* him in a position of honor with his clan.

That position, which he'd always scoffed at needing or wanting, was very important now that 'twas possible.

A new sense of purpose, of possibility, flooded him, making his steps light.

Chapter Eleven

And when James again shall be plac'd on the throne,
All mem'ry of ills we have borne shall be gone.
No tyrant again shall set foot on our shore,
But all shall be happy and blest as before.
"Come, Let Us Be Jovial," *Jacobite Reliques*

BACK IN THEIR room, Traci strode into the latrine, which "graced" the corner of their room. She stuck her arm through the hole in the wooden bench and grasped the small sack she'd tied to the underside. She'd been surprised the first time she'd used the room that there was no smell, for it emptied straight into the loch.

Her larger bag, she'd kept under the bed since having one hadn't been a secret. It held her period clothes and her supplies, though the latter were disguised as seventeenth-century items—precautionary painkillers in a cloudy glass bottle with a stopper, for instance.

She straightened. Iain's head jerked up from blatant butt ogling, and his lips curved, his eyes sparkling with a yeah-ye-caught-me glint. She smirked back and brushed past him, settling herself before the warmth of the peat fire. She pulled out the contents from her secret bag, arranging them on the rug. She picked up her phone, which she'd tucked inside a leather case with a lock.

She couldn't blame Iain for wanting proof. And when he'd been so anxious for her forgiveness when he told her he couldn't trust his heart? Part of the wall around *her* heart cracked. He'd seemed so earnest. But scariest of all, she'd glimpsed a different person behind his devil-may-care attitude. Someone just a little vulnerable.

Iain stood warily by the fireplace, and she waved him over. He eased down beside her, his warmth and scent enveloping her, and their knees touched. He caught her gaze, his eyes a combination of wariness and excitement.

Taking a deep breath, she pushed the power button on her phone and waited for it to boot. The logo flashed onto the screen, and Iain gasped. He leaned closer, and she caught his scent more fully—so intoxicating.

Argh. No.

Highland men were *not* intoxicating. Iain was *not* intoxicating. *None* of this was intoxicating. She would find Fiona and get their modern butts back where they belonged.

After the screen lit up with its icons, Traci retrieved a photo of her standing in front of the same inn where she'd met Iain, but in her own time.

While the building hadn't changed substantially, she'd made sure to include people in the background, a car, its gas station, and the modern sign.

"What is this?" Iain grasped the phone from her hand and peered closer. He stared at her and back at the screen, his eyes wide. "It's a rendering of you. The detail…"

"Yes. Like a painting, but it's done with a…machine. It captures what was in front of it at the time. We call it a camera. So that's me, standing in front of the inn, but in my time, not yours. In my time, it's called the Cluanie Inn. Look closely."

Iain frowned and peered closer. His finger touched the screen, and he jerked back.

"Oh. Sorry. You accidentally switched it to another image."

"It appears to be another image very similar to the earlier one, though your face looks different."

"Yeah," she grumbled. "That wasn't a good shot. I should have deleted it." She reached over and switched it back to the other image. "See the inn? And see how it's changed? It's the same building…" She went on to explain the other objects and the clothes.

"You mean to say that women traipse about in such scanty apparel in your time? I believe I would like that."

She pushed his shoulder. "I bet you would." She leaned over and switched it to several photos back. "If that doesn't convince you, how about this?"

"Oh, Mary Mother!" Iain gasped and dropped the phone, which hit the rug with a dull *thud*. She'd taken a picture of him and Duncan while no one was looking. It'd captured him while he was laughing at something Duncan had said, though the scene was dark because she hadn't used a flash. "That's…that's me." With trembling fingers, he picked up the phone again, pushed it farther away, and then closer. "Uncanny," he whispered. "How does this work?"

"It'd be too complicated to explain, but this contraption captures what it sees at the push of a button. Watch." She took the phone from him, held it up, and snapped a picture of the two of them. She brought it close for him to see.

He backed away, falling back to rest on his hands. "It's scary how accurate that is. Finer than any painter." His voice held only awe.

His face went blank, the muscles in his jaw bunching. "Enough." He shoved to his feet and strode to the lone window, resting his fists against the window ledge. "I believe you." He inhaled and blew out a sharp breath. "Which means neither you nor your sister are spies."

He whirled back around, his face strangely hopeful. "Does this mean you know the outcome of historical events?"

She stood and brushed off her skirt. "Er. Only for really major ones. History is not my strong suit."

"Strong suit? Never mind. I take your meaning." He shoved away from the window, hands fisted at his sides. "Can you tell me if we put the Stuarts back on the throne?"

She shifted and stared off to the side. Ha. Yes, she *did* know the answer to that. "I...I can't tell you."

"Because you don't know, or because you won't tell me."

She looked him in the eyes. "Look. I can't risk telling you. I don't know how this time travel business works. It's not exactly something that's been tested out. Some believe that if history is changed, it could change enough to where I was never born, or worse, some important person isn't born. Others think it's all one closed loop, so that anything I do now was already done by me by the time I'm born. There are many more theories, each more confusing than the other, and it's all just theories. I can't take that risk, because I have *no clue* which time travel theories apply here."

He looked at her, his head cocked to the side.

She smiled. "I know. If I think too hard about it, I feel this heavy, buzzy weight at the top of my head. It's a freaky, weird feeling."

"Aye. It is." He rubbed the crown of his head and smiled. "So, you can't risk revealing anything in case that blinks you out of existence."

"Er, yes. Obviously, I'd like for that not to happen, but I know that's not important on the big scale of things."

"I'd not like to see you blink out either, my wife. Though it's a shame you cannot tell me of the Stuarts' fate, for it would help my clan." He frowned. "Nay. Not worth the risk. Right then."

"Exactly. Now you know why I have to find my sister and return to my time. Neither of us belongs here. It's too risky." Katy's friend Isabelle had stayed behind for her man, but—no. This girl liked her hot showers. Besides, she knew staying here—*in his presence*—any longer than necessary was going to play havoc with her emotions. One-night stands with guys like him were fine, but longer than that? It made her expectations go haywire. She'd accidentally gone there on a rebound from her first serious boyfriend in college—hooked up with a gaming buddy, notorious for his love-em-and-leave-em outlook, and mortifyingly fell for him after a short while. *Oops.*

Iain frowned, but when he didn't protest their leaving, she felt an odd sense of disappointment. Just as she suspected, he wasn't interested in more than flirtation. *And neither was she!*

He crossed his arms. "We need to figure out what to do about your sister."

"What do you know? You didn't answer my question earlier."

He stepped toward her, his face wary. "Now 'tis your turn not to be angry with me. I swear to you, I was not informed of my clan's role until today when my uncle deigned to tell me. And *that*," he said with a bitter laugh, "was only because he wanted information from you."

Shit. She stepped up onto the bed and sat, face in the palms of her hands. "Just tell me."

"That night at the inn, it was the other half of my party who took your sister. Ross meant to take you too, but you disappeared." He barked a laugh. "Now I can guess how."

"What could they have possibly wanted with us?" She dragged her hands from her face.

"To get you out of the way, mainly. You were strangers, poorly disguised as commoners, and cursed with the last name of Campbell, which they overheard when we handfasted. You might not be aware, but there is no other Highland name that could have made you more suspicious. Campbells have become too powerful, and they support the new regime. Ross thought 'twould be better to take you to the chief of the Glengarry MacDonells for safekeeping until…"

"Until what?"

"Now I must ask for *your* secrecy. I'm placing a great trust in you, and…" He broke off and spun back to the window. His hands were flexing, as was a muscle in his jaw.

She shifted forward. "What? Iain, I swear to you, I won't hurt your clan."

c/3

IAIN STARED OUT the chamber window. As far as his eye could track, he beheld only his clan's land. Land that had been governed by successive sons. Until him.

His heart and his mind battled with what to do next. If he trusted her—and against all logic he did—and he was *wrong*...

His clan would never forgive him this time.

They'd barely forgiven him the last time. Only his youth had tempered their judgment.

Always, always, he let his emotions and his gut rule him, and time and again, those decisions proved defective. At the time they seemed harmless, but...

He glanced over his shoulder at his wife. The murky daylight cast her in part shadow, but her eyes were riveted to his, and he saw only honesty and forthrightness in their depths. He felt an inexplicable pull to her, as if her truth were his.

He shook his head. It made no sense.

Och, God. Could he do it? Put his clan at risk. On a decision he made on his own?

He sifted through everything she'd told him, taking care to measure each statement, each inflection she gave her words.

And—piss on a goat—he couldn't find any falseness in her manner or her words. This "time travel" was the only explanation, not only for her sudden appearance, but also for the magical items she'd shown him. Those renderings on the small contraption...

He closed his eyes and tilted his head upward. *Everything* about this felt right to him.

He opened his eyes and contemplated her beautiful face, the air between them weighted with significance. Hell, if he were wrong, could any hot-blooded male blame him? Maybe he was the idiot his uncle believed of him. But she was his woman now, and he'd be damned if he didn't do all he could to protect and aid her.

Lord help him, he'd side with his gut. He'd side with *her*.

He took a long breath and stepped forward. "They took her—and

81

tasked me with keeping you distracted—because we're in the midst of crucial plans to return the rightful king to his throne."

"King James," she whispered.

"Aye. Dundee has been gathering men to test our might against the Williamites, led by Mackay."

"And your chieftain thought we were sent by the…by the Williamites to learn what your plans are?"

"You have the right of it there."

"So my sister is with the MacDonells of…of Glengarry?"

He swallowed hard. "Aye."

She gasped and shoved off the bed. "I have to get her," she said in a rush. "I have to help her." She dashed to her sack and stuffed her belongings inside. She straightened. "Wait. If your clan knew where she was, what was all this about sending out a party to look for her?"

He refused to look away from her. He wasn't the guilty party here, though he felt like it. It was his chieftain. "We had to maintain appearances. And it gave us the cover to send some men to Dundee."

"Your chieftain lied to me about helping search for Fiona."

Shame washed through him. Aye, they'd needed to keep their movements secret from newcomers, but he hated that it was at her expense and that his chieftain had not told her that her sister was safe. "Aye. He did."

"I don't know that I care for your chieftain." She stopped, gripping her sack in her fist. Her stare ripped through him. "Did you know this was their plan? You told me yourself they were sent to look for my sister, and I…I believed you."

"I swear to you, I knew not. I learned of this directly before I found you today."

She nodded and tightened the string, which closed up the opening of her sack. Inexplicably, his chest tightened at how easily she took him at his word. It made him proud and scared at the same time.

"I need to go to her. I don't care if you or anyone else comes, and I won't let any of you stop me this time. I'm the only hope she has of returning to our time. She *needs* me."

She rushed past him for the door, and he grabbed her arm, swinging her back around to face him, bumping her against the bed frame.

"Don't be so bloody hasty. I'm coming with ye," he said fiercely. "But let's do this right. I need to convince the chieftain of your innocence and get permission to retrieve her. It will do us no good to make an enemy of him."

She plopped onto the edge of the bed and blew at a strand of hair that had fallen in her face. Her shoulders slumped. "Okay. You're right. But you can't tell your chieftain our secret."

"Aye, I ken."

"If you can't convince him, I'm sneaking out of here. You can't stop me, Iain."

"I will not try. Have no fear." Hell, he'd aid her in her escape. "If all goes well, we can leave soon. Invergarry castle is not far, and we can be there before dusk."

She took a deep breath, and he'd swear her eyes glistened with unshed tears. She dropped her bag, which hit the rug with a dull *thunk*. "We have to get her, Iain," she whispered.

His heart cracked open a little wider. In an instant, he closed the distance between them and enfolded her in his arms. He placed a comforting hand atop her head and rested his chin there. "We'll get her, my wife. We'll get her. Dinnae fash yourself. And take comfort in knowing she is safe for now. We know where she is."

The weight of his decision, and its implications for his clan if he were wrong, hung heavy in the air. He could almost taste it.

There was no going back now.

No going back on his trust of her.

And more than anything, he couldn't escape the fact that this felt *right*.

Chapter Twelve

Yet friendship sincere, and loyalty true,
And for courage so bold that no foe can subdue,
Unmatch'd is our country, unrivall'd our swains,
And lovely and true are the nymphs of our plains,
Where rises the thistle, the thistle so green.
"The Thistle of Scotland," *Jacobite Reliques*

IAIN STEPPED AROUND the men playing dice in the great hall and rubbed his belly. He'd detoured to the kitchen, for they were leaving for Invergarry before the hour was out, and procured two flagons of deoch-maidne. The afternoon was late, but as the distance was not great, they should reach their destination before dusk.

A strange energy suffused him, and he couldn't quite pinpoint its source. All he knew was that he was eager to begin their journey. Perhaps it was the prospect of Traci being forced into closer proximity, but he felt it was more than that. Perhaps it was only a sense of accomplishment—he'd managed to allay his uncle's suspicions after all. No small feat, that.

A little niggle crept inside that it had been a little *too* easy, given his uncle's suspicions.

As he approached the double doors which led outside, a shadow darted from the side, and a hand closed around his arm, halting him. He looked down into the dark eyes of his chieftain.

"Don't botch this up, lad."

Iain stiffened at his uncle's words, as well as the tone. However, he forced one of his trademark smiles onto his face, though the darkness enclosing the large space probably made it difficult to discern. "How can I? Seems a straightforward business to me. One that even a *donnart* such as myself would be hard-pressed to botch." He added a self-deprecating laugh.

His uncle narrowed his eyes. "You are leading this party. Please take it seriously. I only pray you're right about these women. Retrieve the sister and bring her here. 'Tis better to have them together in case you're wrong." He shoved a parchment into his hand. "Here is the letter for Glengarry with my thoughts on the matter so your way will be clear."

In that moment, Iain pinpointed the source of his unusual energy—'twas the prospect of leading this party. Which was a puzzle. Iain had never taken himself for a leader of men. Hell, he'd been glad when his uncle had stepped in as chieftain after Iain's brother died while fighting Campbells. Better to have no one dependent on him, he'd reasoned— less chance of him messing up anyone else's life.

This time it was harder to hide his annoyance, his tone hard-edged. Especially in light of the gossip he'd overheard from the kitchen maids—more evidence that his uncle was stingy. Good chieftains looked after *all* under their care and did not hoard the clan's wealth. "I believe I shall manage, uncle."

"I pray that you do. It was fortunate for our clan that you had no taste for leadership. Some have the taste, but not the skill. And their clans suffer for it."

Iain's lips thinned, and he gave a stiff nod. "I shall see you anon." He'd been eighteen when his brother died, and there had been a coalition who would have supported him, if he'd had a mind to put himself forward. But his uncle had been someone he'd looked up to all his life. Even Iain would rather have him as their leader. Unlike the English, succession wasn't by primogeniture. If Iain had somehow convinced the leading men to back him over his more experienced kinsman and botched it—a most likely outcome—his people would have given their allegiance elsewhere.

He pushed past his uncle, threw open one of the doors, and quick-stepped down the stairs, breathing in the early afternoon air and trying to recapture his enthusiasm. He'd wished to succeed in this mission for his wife's sake. Now he also wanted to succeed for his own.

‟

WHAT HAD BEEN a clear day had turned to a drizzle as Traci stepped off the ferry and headed for the stables. She shivered and pulled the wool plaid tighter around her shoulders. Her hand wandered to the pouch secured to her belt, assuring herself it was there. She'd hastily sewn her phone and her time-traveling case into it. She'd be damned if she took the chance of having it separated from her. The rest of her belongings were in a sack she'd attach to her saddle.

Having Iain a member of the party had her insides all messed up. On the one hand, it was comforting, because he was someone she trusted, however much she could trust her own instincts there. Which wasn't much.

But on the other hand, he threw off her equilibrium. Especially after today. Up until now, it had been easy to dismiss him as a big flirt like her gaming friend Johnny who'd showed her the ropes in the art of the hookup senior year of college. She'd established some kind of mutual banter agreement with Iain—each knowing the other's flirtation was just that. And flirtation was easy when it meant nothing and kept him, and others like him, at an emotional distance.

But this morning…this morning she'd glimpsed a little more under his shell. And she was simultaneously pulled by that possibility of more and scared of exploring it. Opening herself up hadn't gone too well in the past.

She could *not* get close to anyone here. And God, wouldn't she end up looking like an idiot if she dropped their pretense, looking for more from him, and he didn't drop his. Or worse, decided her feelings were just on the smidge side of too much and pushed her away as no more fun to "play" with.

She'd lose her only ally. Like she had with Johnny.

She swallowed a lump in her throat and took a shaky breath. And then laughed. What the hell was she even doing whining about this? She needed to get to her sister and get them the hell out of Dodge. No bypassing for smooching or—*God*—sex.

She couldn't wait to get her sister and zap back to her old life. Her old life where she could bury herself in her work and not analyze, or even fucking *care*, about what some guy thought about her. Work was the only place where she had any control in her life. At work, she was successful, her instincts were true, and she was respected. And if she overworked, she blew off steam by losing herself in testing their latest RPG.

Ha. Well, first she'd have to talk them into letting her cut her vacation short. They'd insisted she take these three weeks, worried that she'd burn out.

Yes. She couldn't wait to get back to where she felt the most herself.

She stamped her feet as she strode toward the stables, trying to jiggle a little warmth and sense into her veins. She joined the rest of the party, who were busy saddling up the ponies or securing their supplies.

Iain lumbered up then, his stride loose and self-assured. And sexy as hell. Her breath caught in her throat. His features seemed transformed in the diffused, afternoon light. He was more animated than she'd ever seen him, a new confidence affecting the air around him. Almost a defiance. And it changed his features. Before, his features seemed tailor-made for laughing, a smile ever ready, lighting up his face and making him approachable. Now, those same features delineated a sharp, angular jaw that looked as if it'd take no prisoners. No bullshit. He'd been adorable before. Now he was a dark, fierce, handsome Highland warrior.

Chills pockmarked her skin.

He caught sight of her, winked, and the illusion broke. He handed her a cup and downed the contents of the other he held.

She sniffed it. "What is it?"

"We call it Old Man's Milk. 'Tis milk mixed with a raw egg and a dram of whisky."

"Oh God, no." She handed it back.

He laughed and drank hers, then clapped his hands together, facing the others. "Listen up, lads. We leave as soon as you're finished dithering."

"It wasn't one of us who strolled up just now," joked a red-haired, thickly built man to her left.

"I'm here now, aren't I, Gavin?" He grinned and crossed his arms.

It struck her then what was different about Iain—he was excited about leading this party. And from the curious stares he drew from the others, him leading wasn't normal. They were coming around though, as his natural humor won them over. Though Gavin and Lochloinn didn't seem surprised.

"Unless anyone objects overmuch," Iain continued, "let's away."

Everyone nodded and swung up onto their mounts. A stable boy nudged her, and he held out the reins for Glenfiddich.

"Thank you." She searched for a place to step on to mount when warm hands clasped her waist.

"I have ye," rumbled Iain's melodic voice near her ear. His heat warmed her back. With no difficulty whatsoever, he hoisted her up, and she arranged her leg around the side-saddle.

On her arrival, much had been made over her odd saddle, so different from their side-saddles, but she'd told them it was a new style in Cornwall, and they'd accepted it without question.

"What about Duncan? Isn't he coming?" she asked, low enough for only Iain to hear.

"Nay. He did not wish to accompany us, which is strange considering he believes we're…"

"…We're retrieving my sister…" She frowned and glanced back at the keep. "Yes. That is strange."

"Strange indeed." Iain cupped her thigh and squeezed. "We're to follow Gavin east. I'll deliver you safely to your sister. After that, I'll do my best to get you alone so you may depart."

She nodded. "Thank you," she whispered.

He nodded back, gave her thigh another squeeze, and swung up onto his saddle with an ease that said he'd practiced that move. Probably to impress the ladies, and, yeah, she had to admit, it *was* pretty manly.

As if sensing her thoughts, he looked back over his shoulder and winked, the imp. He clucked softly to his mount, and they trotted through the open gate and across the causeway, their ponies snorting into the air, their heads bobbing up and down, eager to be given their heads.

The clatter of the ponies' hooves grew muted as the last of the party cleared the causeway and stepped onto the path around the lake. She glanced over, taking in the lake and the rolling vastness on its far side. She craned her neck up the green ridge they'd descended on their arrival the other day. And over that ridge lay another swath of wild, tempestuous, wide-open Highlands. She shivered.

At least her sister was safe.

❧

SOON THE DRIZZLE stopped, and their party traveled along the rocky shore of Loch Garry and across the glen bordering the river of the same name. Occasionally, the ground dipped into small pockets, blanketed in fog, and Traci shuddered because she couldn't see a damn thing below her knees.

After several miles, her stomach rumbled with hunger, but she kept silent, unwilling to waste time. They would be at Invergarry castle in another hour at most, if she judged the sun right.

They dipped into yet another of these foggy hollows, and Glenfiddich stumbled. She pitched forward, and Traci lost her seat, tumbling into the fog.

She landed with a soft "umph" on her right hip. "Shit." She rolled to a sitting position and placed her hands out so that the pony wouldn't bump into her. If she'd been *astride*, that would *not* have happened. A murky soup of fog surrounded her.

Oh, crap. Her case. She patted her hip and found her bag. Still there and still closed. She gripped the cloth to feel the comforting shape of the case.

"Traci?" Iain's strong, melodic voice rang out.

"Over here." She flipped onto her hands and knees and slowly rose, testing her weight on her ankles. Whew, nothing felt sprained or broken. She glanced up—her head and shoulders now above the fog. She twirled around until Glenfiddich came into view, a few feet away. Iain bore down on her, his pony stepping carefully.

"What happened?" he asked. The other members of the party crowded around her too.

"I'm not sure. Fiddich tripped on something, and I fell."

"Are you all right?"

"Yes. I'm fine."

Iain swung off his pony. He cooed to her mount and bent over near the front side, lifting one of her pony's legs. He repeated the action on the other side.

"*Mo Chreach!* She's thrown a shoe, and we're not like to find it in this cursed fog."

He patted Fiddich's neck and straightened. "There's nothing for it. You'll need to ride with me. Glengarry's blacksmith can repair it when we reach the castle."

He took her reins and attached them to his own pony. That accomplished, he approached her, a grin splitting his face. "You up for a ride? With me?"

"That depends. What kind of ride will it be?"

"One you won't forget, I can assure you."

His innuendos were a keen reminder that he *was* nothing more than a flirt, handfasting or no, their conversation this morning notwithstanding. And she'd do well to remember that. It certainly made it easier to resist him.

"You promise, my husband?"

The men chuckled, and her face flamed. *Oops, forgot about the audience.* Her face heated further, because dammit, she wasn't a blusher. Flirting was her forté, and no one would make her feel ashamed of that. She'd give as good as she got.

"Aye, 'tis a promise. Come, let me assist you onto our delightful, and *shared,* conveyance. You know you cannae resist."

Normally, she'd assume he spoke from arrogance, but she could tell it was all just a fun exchange of words. Like her, perhaps, he used flirtation to keep others at bay?

She stepped close and placed her hand in his, which he held above the line of fog. She ignored the jolt she received when her skin met his. He reached behind her with his other hand. Since it was beneath the fog—and so out of sight of the others—he gave her ass a quick squeeze.

She glared at him, and he winked. "Up ye go."

He grasped her waist and lifted her onto his pony, sitting sideways. "Ready for me, lass?" He winked and swung up behind her, standing straight in the stirrups. "Tsk, tsk, tsk. This willna do." He raised her up, sat himself, and settled her back down, her hip snug against his stomach on one side and the high pommel of his saddle on the other. It put her at an angle that tipped her toward him and of a height with his face. She had no choice but to settle her head against his shoulder so he could see. Their saddle didn't leave a lot of room for any other position.

He snaked his arm around her middle and secured her against him.

"Here, let's get you more comfortable, my wife," he whispered in her ear, his warm tones sending a shiver of delight down her back. His wicked hands clasped her waist. Under the guise of "adjusting" her, he wiggled her around a little more in his lap.

He was incorrigible. If it were anyone else, she'd turn around and pop him right where it'd hurt the most. It was as if he knew she wouldn't object and took full advantage. Or was testing his boundaries with her.

"Aye. There we go," he rumbled. He said, a little louder, "You comfortable yet, my wife? You sure are finding it difficult to settle down."

She dug her elbow into his ribs and was satisfied to hear a soft grunt and another chuckle.

He clucked to his pony, and his thighs tensed under hers as he directed his mount up out of the hollow. The voices of the others fell in behind. She peeked around his broad frame and saw Fiddich following docilely behind.

Soon they reached another fog-drenched hollow.

She asked what she'd worried about earlier. "How do you know it's not just a drop-off into a ravine?"

"Och, dinnae fash. We know these lands. And so do our mounts." He hugged her a little tighter to his body. "See that slightly worn area in front of us? That's a wee path with which we're familiar. It'll take us safely through this patch and up to the other side."

They approached the edge and descended. This time, the fog inched higher and higher up her body. Would it swallow up over their heads? At the height of her shoulders, however, it leveled out. The chalky white tendrils swirled and eddied around them, taking on a different pattern as they sliced through it, their life-sized witch's cauldron.

The whole time she'd been sitting in his lap, Traci had been achingly aware of Iain's solid strength below and beside her. Every time he adjusted the direction of his pony, his thighs tensed and shifted below hers. The heat radiating from him was enough to keep her warm too, as they pushed through the chilly fog.

Again, he tensed below her, and she thought he was adjusting the direction of the pony. But his hand brushed across her waist, and now *she* tensed. He pressed her against him, his erection nudging against her hip, until she was snug against his chest.

What was he doing?

Nothing, apparently. Just getting a little more *comfortable*, the imp.

Every nerve ending was strung taut, awareness zinging up and down her at his nearness. It was strange wading through the fog with only their heads and shoulders above it, and, yeah, she'd not begrudge him huddling her closer against him. Not that she needed the extra security. Nope. But she'd not turn away his warmth.

His hand inched, oh so slowly, up her stomach. She pulled in a shallow breath. He was just adjusting his hold on her, that was all. But it edged up. Up again, almost so incremental she could have been imagining the glacial progress. Except this was Iain.

Gavin pulled up beside them. "Scouts ahead report the way is clear to Invergarry. If we keep to this pace, we'll reach their keep 'ere night falls."

She smiled her thanks to him for speaking in English.

Iain lifted his chin, and again his muscles shifted below her as he angled toward Gavin. "Very good. I know my wife is eager to see her sister."

They talked logistics as they plodded along, their cadences, his warmth and closeness lulling her until she jerked in surprise—Iain's hand had continued its glacial slide up her body and now he cupped the underside of a breast. She darted a glance over to Gavin, shocked by Iain's boldness. But Gavin didn't appear to notice.

She glanced down. Ha. That was why—everything Iain did was beneath the fog. An illicit thrill spiked through her, and she clenched her thighs together.

He wouldn't dare.

But yep, as he continued talking, his strong, warm hand eased up another fraction until he cupped her entire breast.

And pinched her nipple.

Holy shit, she should totally slap his hand away.

But she didn't.

Not because she was afraid to make a scene. She couldn't care less about that.

No. She didn't slap him away because the whole damn thing was such a thrill—her legs atop his strong thighs, the proximity of the others, and the way he slyly used the cover of the fog to toy with her breast.

Well, two could play that game.

Er. Maybe.

She frowned, trying to figure out which of his body parts she could reach.

Chapter Thirteen

❦

I met a man in tartan trews,
I speer'd at him what was the news…
"The Haughs of Cromdale," *Jacobite Reliques*

IAIN GENTLY TWEAKED his wife's perky nipple again and bit back a grin as she tensed.

Gavin continued to drone on, and Iain tried to pay attention, he really did, but with the bit of distraction he had in his lap, could anyone blame him?

As they'd ridden toward their destination, having her bundled and snugged up so tightly to him played havoc on his self-control. To have her in his lap, her lovely bottom pressed so enticingly against him, would drive any man insane. He'd laugh at the first man who'd deny it.

Each mile they traversed, he felt his resolve to resist her drain that much further away. When he'd grabbed a quick bite at the castle before setting out, he'd tried to absorb all that she'd told him and its implications. God, he still wanted her, but learning where she truly came from had made it clear that this was not her world. If he'd been daft enough not to figure that out on his own, she'd cinched it with her stated resolve to find her sister and return to their time.

By the time they'd descended again into another hollow, and the fog covered their bodies, he wasn't at all surprised to find his hand starting to wander.

His body had decided for him. As always.

When Gavin had started with his chatter, his attention was stretched to its limit.

Another pinch, her breath hitched, and triumph surged through him.

He was answering a question of Gavin's when he nearly bit his tongue—she had managed to slip underneath her skirt and brush his cods with her knuckles.

His whole body stiffened, and he stopped mid-sentence.

Gavin shot him an odd look. "What about Glengarry?" he asked, frowning.

Iain cleared his throat, and Traci gave a low, throaty giggle, which shot a jolt of lust straight to his groin. He pinched her breast again in retaliation. "Remember 'tis only our chieftain we've convinced of my wife's innocence." Again unease settled in his gut at how easy it had been.

"Do you expect trouble?"

"We should always expect trouble, I think."

A strange look crossed Gavin's face. He nodded and allowed his horse to fall behind. Iain brought his hand, reluctant to leave such a luscious handful, to rest on his thigh. But they'd soon be ascending.

He chuckled when their ascent finally dawned on his wife. She scrambled to straighten her skirts.

ഉ

DUSK CAME EARLY as the last rays of the sun fractured over the mountain tops behind them. As they trotted along the northern edge of the foothills of Ben Tee, an imposing five-story stone castle rose from a jagged rock. Castle Invergarry. The calm waters of Loch Oich sparkled in the background.

This was a site Traci had visited with her sister, so seeing it whole instead of a crumbling ruin was incredible. There were far fewer trees, and a wide swath of green pasture led up to the entrance of the castle's curtain wall. A scattering of oblong stone cottages dotted the land to the right, and the Highlanders' particular breed of cows—black and hairy as heck—dotted the area to the left.

Iain's arms tightened around her waist as their pony ambled down the hill to the glen leading up to the castle's entrance. She was grateful for the reassurance. Any time she interacted with anyone from this time, she ran a risk of exposure. But her sister was in there. Soon she'd have her safe at her side, and they could zap back to their own time.

"He's expecting us, right?"

"Aye, he is at that. But be aware, he shares the same suspicions my uncle had. We will need to allay those."

"What if he doesn't believe me? We were lucky with your uncle."

"Och, 'twas not hard for me to convince him that such a one as you, with your bonnie face and manners, was not a wicked spy." He rubbed

94

her hip, but while his voice was light, she detected a thread of unease. "Besides, all we require is the chance to get you with your sister. I think I can at least get you alone with her. And then you can…"

She only noticed the hesitation because she was pressed against him and she felt his swallow.

"You can ignite your magic and return to your time."

She pulled in a deep breath. "If we don't get a chance to talk alone before then, I want to thank you for all of your help. I couldn't have found her without you. I'd have been lost. And Lord knows what would have happened to Fiona."

"The MacDonells are a good clan. No harm would have come to her. Our clan is bonded to theirs by manrent."

"Manrent?"

"We are pledged to serve them in exchange for protection. She's in good hands."

"And she *does* love Scotland." Traci laughed. "In fact, I wonder if she even *wants* to go back. I guess we'll see."

By then, they'd reached the glen, and the others in their party had bunched around them, so she didn't talk further. The gate opened ahead, and out rode a dozen men on Highland ponies.

Iain pulled up on his reins, and the others halted. Right next to a tannery. Ugh.

Wood-lined streams snaked and intersected a patch of ground on the bank of the River Garry, and hides in various states of being skinned and tanned lay stretched over wooden poles. Traci gagged. The smell was absolutely vile. Worse than any porta potty at a summer music festival. Her eyes watered from the ammonia. The workers at the tannery, indeed all the villagers she could see on both sides of the road, wore less colorful plaids. Most were a natural, off-white color, the variegated stripes barely visible. She'd noticed the same thing at Dungarbh—it seemed the poorer classes in both places sported less colorful tartans. Perhaps they couldn't afford the dye?

The welcoming party—God, she hoped that's what they were—pulled up in a flurry of hooves, their ponies nickering and prancing in place before them. She stretched up, surveying the party for a peek of her sister. No such luck. But that was okay. She was close. If all went well here, they'd soon see her. Had it only been four days ago that all this mess had started?

The leader, a huge Highlander with a broadsword hanging from his belt, wore tartan pants and had three eagle feathers pinned to his blue bonnet, while the others were dressed in great kilts. A string of Gaelic followed, Iain answering back. Seeing this party of nobles in their bright tartan patterns next to the drabber versions of the villagers lent credence to her theory of a class distinction.

The exchange between Iain and the welcoming party seemed friendly. Couldn't they hurry up with all the posturing so she could get to her sister and this whole escapade could be over?

It was friendly enough until all the muscles in Iain's body stiffened. "*Mo Chreach!*" he said, in an explosion of breath.

She'd gathered enough Gaelic to know that was an oath. Chill bumps pricked her skin. "What's going on?" she whispered.

"Your sister is gone."

Chapter Fourteen

၁

Pox on every sneaking blade
"Here's to the King, Sir," *Jacobite Reliques*

$\mathcal{A}$ N HOUR LATER, Traci was tucked between Iain and Gavin in the great hall of Invergarry Castle. It was easily twice as large as Iain's main hall. The high-backed wooden chair seemed to swallow her up, a feeling enhanced by being between the two tall forms of her protectors. It was a strange sensation, feeling small and delicate.

Thankfully, Iain had convinced the clan chief and the rest to speak in English, so she was able to follow the conversation. It wasn't lost on her that it was only the three of them from their group sitting at the table with the MacDonell chief and his men. The rest of their party stood behind them, alert.

Iain set down his flask of whisky. "My uncle and chieftain sends his greetings. I thank you for your hospitality and the repast. Now that our bellies are full and our throats wet, I wish to beg your forbearance further that you might tell us news of Fiona Campbell, my wife's sister." He wrapped an arm around her shoulders and pulled her tight against him.

At first, she was annoyed that he kept going on with the wife business, but then she realized that his gesture wasn't a simple one. He was letting them know that she was part of his clan. And so under their protection.

The chief frowned. "So you're the one who married the sister. We didn't credit her tale. She spoke of a handfasting, but truth be told, her story was muddled and her speech strange. You did the right thing, coming here."

"How did she escape and when?"

"She slipped away when she was with the ladies taking the air two days past."

Traci opened her mouth, but Iain's hand clasped her thigh and squeezed.

"Why didn't you send word at once?"

"We wanted to find her first. I had men track her, with the intention

97

of bringing her back, but they returned not an hour before your arrival." He leaned forward and pushed his flask out of the way. He cocked his head toward Traci, and directed a stream of Gaelic to Iain.

What the hell?

⁊

Iain tensed as the MacDonell switched to Gaelic. Next to him sat his son and heir, Alasdair. Iain had always gotten along with Alasdair, and he hoped he'd be able to swing him to at least a sympathetic stance.

"Nay, she cannot understand our speech," Iain gritted out, answering in *Gàidhlig*.

The chief leveled a stare at Traci and then leaned back. "Well, then. This Fiona Campbell confirmed your Ross's initial assessment, for our search party witnessed her prancing into Urquhart Castle."

Dread pooled in his belly. *He* knew it meant nothing. "That's not conclusive."

"It's conclusive enough for me. All in the Great Glen know the chief of the Grants is siding with the usurper William. There's talk of laying siege to his castle. That she walked in there, bold as you please, says plenty."

Alasdair leaned forward, a frown pinching his brow. "It does appear suspicious. You must see that."

Iain had to tread carefully here. He couldn't just order their overlord to believe him, to believe in Traci's and Fiona's innocence. Much was at stake, and tensions were high all across the Highlands with the rebellion. "I cannot vouch for Fiona…" *St. Columba preserve him.* He hated to cast her in such a light, but Traci was here right now, needing protection, and Fiona wasn't. "…but I can vouch for my wife. She is no spy. I swear by the hand of my grandfather that this is so."

That would buy them only a little time. Such an oath was a strong one to a fellow Highlander, though he doubted a Lowlander, or the English they imitated, would be as moved. The chief wouldn't dare risk enmity with Iain's clan and deny his trust. At least not right away. He only needed a little time, though. Time to plan their next step.

Again, the chief raked her with a glare. He lurched to the side and snapped his fingers. "More whisky."

While the chief was distracted, Iain leaned down to Traci's ear.

"Yawn," he whispered.

He straightened as the chief faced them again. Traci's hand squeezed his where it rested on her thigh. He dutifully witnessed her yawn. "My wife is exhausted," he said in English. "She's had a trying time, and with this unwelcome news of her sister, I feel it has quite overwhelmed her, poor dear."

He stifled a grin as Traci muttered under her breath. Then he nearly gasped as her grip on his hand tightened to a painful degree. "May we trespass further on your hospitality and abide here for the night?"

The chief gave a measured nod. "Of course. Your men may bed down in the hall. You and your wife may take the guest chamber in the southern wing. We will resume our discussion in the morning and settle matters about your wife."

Iain handed over his uncle's letter to help make his case and took his leave. Uneasiness swirled through him. He did not care for how that was phrased. Nay. Not at all.

◌◌

TRACI STRETCHED HER legs before the fire in their room. Iain had just finished catching her up on what the chief had said in Gaelic, when Iain strode to her, knelt, and gripped her shoulders. "I will do all in my power to get your sister. That she's with a clan we are not at peace with will be no small obstacle. But I will do my best. I promise."

He held her gaze, and she stared into his light blue eyes. Again, he was exposing a new side to himself, and a part of her weakened. He *knew* he couldn't guarantee the outcome, and admitting as much must have been difficult.

"Thank you," she whispered. "Do you think the chief will let me leave? He seems suspicious."

Iain picked up the fireplace poker and stoked the freshly laid fire. "I know not. The oath I swore to your innocence is a strong one. I'll just have to convince him, as I did with my uncle. We should—"

A hard knock rapped on their door.

Iain pushed away from the fireplace mantel and strode to the door. "Who is it?"

" 'Tis I, Duncan."

Duncan? Iain yanked open the door, and Duncan pushed his way past. His handsome face was set in a grim line. He shut and barred the door. "I came as fast as I could," he rasped in English.

"What news, cousin? Did something happen with mine uncle?"

"Your uncle is hale and hearty, but my news does concern him. Give me a drink first. My throat is parched."

Iain shoved a flask into his cousin's hand. Duncan drained it with one swallow. "We must leave at once. You were sent here under false pretenses."

Traci jumped to her feet. "What do you mean?"

"Aye. What is this about?" growled Iain.

"Only that your uncle lied to you. Glengarry demanded your presence here. Our chieftain was handing over your wife to Glengarry for safekeeping until this whole rebellion was settled. The letter you carried stated you are in compliance and are here under his direction. He only feigned belief in her innocence."

Iain's hands tightened into fists. "And he kept this from me?"

"Aye. I thought it was only because he knew you'd never go along with it. I'm not as sure of her innocence meself. But then I learned that he also kept it from you so you'd arrive here, seemingly in compliance, and when you tried to leave with her and Fiona, you'd appear fickle and unreliable. For Glengarry would confront you, and your uncle knew you'd resist them being detained."

"What?" Iain's voice could barely be heard over the crackling of the peat fire. But she heard it. And heard the pain laced in that simple word.

❧

DISBELIEF WARRED WITH anger in Iain's breast. He'd been hoodwinked? By his own uncle? As he parsed through Duncan's words— and, aye, as hard as it was, he believed his cousin—he saw that his uncle meant to make him look the fool.

He sat down hard on the settle by the fire. "Why?"

Though Duncan was five years his senior, they'd formed a tight bond forged on the practice field and the few skirmishes they'd been involved in over the last eight years.

He was the closest Iain had now to a brother.

Duncan leaned against the door and crossed his arms. "My guess? He's threatened by you."

Of all the things he'd expected to come from Duncan's mouth, that was not one of them. Iain barked a laugh. "Be serious, cousin."

"I am. Especially now that you've handfasted. And to the mighty Campbells, no less."

"What could—?" He stopped himself. "He believes I'll challenge him for the chieftainship."

"Aye. 'Tis rightly yours. If you put yourself forward, you'd have support."

A strange reality seemed to shimmer and solidify in Iain's mind. One where he'd been an unwitting player in a game only his uncle thought they were playing. Iain had no desire to be chieftain. Leave that responsibility to someone who wanted it. Who could be relied on.

Which wasn't him.

He shook his head. "He *knows* I have no wish to be chieftain."

"He takes no chances, and, to be honest, you play right into his hands."

"I couldn't have foreseen his betrayal with Traci."

Traci approached and stood beside him, facing Duncan.

His cousin flicked his gaze to her and back. "I refer to your reputation. He manipulates you, and you don't even realize it. He casts you in the role of court jester, and you oblige." He shoved away from the wall and uncrossed his arms. "Look. We have no time to palaver. Glengarry has already retired with his wife." He switched to *Gàidhlig.* "His son Alasdair left with their contingent of men to join Dundee. I told his men you'd asked me to join you as soon as I could, and they directed me here. But I think 'tis wise—"

"That we leave immediately. Aye," he finished in English and turned to Traci. "Get your things together."

"There's not much anyway." She grabbed her sack from under the bed and stood next to him. "Ready. Where are we going? If you're going back to Dungarbh, I'm not going with you. I need to go to Urquhart Castle. I need to get my sister."

Duncan spun and faced Traci, his face turning pale. "What? She's not here?"

They quickly filled Duncan in, with Traci carrying the bulk of the recital. All the while, Iain's mind turned, sifting through possibilities.

When she finished, Iain grabbed his baldric containing his sword. "We need to orchestrate this carefully. We cannot just leave in the dead of night. It would be an insult to Glengarry's hospitality and would endanger your standing with our chieftain as well. And my uncle has made Glengarry believe I'm in agreement on this spy business. For me to leave, seemingly to prevent Traci from being detained by him, would still achieve my uncle's goal: to make me appear a fickle fool at best or culpable at worst."

Duncan nodded. "Gavin and the others believe you are here to turn her over as well. What do you suggest?"

Et tu, Gavin? Something of his thoughts must have shown, for Duncan added, "Gavin did not know your uncle's full plan. He believes you're handing her over willingly."

That made him feel marginally better. "While it is unfortunate Fiona escaped, this will perhaps lend a better light to our late-night flight. We can use your arrival as cover—you have brought additional word of Fiona's whereabouts, and we were eager to depart and bring her back into the fold before the trail grew cold. And we need Traci's presence to coddle the sister into returning with us."

Traci gripped her knees. "But your chieftain would know Duncan wasn't privy to news of Fiona."

Duncan rubbed his jaw. "I told him I had business in the village."

Iain crossed to the fire and picked up the poker. He turned it in his hand. "And while there you could have heard news that prompted us to act. It doesn't have to match up perfectly—the story could plausibly have been miscommunicated back to the chieftain." He jabbed the poker into the fire. "What else? Are there any other angles we should consider? We're leaving without our men, because…"

"They're drunk."

Iain lifted his head at that.

"They are. I passed them on the way in. To them, their mission is over, and Glengarry is generous, unlike our chieftain."

So his suspicions were true. "Even Gavin?"

"Aye."

"We'll need provisions."

"Caitrina," they both said at once.

"Who's Caitrina?"

Iain returned to Traci's side. "She's a cousin who married a tenant of the MacDonell and owns a farm on the north side of Invergarry's glen. We'll have to pass it after we ford the River Garry."

Duncan rubbed his chin. "It will be a full day's travel 'ere we reach Urquhart Castle's environs, but only a half a day left in our own lands. What excuse do we have for crossing into the Grant's lands?"

"The simplest, I think," said Iain. "We search for our lost kinswoman. No one will doubt our tale since we have a woman traveling with us. Were we raiding, we'd not. And we'd have more men."

"That could work," Duncan said.

"All right. Today is the twentieth of July. That should give us seven days to look for her, before we need to head to Struan for the gathering on the twenty-ninth." Iain leaned the poker back against the wall. "We ready?"

Duncan nodded, and Traci said, "Let's do this."

અ

IAIN GRABBED GAVIN by his shirt collar and shook him. "Listen up. I'm leaving you in charge of the men. Give our thanks to Glengarry for his hospitality, but we had to leave."

Gavin's eyes were glassy from drink. "What about her? Glengarry expects her to remain here."

Again, humiliation burned through him that he'd been set up to play the fool. "Glengarry'll have to wait." He nodded toward Duncan. "He learned the sister has left Urquhart. We mean to apprehend her."

"Can you not do that without her?"

Iain cast a quick glance at Traci, who stood in the shadows, arms crossed, defiance etched in her stance. *That's my* nighean. "Nay. We need her as bait."

"At least wait till morning. Our men will be sober then, and we can lay in supplies and aid you."

"Delay will not aid our quest. The trail grows cold already. We mean to leave now and ride hard. Besides, I need someone I trust to smooth any ruffled feathers the MacDonell might have. Assure him of our return. When your men have sobered up, inform our chieftain of our whereabouts and that we will return anon."

"Aye."

"Repeat it back to me."

After Gavin repeated the instructions to Iain's satisfaction, he slumped back onto the bench he'd occupied by the fire when they'd crept downstairs.

Iain nodded to Traci and Duncan. The easiest part out of the way, they made their way out of the main hall and headed to the gate. They took a gamble, but they couldn't leave by subterfuge. They stopped at the stable while Duncan retrieved their ponies and the one she called Fiddich.

In the end, the guard at the gate proved easier to convince of their mission than Gavin. It helped that he had no knowledge of the fate his chief had planned for Traci. He only knew that Iain and Duncan were allied clan folk and he had no reason to question them.

Iain helped Traci into her saddle. Urquhart Castle was a full day's ride from here, northeast along Loch Oich and then up the greater part of the length of Loch Ness. The stop at Caitrina's would be necessary but with luck, they'd reach Drumnadrochit near Urquhart before nightfall.

Chapter Fifteen

Far dearer to me are the hills of the north,
The land of blue mountains, the birth-place of worth
"The Thistle of Scotland," *Jacobite Reliques*

THE FIRST RAYS of dawn streaked across Loch Oich and the glen when they crossed the River Garry. Traci adjusted her seat in the saddle.

Iain pulled his pony to a stop. "Let's refill our flasks before we continue farther." He dismounted, and a sharp breeze whipped by, snapping Iain's plaid against his manly form. Behind him stretched a haunting, bleak, but strangely soulful landscape. From her angle—it *had* to be a trick of the light—he seemed to slightly *glow*. And she'd swear that wind carried a faint sound of bagpipes, worming their way into her with their siren call of her Scottish ancestors and all that crap. A chill, deeper than the wind warranted, skittered across her skin.

God damn it.

She tore her gaze away and frowned. Duncan swung off his pony and joined Iain at the river, their movements breaking the strange spell.

"How far to Caitrina's?"

" 'Tis only over that hill. We'll be there shortly."

True to his word, they soon reached the heart of a modest farm. Traci eased off Fiddich and stumble-landed near Iain and Duncan and their mounts. They had a whole day of this? She rubbed her already sore butt. Their ponies' breaths formed steamy puffs in the chill air, and Traci tugged her plaid wrap tighter around her shoulders.

Iain brushed past, increasing her awareness of him. He gathered their ponies' reins and looped them around a fence rail. "Caitrina should be up doing chores. Let us make this quick."

Traci followed behind as they advanced through the outer edges of the farm. This was a working farm, with no thought to such a concept as curb appeal, and so various buildings and equipment encircled the modest cottage where they made the most sense. Though chaotic, the farm was tidy. Efficient.

And pungent. She pulled a corner of her plaid over her nose.

Docile, hairy, black Highland cows, their eyes large and innocent, stared from a nearby paddock. Across the lane, a small enclosure contained several grunting pigs delighting in a mud bath.

"Voices ahead," Duncan called back. He waved to the stone building near the cows, and they stepped through its wide entrance.

Traci shivered and rubbed her arms at the temperature drop. Nearby, two women milked a pair of cows, their rhythms creating an oddly soothing, alternating beat as frothy milk squirted into the pails.

Duncan and Iain greeted them in Gaelic, and the older woman stood and wiped her hands on her apron.

Iain leaned over and said in an undertone, "That there is Caitrina, and I'm about to introduce ye." He chatted to Caitrina, and Traci's name cropped up just before he draped an arm around her and squeezed her to his side. Probably just told her they were married, the imp.

Traci gave him an arch look and stepped forward. "Greetings," she said in Gaelic as they'd taught her and held out her hand. Caitrina startled at the offer of a handshake, but she grasped her hand firmly and shook. Before Caitrina released her grip though, she turned Traci's hand and brought it closer. She said something in Gaelic.

Traci raised an eyebrow at Iain.

"She says yer ring is lovely."

Oh. "Tell her thank you."

As agreed, Duncan took up the negotiations so Iain could translate. They hoped to trade on future goods from their clan's stores, but at that, she balked.

"She doesn't trust my uncle. Said he doesn't treat his tenants well, and that's why she moved here. And she won't gift the supplies as she has the mouths of ten grandchildren to feed."

Duncan and Iain tried to charm the woman, but it was obvious she wouldn't budge. Then Caitrina gestured to Traci and said something more, but both Duncan and Iain shook their heads, adamant.

"What's she saying?"

"She says she'll give us what we require if she can have yer ring."

Traci's heart lurched, and she instinctively raised her hand and hid the ruby ring with her other hand.

All the old feelings burbled up. The ones she'd long ago buried the night her first serious boyfriend had revealed he only saw her as a Friend With Benefits. God, she'd been such a stupid sap about him, imagining they were embarking on their lifelong love story. College had been such an awakening for her, but like all awakenings, a part of it was painful.

She'd finally come into her own, away from her family. And she'd found a solid core of friends who shared similar views. One of those friends had been Brad, a pre-law student destined to work at his father's prestigious law firm back in Boston. She'd opened up for the first time in her life to someone. It had been freeing and scary and magical.

They'd soon become an item. But when she discovered he was taking his fellow pre-law student to an important schmooze event instead of her, the scales had come off. She'd been so shocked, she'd confronted him about it.

And what hurt the most? He was genuinely baffled. Had no clue she'd seen their fooling around as anything more than what it was. He'd given off the distinct vibe that to be seen with her at that event would have *embarrassed* him.

She'd been so disillusioned—with herself and with men—she'd rebounded by hooking up with her gaming friend Johnny the flirt. Then read more into that! And eventually lost him as a friend.

No. The ring was her cautionary tale.

"Don't worry." Iain's gentle voice brought her out of her memories. "I told her ye wouldna part with it."

"But what else can we do?"

"We can cross the ford and hunt in a nearby forest."

"How long will that take?"

He sighed and looked to the side. "It depends on our luck, but it can eat up our day, especially to dress our kill and cook it."

Traci glanced at her hand, the redness of the ruby deeper in the murky light of the barn. Could she part with it? Seeing it on her right middle finger helped ground her. Reminded her that men were not worth the trouble.

The three of them now stared at her, Caitrina in anticipation, and Duncan and Iain with unreadable expressions, while the *squirt-squirt-squirt* of the lone milkmaid's efforts filled the silence. Traci swallowed and gripped the ring.

Hell. It was just a stupid bauble. She was stronger now, right? And if it got them to Fiona quicker… She tugged it off without sparing it a glance and handed it over to Caitrina with a curt nod.

⟡

THE SUN WAS directly overhead when Iain reined in his mount at the fast-flowing River Moriston. As he had figured, they were delayed at Caitrina's for part of the morning. But they'd made good time since, though they'd crossed into Grant territory a while back. Somehow with this adventure, he needed to see them safely through Grant's lands, find Fiona, and keep Duncan in the chieftain's good graces.

He turned his pony westward, seeking the ford crossing. 'Twas risky, taking this one, but to cross at the safer ford would delay their journey. Iain crossed first, and Duncan took up the rear. His pony had just navigated onto the rocky bank when a whinny and a panicked shout pierced the chilly air.

He whipped around. Their sole pack pony had lost his footing and was being carried swiftly downstream. Iain dug his heels into the flanks of his own mount and galloped down the bank.

When he passed the floundering pony, he reined in his own and leaped from his back into the swift stream. He nearly gasped under water at the cold shock to his body. When he breached the surface, the pack pony swooshed by, struggling to stay upright. He had to act quickly, for they'd soon be flushed into the larger waters of Loch Ness. He swam hard across the current. The water chilled his limbs, making his muscles heavy, and he pulled a portion of river water into his lungs. He coughed and turned on his back, using his remaining energy to cross the river.

A few feet ahead, the pony's lead bobbed and thrashed in the current, but Iain didn't dare grab it for fear of harming the pony. Limbs straining, he put on another burst of energy and reached the beast's side. He grabbed the bridle and, arm around his neck, helped lead the panting animal across to the northern shore.

When the pack pony's hooves hit the bank, Iain let go and allowed the pony to pull himself wearily to shore. Iain grabbed a rock and used the torque to swing his body onto the embankment, where he elbowed onto firmer ground and fell onto his back, his chest heaving.

108

Footsteps pounded up the bank, and Traci's face loomed overhead. Her braid tumbled forward and bumped his chin. "Are you okay?" Her lovely eyes were wide with panic.

"Aye, just a—" He coughed. "Just a wee bit bruised. Thought I'd make sure the sky was still up where it should be, that's all." He took an embarrassingly long gasp for air. "No cause for alarm, I assure you."

She rolled her eyes and put an arm behind his shoulders, leveraging him into a sitting position.

He winced, holding his side. "I guess the sky can wait then. Let me see to the pony."

She puffed near his ear. "Don't act so tough. Rest a moment, and get your breath. Duncan is seeing to it."

It was *his* responsibility. He rose onto shaky legs and straightened to his full height, though he really wanted to rest his hands on his knees. For just another moment.

Indeed, Duncan had the pack pony secured, and it was soon plain to see that it was uninjured, but the supplies it carried were missing.

"Our food is gone," Duncan said, walking toward him, his voice grim.

"*Mo Chreach.*" He scraped a hand through his hair and tugged. "All right. We're stopping here then, and we'll take turns hunting to restock."

℥

TRACI STRETCHED OUT her legs, massaging her thighs and calf muscles through her skirts. The bottom hems were wet from the river crossing, so she toed off her shoes, arranged them near the fire, and spread her skirts as much as possible.

Contemplating Iain's back, she shivered. But not from cold. She depended on him, and Duncan, for her life and health. His struggle to rescue that pony had driven it home. He'd been so decisive and masterful, it took her breath away.

But her heart had also been frantically pounding the whole time. What if something happened to him in that water? Nothing had happened, but the possibility still hung heavy, like an oppressive weight on her shoulders weighing her down and making her heart beat a bit too fast, her skin go a bit too clammy.

Her only ally could be swept away by a twist of fate.

She was essentially alone in this vast, wild land. What the hell was

109

she doing? All of it was her fault. But she'd make it right. She leaned forward and massaged a lower calf, and her gaze snagged on the light band around her finger where her ring had been. Traded for food that was long gone. But oddly, she felt nothing. Kinda hard to get worked up about a stupid talisman when Iain could have died.

Her head jerked up at raised voices—Iain and Duncan exchanging heated words. She scrambled to a stand and marched over. "What's going on?" She couldn't understand a word, since they were speaking in Gaelic.

Iain turned to her and said in English, "Duncan believes we should head back to Dungarbh and reorganize."

A panic fluttered in her chest. "No way."

Duncan crossed his arms and faced her. "Lassie, you dinnae understand. We are deep into Grant lands, and we are not very friendly with that clan. What food and supplies we had just traipsed down the River Moriston and became a wee snack for old Nessie. If we leave now, we can be back on our own lands before sundown."

Iain stepped forward. "And I made a promise to this *lassie*, who is my wife by the by."

"You can still keep that promise. But we need supplies. If we go back, we can augment our party with more warriors."

A worried frown crossed Iain's face, and he glanced away.

She took a moment to compose herself. Perhaps even channel her friend Katy, who always kept a cool head. Yeah, now was not the time to pop off on a couple Highland warriors. Especially ones as big and muscular as these.

She suppressed an inappropriate giggle because, with the exception of Iain and Duncan, the whole lot of warriors she'd met so far would have won her bet with her sister if she were here. Large and impressive they were, but hot? No.

She shook her head. Okay. Apparently she was *not* capable of channeling her friend Katy during a serious moment.

Focus.

Duncan continued, "I believe Fiona's innocent too, but we can't find her without supplies."

Still Iain said nothing, and all of her pent up frustration bubbled up. She raised her chin. "Damn it. If one of you will give me directions to this castle, I'll go there myself."

Katy, I tried to be calm, cool, and collected. I really did.

But a frantic energy had been building inside her and screamed to escape—increasing as time wore on and she couldn't *do* anything. Made her jumpy. Made her not be able to *think*. Made her want to ride, hell-bent for leather, through this rocky, raw land and get her damn sister. Gah!

She shook her hands at her sides to release some energy while she waited for a response. They just gawked at her as if she'd sprouted a second head.

She pursed her lips together and glared.

"Now don't be hasty, love." Iain grabbed her arms.

She yanked her arms from his grip. "I'm not your love. Don't patronize me. You *know* what's at stake for me."

He lowered his voice so only she could hear. "This isn't an easy decision. More is at stake than just you and your sister."

"That's fine. Go on. Do your thing. But the *only* thing that matters to me, the *only* thing that is at stake for *me*, is Fiona. And I'm *not* abandoning her here."

He regarded Duncan, his mouth set in a hard line, and returned his blue gaze to her.

She huffed out a breath. "Oh, grow a pair and make a decision, will you?"

"Grow a pair?" he asked slowly. "I don't take your meaning."

She gestured in his southerly direction. "Balls?"

Duncan snickered, and her face flushed. Iain's eyes grew steely. But it was erased in an instant, and he tipped his head back and laughed.

"Aye, you're a wonder, my wife." He tucked his thumbs behind his sporran and rocked his hips forward. "You're well aware, ye are, that I have a fine pair. I don't know what you're going on about." He winked.

Duncan laughed, and she shook her head ruefully, a smile reluctantly tugging at her lips. He *was* all back into his normal jocular, flirty self, except something made her look closer.

His eyes were smiling, as was his face. His body was relaxed. But. A tiny sliver of doubt and vulnerability lurked in his gaze. She normally would have missed it, but something made her assess him more closely. And...perhaps...she recognized herself in his stance.

She hid behind quips and flirty behavior. It was easier to keep a distance, keep from getting hurt.

"Yes, I am. But I think..." She stroked her finger down his arm. "I need a refresher? Give us a moment, Duncan, will you?"

"That's all he needs is a moment."

"You're confusing me with yourself, old man," Iain yelled back over his shoulder.

They walked in silence through the rocky glen until they reached an overlarge boulder. She scooted behind it and started to sit, when he swung her about until she was pressed between the boulder and his hard body.

"So," he said, his eyes roaming down her body and back up in a slow perusal, which carried a shocking amount of heat, dammit. "Finally admitting you can no longer resist? I knew you'd come around."

She swatted him on the arm. "Be serious, Iain."

"I am being serious. In this, I'm always serious."

"No, you're not."

He smiled. "You're right. I'm not."

Again, a slight shadow crossed his face.

He leaned down, his eyes locked on her lips, and she shoved him back. Not enough to actually budge the built-like-a-castle Highlander, but enough to get her point across. Besides, he was sopping wet.

"Stop it, Iain."

He raised his hands, palms facing her. "I'm stopping. If you're going to be a stubborn lass, there's naught I can do about it, that's for certain."

"No. I mean, stop with the act. We're alone. No need to keep up this pretense."

Now he cocked his head and frowned. "'Tis no pretense, lass. I find you attractive. Very attractive. And I know you feel the same about me. Soo…"

He leaned forward, crowding her against the rock and his strength, his masculine scent swamping her senses.

God, she already couldn't think straight with him like this. Against her. She shoved again.

"I'm serious, Iain. We need to talk. Now's not the time for this."

"Fine." He stepped back. "What do you wish to discuss?"

"My sister!" She placed her hands on his shoulders and locked her elbows. "I meant what I said. I'll take Glenfiddich and find her myself."

"You are *not* wandering off on your own in the Highlands."

She rolled her eyes. "Okay, okay, let's just fast forward through all the male posturing. I get it. It's dangerous. I could get hurt. I get it. I *get it*, Iain. But don't you see? That's how important it is to me. If it's dangerous for me, it's even worse for her. She could be hurt."

And now, God, her voice rose in pitch and got a little wobbly there at the end. She clenched her jaw tight and took a deep breath through her nose.

To her further horror, she choked back a sob as she said, "And it's all my fault."

Chapter Sixteen

How base his ambition, how poor is his pride,
Who would lay the high name of a Scotsman aside…
"Though Rugged and Rough Be the Land of my Birth,"
Jacobite Reliques

RACI'S DISTRESS—ACH, IT tore through Iain. As if his poor heart went all squashy and helpless, like some puffed-up Englishman.

By God. She looked close to tears.

What he'd have normally done—crack a joke to take the other person's mind off their trouble—just didn't feel…right. However, he was helpless to know what to do in its stead. He just felt in his bones that now would *not* be the time to pour on the full force of his considerable charm. Aye, he was humble.

At a loss, he placed his hands on her rigid arms, which still held him away from her, and rubbed slowly back and forth. "How…?" He cleared his throat. "How is it your fault?"

He'd listen. For once. Her distress cut through his senses, dulled by the frantic rescue. His skin had long dried, and he barely noticed his wet *féileadh*.

Her breath shuddered through her, and she looked to the side, avoiding his gaze. She bit her lip and looked down.

"My sister had…" She took another shuddering breath. Combined with small tells—tightened jaw and fists, a measured, flat tone—it bespoke the struggle she waged to stay calm and in control. "She had this silly idea that all Scottish men were hunks in kilts."

"Hunks?"

She gave a watery smile. "Hot."

He shook his head.

Inexplicably, her face turned red, which seemed to annoy her. "An expression that means the men are incredibly good-looking."

"Ah, I ken your meaning." He gave a little smile.

"Anywho. She…well, my whole family is obsessed with Scotland. Even though we've lived in America for over three hundred years. It might be hard for you to imagine, but in my country, in my time, we have this celebration every year called the Highland Games, and my family always participates. They're quite nuts about it actually. Campbell tartans for throw pillows and curtains. Scottish dancing lessons. All of it. And I…" She glanced away.

He rubbed her arms again, and she softened her hold. Enough so he was now pressed against her lovely form again. He cupped her upper arms and squeezed. "You…?"

Her face flushed red again. "I hated it. It all seemed so pointless. And, I guess, part of me resented it because I had no choice in the matter. My brother and sister and I were trotted out as cute little Scottish kids to put on a show and make our parents proud. I felt like a damned performing monkey. Yet, anything I had an interest in, they just…pretended wasn't the case. It was as if I were invisible."

Her lips rolled into a thin line, and she puffed out a sharp breath. "I feel so damn ungrateful for complaining about it, because really, how spoiled does all that sound? I had a family who cared for me. Fed me. Sheltered me. All they asked in return was that I make the Campbell clan proud every year at the Games. But…I was a kid." She shrugged. "I didn't know until later how good I had it. How safe I was."

"How did all this bring you here then?"

"My sister came to visit me in London. She lives in America and wanted to see Scotland, because, unlike me, she and my brother are just like my mom and dad—"

"Bewitched by Scotland."

"Yes. And she was loading up on all the Campbell tchotchkes—"

"Tchotchkes?"

She waved a hand. "Stupid items. All of them smeared with the Campbell tartan, or the Campbell motto, or some such shit. She'd already been here for five days, and we had fifteen more days of this. Touring around. Looking at Campbell monument this, or Campbell castle that. If I had to go in one more tourist spot, I was going to scream."

She paused, and Iain took the opportunity to interject. "I don't understand most of what you say, but I think I understand. You were getting increasingly frustrated with your sister's activities, correct? And you and your wishes were invisible again."

She choked back a sob. "Yes," she said, her voice laced with tears.

Seeing this tough woman turn emotional left him feeling anxious. That tough veneer, combined with her easygoing banter, he understood and knew how to play off of, but this? His experiences with women were either the high-strung, emotional types like his mother, or the tough-as-nails kind like his aunt. To see the latter become the former?

But he knew that, unlike his mother, Traci didn't wish for him to distract her with cheer.

At a loss for what else to do, he continued to gently rub her arms and whispered, "Go on." He could tell she hated getting emotional, so he opted not to draw attention to it.

"That night I suggested we party a little. I just wanted a break, you know? So we bought some good Scotch and holed up in our room at the B&B."

"B&B?"

"Bed and breakfast. It's like the inn. It's where we were spending the night. Anyway, we got to drinking, and one thing led to another, and I bet her I could prove...prove..."

"That we Scots are not 'hot' in our plaids?"

She chuckled. "Yes. I bet her a good chunk of money too. She already had some period clothes because she'd bamboozled me into going to the Highland Games on the Isle of Skye, so we changed, picked a time that fit our outfits, and, well...you know the rest."

"That's when I met you then."

"Yes."

A thought occurred to him. "Wait. So the myth you were referring to, it wasn't the Loch Ness monster?"

As he'd hoped, her cheeks again flared red. Lord help him, but he enjoyed causing that reaction in her, more so because he sensed it was not something she normally did.

Her mouth set in a mulish line.

He nudged her with his hips and chuckled. "Admit it, lass. What was the myth?"

"I think you know," she grumbled.

"Truly, I'm at a loss." He kept his voice innocent.

She glared at him. "That hot men in kilts existed." She said each word as if it cost her much to admit each one.

"And what's your stance on that myth now?"

She jutted her chin in the air. "Your clansmen, I hate to tell you, are not hot."

"I'm glad to hear you say so. Do you include me in their number then?" He stole a glance at her lips.

"You're going to make me say it, aren't you?" she asked, her voice half-exasperated, half-laughing.

He leaned down the scant inches required to bring his mouth near the soft shell of her ear. "Aye. I am. Tell me, my wife. Do you find me…'hot'?"

She trembled slightly in his arms. Her sweet breath puffed near his own ear when she whispered, "Yes," causing his own lust to flare.

"Yes, what?" He nibbled on her delicate ear lobe, and triumph surged when she groaned with desire.

"Yes, I find you hot, damn you."

To his complete and utter shock, she grasped his rod and cods in her wee hand. Pain mixed with pleasure.

And it wasn't in a prelude to play, the minx. It was out of frustration, anger, and a way to make him shut up. He'd bet their best steer on it.

He chuckled and drew back, and she threw him a saucy grin. "You're pushing your luck, buster."

"Aye, maybe I am. Or maybe you have me right where ye want me." He thrust his hips forward, pushing against her so her hand and his now-hard cock were pressed between them.

Her eyes darkened, and her breath came in quicker gasps. But he waited, his face, his lips inches from hers.

Her hand shifted, softened into a caress, and he groaned. He plunged his fingers into her hair, digging into the loose braid. He captured her mouth and ground his hips against her hand, against her hips. She pulled her hand away and gripped his head too, as their mouths fought each other, each trying to control the kiss, each frantic to take a little from the other. To have the last say.

Blood pounded in his ears. Her lips parted, and he plunged his tongue into her warm, sweet mouth. Ah, God, he'd missed her taste. She was driving him half-crazy.

If she was going to leave—if he only had a moment with her—then damn it if he wouldn't take what she was willing to give. Need and urgency had him trembling, and their movements were still frantic, their teeth bumping.

She fired his blood like no other lass. And he refused to think what that would mean for him when she left.

He kept one hand at the base of her head and angled her for better access, their tongues fighting, tasting, clashing. He dragged his other hand down the lovely, soft column of her neck until he cupped one voluptuous breast.

She groaned, and he plumped her lush softness, pinching the tip, rolling her stiff nipple in his fingers. His hips grinding against hers. Their faces dipping and tasting each other, over and over, as they fell into a rhythm. A rhythm he wished to God he was performing with his cock. It lay, hard and heavy between them, pressed into her belly.

A crazed part of him wanted to lift her skirts, shift aside his plaid, and plunge into her warm, tight channel. Again and again. Until she cried his name.

And then he did hear his name shouted. But it wasn't from her, since she was still enthusiastically engaged in devouring his mouth.

"Iain. Finish up with your wife, will ye? We need to get back to MacDonell lands," Duncan shouted.

She stiffened against him, and he stilled as well.

Damn ol' Nessie's blowhole to hell.

Breathing hard, he unclasped his fingers from her breast and stepped back. She was panting as well, her face glazed with want. Want for him.

God *damn* it.

He'd again lost control with this woman. Porridge for brains, he had. They hadn't even discussed what to do next. And 'twas clear, where she was concerned, he couldn't think clearly.

She continued to stare, but she calmly tucked a stray strand of hair behind her ear and straightened her clothes.

"Give us a moment, would ye, Duncan? We're still discussing matters."

"Is that what you call it?" His cousin's voice echoed down the ravine.

"Leave off," he barked. "I mean it. Another moment is all I'm asking."

Duncan grumbled, but his footsteps retreated.

Iain stepped toward Traci, and she straightened, wariness tightening her limbs. "I'm not going to touch you again." He stopped his hand en route to stroking her cheek and balled it into a fist. "But I *am* going with you, and I'll take no argument."

"What about Duncan?"

"I'll tell him our plans. If he wishes to accompany us, he can."

Her pretty eyebrows raised slightly. "So you'll still help me?" The trace of disbelief in her voice slayed him.

"Aye, I will. I'll not leave you. I'm in, for better or worse, though I hope it doesn't come to the latter."

She pushed away from the rock. "Okay. Then go do your thing and convince him to come. I think we need everyone we can muster."

"Do my thing?"

"Yeah, you know." She waved a hand at him. "Your thing."

As he could only stare, at a loss as to her meaning, she cocked her head to the side. "You don't see it, do you?"

"See what?"

She stepped forward and put her hands on his arms, squeezing them. "You're a natural leader."

He gave out a bitter laugh. "Far from it."

She searched his eyes, and he resisted the urge to squirm in place. It unnerved him, how she seemed to stare right down into his soul.

"You really don't see it." Her voice held a trace of disbelief. "I noticed it when we left yesterday afternoon. You put everyone at ease, and they all looked to you as their leader. And then when we were debating our exit strategy from Invergarry."

This time he couldn't help but shift in place. Restless. "They had no choice. The chieftain put me in charge."

She shook her head. "Perhaps that's why they showed up at the stables, saddled and ready. But when you appeared, I *saw* them, Iain. Their postures changed. There was an air about you. And they sensed it, even if they didn't know what it was. But I could see them looking to you, trusting you. Duncan might disagree with you on tactics now, but he respects you."

His lips thinned, bitterness twisting further through him. "Until I *proved* my leadership abilities today beyond a shadow of a doubt."

This was exactly why he'd avoided any responsibilities in the past. Better to skim along in life, take tiny, happy sips of what it had to offer, and move on.

She frowned. "The river crossing?"

"Aye."

"That wasn't your fault."

He swallowed hard, but for some reason, it wasn't difficult to bare this to her. "It was, though. I should have secured the packs better, or taken the time to go to the shallower ford—"

She placed a hand on his cheek. "You're only human, Iain. Don't be so hard on yourself."

"It proves I have no business leading men."

"But—"

He pulled away. "Nay. I'll hear no more on it. I'll help you, have no fear, but a leader I'm not."

She stared at him a moment, then brushed past him, shaking her head. "Fine. Believe what you want. Let's go."

He watched her retreating back, the sway of her generous hips. "Aye. Let's go."

Chapter Seventeen

❦

My tartan plaid, my ae good sheet,
That keepit me frae wind an' weet,
An held me bien baith night an' day,
Is over the hills, an' far away.
"The Wind Has Blow My Plaid Away," *Jacobite Reliques*

"Iain?" Traci whispered.

Without expressing anything out loud, they'd arranged their pallets together by the fire that night, and they were both huddled under his plaid. She'd been surprised when he'd wet it in a stream when they made camp, but he'd explained that it expanded the wool and shielded them from the wind. She had to admit, it made an odd but effective windbreaker. Kept midges out too, he'd explained, but thank God she didn't have to test that out as it wasn't yet midge season.

After slaying and dressing a deer earlier that day, they'd pressed on toward Urquhart Castle. Iain had managed to convince Duncan to forge ahead without having to resort to spilling her secret. Now Iain lay stretched out behind her, his strong arm looped around her waist, holding her tight against him. She'd protest his presumptuousness, but she found she liked it. Allowed her to pretend…

"Hmm?" His voice rumbled along her back.

Duncan had the first watch and had slipped into the night. Duncan wouldn't admit it, but she was getting better at reading the close-to-the-vest Highlander, and he was worried about Fiona too.

She shifted around in the cocoon of their plaids and faced Iain, though she could barely see him in the dark. Telling him about her family this afternoon had given her time to reflect—about herself and about him. And during their long ride today, a new thought had occurred to her: if her parents had wanted her to conform, then why was she the only kid in the family with the non-traditional name? It was as if they didn't expect her to fit in from the start. Had she always subconsciously felt that difference?

But she'd also had time to study Iain, and now, lying beside him with the blanket of stars arching overhead, a new memory from their first night had surfaced—of her babbling about stars and connections. While she couldn't remember the conversation word-for-word, a warm sense of closeness flooded her. That memory, and her earlier study of him, had left her with one thing—well, one *major* thing—which still puzzled her. "Why do you doubt yourself?"

He stiffened, and though she didn't feel him ease away, she sensed it.

"I have no doubts, my wife. What is there for me to doubt?" He circled his big hand around her waist and nudged her forward into his body.

She shoved against his chest, while also tamping down on the visceral pull she always felt around him. "Yeah. I know you have no doubts on that score, big guy."

"I'm glad you're aware of this fact. I was beginning to doubt *you* knew."

"Be serious."

"Why?"

"I know, silly, right?"

"I certainly think so, aye."

She rolled her eyes. "Humor me."

"Do you have a reward?"

"I can probably think of something."

"I can as well, my wife. I can as well." He gently nudged her with his hips.

Heat flared through her, but she shoved it down. She'd glimpsed something beneath his always-joking façade, and she was curious to see if it was a fluke. She knew what he was trying to do now—deflect her. Besides, she'd vowed not to indulge while her sister was in danger. Their interlude earlier today had left her feeling justifiably guilty.

"Duncan followed you, you noticed."

"Are ye sure he wasn't following my bonnie wife?"

"Yes. I know you don't see it, but you do have a natural talent for leading. Why do you doubt that?"

He blew out a breath and rolled onto his back. He placed a forearm over his forehead.

She levered up and propped her head in her hand. "What happened? I told you my pathetic sob story. Yours couldn't be any sillier. Spill."

"So, it's like that, is it? You showed me yours, and now I have to show you mine?"

"Yes."

He looked at her from the corner of his eyes and then returned his gaze to the star-studded sky. "My father used to be chieftain. Since I wasn't the eldest, he left me to fend for myself. Which suited me fine as a lad. I could hunt and fish and pester the lasses as much as I pleased. Life was grand. But as I grew older, I…I don't know, I guess I wanted more. To do more. So I pestered my brother and cousins during their training and insisted on learning to be a warrior too."

When he stopped talking for a bit, she prompted, "What happened?"

"Like everything in my life, it came easy to me. So when it came time for me to join them in a raid, I insisted I was ready. Walked around all puffed-up."

"How old were you?"

"Fourteen."

Whoa. "And they let you join them? On a raid?"

"Aye, they did. Mind you, raids are simple affairs. No risk to it. A pastime, it is, shuffling cattle back and forth between the clans. At least it used to be."

"What happened?" she whispered.

"What was to be expected, I guess. We'd joined the MacDonalds in raiding a Campbell holding to support the Macleans of Duart and harass Argyll for his attempts to invade the Isle of Mull. We were on our way back when I decided to do some target practice while we rode. Showing off, you know. My father rode up to my side and cuffed me hard enough to throw me off my horse." He swallowed hard. " 'Twas jumbled after that, but the end result is vivid enough—my father on the ground, blood pumping out of his thigh. I'd shot him. The gun had gone off and I shot my own father. And he damned me for a fool with his last breath."

She swallowed hard and touched his chest. "Oh, Iain. That's horrible—"

"Aye. 'Twas. No denying." He pulled in a deep breath. "Well. Now you know my sorry tale, we can bring in the keening women."

"Don't," she whispered and curled her fingers against his chest.

"What?" He looked at her, humor written all over his face. Except for his eyes. Pain lurked there.

"Retreat."

His jaw flexed. "Who's retreating? I told you what happened, like you asked. It's as simple as that."

"Is it really?"

"Of course." Now he crossed his arms while he lay there on his back and resembled a little boy in a way, who'd just been thwarted and didn't like it one bit.

"What was he like?"

"My father?"

"No, your childhood horse. Of course your father."

He sighed and clasped his hands behind his head. He was quiet long enough that she thought he wouldn't answer. Then his voice emerged, low and tentative. "He was a stern but fair chieftain and father. A good leader. He'd raised my brother to follow him as chieftain."

She frowned. "What happened? Why is your uncle chieftain then?"

"He died several years after Father's death. I was too young. Plus by then, 'twas obvious I was not chieftain material. My uncle stepped in and has led the clan since."

"How'd your brother die?"

He pursed his lips. "Fighting the Campbells. By then, the Earl of Argyll had succeeded in taking Mull."

"I'm sorry."

He shrugged. " 'Tis how it can be, at times. My uncle did send me to Edinburgh to attend university, now that I was the eldest."

"What does that have to do with anything?"

" 'Tis the law. Oldest sons of Highland chiefs must attend school in the Lowlands, and he opted for university. I won't lie, I enjoyed my years there tremendously. There was an energy there that was palpable. But I…I really didn't have a reason to stay afterward. The energy was addictive, but I was only a spectator. So I came home. But…"

"But what?"

"But I don't fit in here either," he said in a low whisper.

❧

IAIN GROANED AT what he'd nearly admitted. Was bad enough what he did end up saying.

But the truth almost escaped his tongue: that he wished for more with his clan. Because was this all there was to his life? Eating, drinking, fucking?

Somehow, he'd been pushed into that role, and he'd be damned if he could figure how to break out of it. The role had become a cage in which he rattled around. Looking out of the bars at others who had companions and families. Children they could love.

Most of the time, he ignored those bars. Kept his back to them and enjoyed himself. After all, life was short, was it not?

Every once in a while, though, he looked over his shoulder and caught a tender glance from a husband to his wife, or a chubby child wrapping his wee, pudgy arms around his father's leg and holding on as if his father were the wee one's anchor.

And something inside him…ached.

He'd whip his head back around then and crack a joke, determined to make the most of his lot. It was more than what his brother had been given.

Nay. He'd not be confessing this to a soul. They'd think him as cocked up as a Highland cow mooing down a dirty London lane.

He faced Traci and propped himself up by his elbow, mirroring her pose. "So. We're both misfits then."

She nodded. He couldn't read her thoughts, but he feared they contained pity, and that he couldn't abide.

He pushed her shoulder, turning her around until he could tuck her up against his body.

He'd ached to have her stretched out beside him, to feel her warm skin against his, but truth be told, this wasn't the reason for his action. He wanted her penetrating stare directed away from him. She saw too much.

She sighed and held herself stiffly at first, but he didn't press any further, and soon she relaxed against him. Honestly—and he'd chop off his left cod before admitting this to any of the men—it was pleasant to be just lying here with someone. Lord knew he was tired.

And it wasn't just someone.

It was Traci.

Traci made him feel comfortable when he allowed himself to be still and let her presence soak into him. He'd discovered this accidentally when she'd ridden on the pony with him to Invergarry. They'd ceased talking and…relaxed into each other.

It was an odd sensation. Part of him still prickled with awareness and restlessness all over his skin, sure, but he had no urge to brush her hair aside, skim his lips along her smooth, creamy shoulder, and whisper a soft, seductive word or two into her ear.

Nay, that wasn't exactly right, as the hard evidence against his stomach could attest. But it wasn't the *only* urge. He ignored the restlessness, allowed himself to settle beside her, against him, and just...be. Which was a wonder in and of itself. Never had he wanted to just...sleep next to a woman.

Somehow, being beside Traci allowed him to snatch glimpses of himself, and he didn't want to chase it away now that he'd glimpsed it.

Maybe if he remained still long enough beside her, he'd find out... find out who he truly *was*.

Because, while he had a role in his clan and filled it well, it wasn't how he wanted to fit in.

Chapter Eighteen

My love has breath o' roses,
O' roses, o' roses,
Wi' arms o' lily posies,
To fauld a lassie in.
"Merry May the Keel Row," *Jacobite Reliques*

"I CAN'T GET a straight answer from any of these villagers." Duncan thunked down his mug of ale and swung onto the bench in the tap room of the alehouse in Drumnadrochit. Though roughly forty-five minutes from the castle, it was the nearest settlement besides the one directly before its gate.

Traci slumped against the wall and sipped from her own mug.

Iain squeezed her thigh in reassurance. They'd been in Drumnadrochit for most of the morning questioning the villagers, but so far no luck.

She set down the mug. "What are you hearing?"

"Some saw a strange lass enter the castle, but I can't get agreement as to whether she entered on her own or with a party of men."

"The same with us," she sighed. "Maybe there are two different women, and their comings and goings are getting intertwined."

"That's a possibility," Iain said. "I talked to the castle servants when they visited the village. The good news is, there are no tales of an abducted lady or one who is in distress within the castle."

Traci nodded. She should be relieved, but it was all a lot of noise. Every hour that passed, the possibility of locating her sister seemed farther out of reach, and yet she couldn't give up.

But what else could she *do*?

"In other news," interjected Duncan, "my lot seemed fearful of some new *gruagach*."

Iain grunted. "Superstitious bunch, villagers are."

Duncan shuddered. "This *gruagach* would put a chill down anyone's spine. According to the tales, its dress is tattered and mildewy, and it moans something awful. The racket has quite terrified the kitchen staff."

"What's a *gruagach*, and why the kitchen staff?" Traci only half listened as she traced swirling figures in the water rings on the table.

Iain waved a hand. "What you English might call a brounie. They are scary creatures with lots of hair, and they haunt buildings and rivers and waterfalls."

"Aye. Seems their new, otherworldly guest has taken up residence roaming the hall outside the larder."

Traci propped her elbows on the table and cradled her head. "Well, this is all very interesting, but it's not helping us find Fiona. Aren't all your castles haunted anyway? Doesn't seem like something to get worked up about."

Duncan chuckled, the sound rough. "Worked up about? You have the oddest expressions, but I ken your meaning. Pay no attention to me. We'll keep trying."

"For how long, though?" She turned to Iain. "Can't we just go up to the castle and ask to come inside?"

"It's not that simple, lass. We risk much being in this village as it is. Our relations with that castle's lord are not an easy one. We cannot traipse up to their gate and request entry. Especially if our only question is to ask if they've taken your sister."

"But what if we don't learn anything this way?"

"We'll think of something."

"If my sister's in there willingly, I can't imagine she'd continue for much longer. She'd go back to the inn to find me. I know she would." At least she thought so. "But if she's held against her will…?"

Duncan's voice was gentle. "We haven't heard any evidence that that's the case."

"I know. I'm just worried."

Iain put his arm around her shoulder, and she hated that it felt good, but dammit, it did. "We'll find her. We have kin nearby and can work out a way in when it comes to it. Have faith, my wife."

She wanted to "my wife" him with a punch to the ribs, but it wasn't his fault. She just felt so useless. Ineffectual.

And she *hated* feeling that way.

To calm herself—who was she kidding—to *stop* herself from pushing the table away from her, grabbing a sword, and storming that friggin' castle like some avatar in one of her computer games, she pulled in a deep breath and allowed Iain's presence to soothe her. He might be a big flirt, but right now, he was *her* big flirt, with a nice, muscly, protective arm slung over her shoulders and a wonderful scent of Highlander pervading her senses.

∽

TRACI'S LIMBS ACHED from slogging all around the village, up and down the rocky inclines and paths, talking to anyone and everyone who'd listen. She was useless in questioning villagers on her own, since she didn't speak the language, but for this afternoon's jaunt, she'd requested to go with Duncan instead of Iain.

Iain looked a little hurt but quickly joked it off and set off in one direction.

It was for her own preservation really. She'd been getting too comfortable with him and could feel her heart becoming more and more squishy. Besides, she wanted to spend more time with Duncan, because she suspected something had happened between him and her sister that night. But he rebuffed her every attempt to pry with the ever practical admonition of, "Let us concentrate on finding Fiona."

She rapped on yet another door of a cottage on the outskirts of Drumnadrochit. Like the others they'd visited, it was a quaint stone house with a thatched roof which thickness and profile reminded her of drawings of houses in the fairy tale books she'd read as a kid.

Chickens clucked and pecked the ground behind her, and off to the right, pigs rooted in an enclosure. She shivered and glanced at the sky—the sun was edging down. This might have to be their last stop.

A gaunt woman with a baby on her hip, and a tousled-blond toddler hugging her leg, opened the door. And like the others, greeted them in Gaelic.

Duncan asked his usual questions, and they conversed for a short while until Duncan turned to her. "She also saw a woman matching your description enter the castle but has heard nothing of her afterward."

"She took that long to say that?"

Duncan chuckled and rubbed his cheek. "Nay. She also asked me about the *gruagach* and if I'd be so kind as to curse it back to where it came from."

"Again with this *gruagach*."

"And a *Sasannach* one at that."

"What do you mean?"

"She says it speaks in your English tongue."

She groaned in frustration but stopped. "Wait. Ask her what this *gruagach* looks like."

He raised a brow but spoke in Gaelic to the woman. She motioned with her free hand around her head and replied in a stream of lilting words.

"The creature is short, with tattered white robes, and its hair is crazed."

"Can you ask her if there are any other details she can recall? What does it say?"

Duncan asked and then turned back to her. "Only that it keeps repeating a phrase."

"What phrase?"

"She doesn't know since it's in your tongue."

"Can you ask her to repeat the sounds?"

He asked, and she nodded and said in the tone of someone mimicking something they'd heard often but didn't understand the meaning, "Ai yam the coast of grismasbast."

Traci frowned and rolled the words around in her head. The hairs on her neck lifted.

It *was* her sister!

Her knees nearly buckled in relief.

She grabbed Duncan's arm. "Tell her thank you. We need to get back."

He nodded, and they retraced their steps to the village center. "Duncan, that's my sister. She's the *gruagach*. Let's find Iain. Can we get into the castle now?"

"How do you know?" While he played it cool, she detected a trace of hope in his tone.

"It's what she says. I'll tell you when we find Iain. We can't lose any time. We have to go in there now."

"Wait. Let me talk to someone I met on my rounds this morning to see if we've raised any suspicions. You find Iain, and we'll make a plan. The gates close in an hour, so let's talk tonight, make plans, and act first thing in the morning."

Traci gritted her teeth in frustration but saw the logic in that. By now, they were at the back of the alehouse.

"I'll take my leave of you now. I'll seek you both out inside upon my return."

"Thank you, Duncan." She scrambled over the stile in the fence and stepped around the dovecote. Up ahead, several village girls sat atop the fence, their heads bent together, staring at something off to the left that was blocked from view by the stables. Whatever it was had their faces flushing and giggles erupting every other moment.

Never mind them—she'd just nip around the side of the stables and use the well water to wash her face and hands before seeking out Iain. The news that her sister was *safe* quickened her steps.

She skirted along the back side of the stables—the girls now out of sight—and turned the corner where the well was located. She pulled up short.

Ha. Now she knew what had caught the girls' attention.

Iain stood by the well, his body soaked with water, the rivulets and drops glinting teasingly off his muscled back in the late afternoon sun. Was he nak—? No. He had on his kilt, but *still*. He might as well have been naked, for the cloth was sopping wet and clung to his muscled butt and thighs, leaving *nothing* to the imagination.

She dragged in a slow breath and willed the blood to stop its stupid rushing through her ears. Her traitorous nipples tightened and poked against the smooth linen of her dress.

He bent over, giving her an even more indecent view, and grabbed a sponge from a bucket. With the slowest, most luxuriant strokes, he glided the sponge down his left side, then across his front, though she couldn't see what he did.

Oh! But those girls could! What a show off.

God, and who could blame them? She settled in for the show, propping her shoulder against the corner of the stables. After all, she needed to speak to him, and what harm would ogling do? He obviously didn't care who watched him bathe, and she'd be damned if those girls were the only ones to enjoy the show.

For it was a show. The flirty devil knew those girls could see him. How could he not? He took his time with that stupid sponge too. With each slide down a muscled bicep, with each slide across a broad shoulder, something inside her grew more and more agitated. At first, she thought it was impatience—a wish to have that sponge in her hand, feeling it squish and flex between her fingers as she trailed it along the dips and ridges of his skin.

But as she pictured it and the feeling grew darker, she stilled, horrified.

Good God. She was *jealous.*

She wanted to be the only one gazing on him and wishing she could hold the sponge. *She* wanted to be the only one realizing he'd smell just a little different, with the heat from the sun on his skin, the tang of the soap.

Move. Slip back around and go into the inn and wait for him.

But her feet didn't budge. And her shoulder didn't budge from the wood as she took in her so-called husband taking a bath in his kilt by the well. And the full extent of how deep she'd let herself get hit her.

He upended the soap bucket, the water gushing out in a miniature facsimile of an ocean wave, eventually lapping against a nearby boulder. He rinsed it with water from another bucket, then attached it to the well rope. He lowered it, then pulled on the rope, his muscles flexing, and hummed a jaunty tune. Once the bucket was back up, he hoisted it over his head. For a moment, he paused, the muscles in his biceps bunching. Then he tipped the bucket, and the water poured over him in one powerful splash.

She stepped back, though she wasn't in danger of getting wet.

Again, rivulets coursed swiftly over his skin, soaking him, making his great kilt cling even more enticingly against his splendid form. Then, like some California surfer dude, he tossed his head, flicking back his hair. Inexplicably, anger threaded into her jealousy—this was all just a spot of fun for him. He had no idea she was behind him being rocked by this new discovery.

He paused for a moment, still in the sun. Again, she told herself to slip away—he and his ego didn't need to know he'd had one extra female gaze on him. Or how it had affected her. She glared in the direction of the ogling girls.

His head turned sharply, and he speared her with his piercing blue eyes. They were unreadable, and *now* her feet moved. She took a step back, and another, while he only stared at her, unmoving.

Until he slowly pivoted and stalked toward her.

With each step he took toward her, the kilt slowly tented, despite the weight of the wet fabric, his gaze locked on hers. She found herself rooted to the spot.

Chapter Nineteen

ↀ

White was the rose in his gay bonnet,
As he faulded me in his broached plaidie...
"Carlisle Yetts," *Jacobite Reliques*

ENOUGH WAS ENOUGH, Iain thought, as he stalked toward his wife. Aye, he'd known the second she'd appeared behind him as he bathed. He always knew when she neared. Somehow the air sharpened and...touched him, a featherlight weight, as if his skin prickled at her nearness, eager to have her closer, to have her skin touching his. To close the distance.

It was the most maddening thing.

Always, he answered that call—got closer to her—but stopped short of touching her as he ached to. Except for the stolen moments he'd taken full advantage of in the last few days.

But as he'd stood there, his back to her, holding the sponge and again flexing and showing off for her like the daft fool he was, he found he'd grown...what? Angry?

Was that what now galloped through him, making his blood pound? Anger? Frustration? Or some kind of premonition, some kind of fae sense telling him they'd soon find her sister.

And Traci would be gone.

Gone from his life forever, in some future world he couldn't even begin to understand.

But when he'd turned, caught her jealous gaze, and seen her quickly cloak herself with cool indifference? His emotion, and its cause, clarified. Anger.

Anger at her denial of her feelings for him.

Anger at himself for not being enough to push her past her mask.

Anger that he had not the time or skill to woo her properly.

But anger switched to determination.

Now he stalked toward her, his blood singing in his veins. His cock hardened further at the naked lust visible in her eyes before she quickly veiled it.

He didn't stop until he was a scarce inch from her body. He looked down at her. He wasn't trying to intimidate her. Nay, he was doing his damnedest not to shove her against the stables, lift her skirts, and plunge into her. If he lifted his hands and touched her… Well, he didn't trust himself.

Their breaths filled the charged space between them. She straightened to her full height, which brought her to that perfect distance below him, her mouth inches away, spannable by a mere duck of his head.

"You know what I think?" he asked, his voice surprisingly husky. Damn, what this woman did to him.

She swallowed. "What do you think?" she whispered, her voice shaky.

He forced himself to flash his woo-the-lassies smile while inside his heart pounded, pounded. He bent forward until he was right by the delicate shell of her ear, the dark red wispy strands of her hair tickling his nose as they curled around her ear. He inhaled her scent, now mixed with the heat of the sun on her skin, and felt himself harden impossibly further. "I think you want me."

He'd swear she trembled for a lovely wee moment. "You do, do you?"

"Aye. Surely you know I'm gone for you. It's making both of us addle-pated."

"It is?"

"Aye. Even now, you're repeating my words like a parrot."

She snapped out of whatever spell she'd been under and placed her hand on his bare, wet chest, as if to shove him from her. She quickly removed it, as if he'd seared her, and ineffectually moved her hand around the area between them, as if seeking a safe surface to shove him away from. She gave up, stepped back, propped her hands on her hips, and looked him in the eye.

"Don't you be working your wiles on me."

He smiled. "My wiles?"

"Yes. You and your brogue, and your…your muscles…"

"And my kilt?"

Now she did shove against his shoulder, and he grinned, some of his anger, his worry, his frustration ebbing away at their familiar banter. Leaving only determination.

"Yes, you and your stupid manly muscles in that kilt. Happy?"

He glanced down at the tent in said kilt. "Aye." He looked back up and winked at her.

"Oh my God, you're impossible."

"I like to think so." He stepped forward.

"Wait. Hold up, big boy. I need to tell you something."

That fae premonition returned, trickling down his spine, and suddenly he didn't want to hear what she had to tell him, because he knew what it was—she had found her sister, and she'd be gone soon.

"What do you need to tell me? You've already confessed you find me… What was it? Ah, yes. *Hot*. In my kilt." He threw another grin at her, but even he could feel the desperation in it.

"Can you not have a serious conversation?"

"Not where you're concerned." He slipped his hands up her arms and cupped her shoulders, and again she trembled slightly. "My brain, as I've said, is addled. We're both edgy. But I'll tell you what little my wee brain has been able to figure out." He brushed his hands up the delicate column of her throat until his thumbs framed her face, his fingers cupping her jaw.

"What's that?"

"We need to give into this attraction we feel toward one another."

Her breath gave an endearing hitch. "Oh yeah, why is that?"

"We're edgy. Unable to think clearly. We need to give in for the good of the mission."

She smirked. "The good of the mission, is it? You'd be willing to make that sacrifice, huh?"

"Oh, aye. For your sister, I think it's important we're able to face this with a clear head."

"And you think…" She stepped forward until her hips bumped into his, and his hard cock juuusst barely nudged against her belly. The barest whisper of pressure against it, and his lust ratcheted up another notch. "You think if we indulged—if we had wild monkey sex—it would help us find my sister faster?"

"Aye. I don't know how monkeys do it, but the wild part sure sounds enticing."

"And you're willing to make this sacrifice. For me?" She pushed her hips closer and eased away, the tease.

He grinned, but it was a desperate grin for he wished to *not* be silly. What he felt was nothing close to that emotion. He was helpless, trapped with this banter because it was what he *knew*. But it was a cage of its own, wasn't it?

He brushed his lips across her jaw until he reached her ear. "Aye. I'm willing. It'll be mighty *hard*..." He nudged her back and withdrew. "...but I'm more than willing. For your sister, you see."

"Mighty big of you."

He stroked his hand around her waist and gripped her delicious rump. He tugged her closer until he'd pressed her fully against him. The pressure-pain was sweet as his cock pulsed between them. "I'm glad you noticed."

She groaned. "Oh, that was bad. But I walked right into that one," she whispered.

"Aye, you did." He walked her backward until she bumped against the wall of the stables. She hit the side with a soft *oof*.

He pinned her against the wall with his hips. Her eyes latched onto his, and he gently stroked his knuckles up her neck, along her jaw, and across her soft cheek. Her pulse jumped in her neck, and their breaths grew ragged.

Aye. He was done with holding back. If she wasn't staying, if she couldn't—wouldn't—admit her feelings, he'd show her what she'd be missing. Show her what she could have with him. And selfishly, no way could he let her leave without touching her, tasting her one last time.

"You're so..." *Beautiful*. "...smart to recognize what needs to be done."

"Is that what you call it?" Her voice brushed against his cheek as he lowered his mouth.

"Aye. Brilliant," he murmured.

"I suppose that makes you brilliant too."

He brushed his lips against hers, and his heart soared at her sharp intake of breath. "If you say so." Another brush of his lips, but that wasn't enough. Not enough at all. He bent his head, nibbled at her lower lip, and took her mouth more firmly, tasting her, treasuring her. Oh, God, her taste. He'd been right—he could taste the heat of the day's sun on her skin.

He pushed his fingers up the back of her neck until they dug into her luscious hair. He cradled her head more firmly and tilted it to that wonderful angle he'd discovered before. Her mouth parted.

Needing no further invitation—he wasn't that daft yet—he swept his tongue inside. His knees nearly buckled with the tasting of her again. More. *Dhia fhèin*, he wanted, needed more. She brushed her hands across his back and held him tighter against her body. Their mouths grew more urgent as they stroked and tasted and feasted on each other, all their pent-up longing finally finding expression.

Her hips undulated against his, and his urgency spiked.

Oh God, he had to feel her sweetly gripping him again as he plunged inside her. His hands dropped to her hips to shove her higher against the wall and do exactly that when some vestige of sanity screamed at him.

He tore his mouth from hers, and they were panting, her eyes wild on his.

He snatched her hand and tugged her toward the back door of the inn. He'd get her to their bed, show her what she'd be missing, and beware anyone who stood in his way.

Except for that small puppy in his path licking his own underparts. He stepped gingerly around the fellow and tugged on Traci's hand as he once again aimed for the back door.

ↄ

TRACI STUMBLED UP the path behind Iain and bumped into him as he pushed open the heavy oak door. Her hand clutched in his larger one, she followed him into the dim hallway of the inn. Already, she'd swear that his skin was drying off from the sheer amount of heat he put off. Urgency and need raced through her, pulling her emotions along in their wake until she felt caught up in a giddy rush—for this felt *personal*. As they'd bantered by the barn, it seemed to hold a different edge, and she got the distinct impression it was *her* he wanted to be with. *Her* he cared about.

If she was right and her sister was the *gruagach*, they'd find her soon and she'd leave. The heady giddiness morphed into panic.

No. She shoved the panic and the other emotions to the side. She was indulging, that was all, because *she* wanted to and, yeah, because she'd gone and let her imagination run a bit ahead of itself earlier. This *was* an indulgence. For both of them. Nothing more. And because of that, she was on safe ground. She knew the rules from the outset. This meant nothing.

They'd reached the foot of the stairs when Duncan stepped out of the tap room. "Iain. A moment, please?"

Iain practically growled at Duncan. "Be gone."

Duncan reared back, surprise written across his face, but a sly smile stole across his rugged features. He held up both hands and stepped backward.

Iain tugged on her hand again, and they bounded up the short flight of stairs to his room. Her heart beat so hard, it felt as if it was as loud as the pounding of their feet on the wooden stairs. Yep, pure indulgence. That was all this was. He shoved open the door so hard it banged against the wall and sprang back to his palm with a resounding *smack*.

Inside the room, a maid was straightening the bed, and she yelped in surprise. One look at Iain, and she ducked her head and power-walked out of the room.

Traci snorted. It was just too delicious, seeing this Highlander go all He-Man, scaring the staff. Even more so because it was so unlike Iain. Normally, he slipped through the world with a wink and a soft laugh, putting everyone around him at ease.

He kicked the door shut and lifted her clear off her feet and into his arms. "No laughing, my wife."

"I'm not."

"So you randomly snort like a pig?" Humor laced his voice.

She gave him a mock punch in his pec, which was, yeah, right by her cheek. Sigh. "Hey, who you calling a pig?"

"So you *were* laughing…" In two long strides he reached the bed, and then she was airborne and weightless for about two seconds until the bed's soft covers *poofed* around her, cushioning her fall.

He landed on the bed beside her. "I might have to punish you for that."

"You don't like to be laughed at?"

"No man wants his woman snickering as he's wooing her."

"So…what moves have you got, big guy?" She nudged his hip with hers.

"Patience. Patience. I'm still wanting to discuss your punishment." He swung a leg across hers and planted his hands on either side of her shoulders. He arched back, the hard ridge of his arousal pressing against her hip. She tried to scoot sideways a tad to get that delicious weight resting right where she wanted him, but he was like a solid mountain.

"Hmm." His gaze roamed across her chest and down the length of her body and back up again, making her squirm all over.

How had she resisted him this whole time? No matter. They were here now. And she'd take advantage of it.

What hot-blooded woman wouldn't?

"My punishment?"

"I'm thinking…"

Chapter Twenty

TRACI POKED IAIN in the chest. Any excuse she could take to touch the delicious expanse. "I think you're taking too long."

She wouldn't dare voice it out loud, but seeing him take up most of her view above her—broad shoulders, tree trunk arms caging her on either side—made her feel simultaneously aroused, protected, and…restless.

"You do, do you?"

She shoved against him, and this time he let her. She flipped him onto his back and straddled his hips, making sure to adjust and wiggle and generally take her time getting in the right position on top of him. Already, she could feel his damp kilt seeping through her skirts.

His eyes slammed shut and his head arched back, and she bit her lip to keep from laughing.

He groaned. "Ah, woman. Stop your torturing."

"You're a soft one, aren't you, if this is torture?"

His eyes snapped open, his blue eyes hooded, piercing hers. "Does *any* part of me feel soft to you, woman?" His voice was husky, and he punctuated his words with a hip twist.

She snorted. "No. I have to say, there's nothing remotely soft about you." She skimmed her hands up his muscled torso, and his skin bunched and flexed under her palms.

She brushed across his arms to his hands and raised them above his head until it brought her mouth inches from his, loving how the position sculpted his biceps, pecs, deltoids—heck, all of the lovely muscles that dipped, curved, and flowed from his chest to his forearms. Greek statues had *nothing* on a Highlander.

He shifted his hips beneath her, just a subtle I'm-here grind against her most sensitive spot. She sucked in a sharp breath as a jolt of pleasure flowed up her center. His breaths, coming faster now, fanned across her cheeks. She captured his mouth in hers. He groaned and took possession of her mouth, thrusting with both tongue and hips.

Sensation and pleasure and a restless energy fizzed through her veins, increasing her desperation. This guy revved her up faster than any man had ever done. Taking control like this was how she always approached sex with a guy, her way of making sure he was aware that she was going into this with purpose, thank you very much, with no chance she could be seen as taken advantage of. *She* was in control and knew how these interactions went. She was *no one's* fool.

Iain seemed to love it, though a part of her imagined what it'd be like to submit to this strong Highlander in bed. Warmth shot through her, and she shuddered.

She nipped his bottom lip and pulled away, catching this gaze. His eyes were dazed, and his chest heaved, each breath he took a slight brush-and-pressure against her sensitive nipples. Oh God, yeah. She released his hands and retraced a path down his arms, moving her body down his.

When she reached his glorious chest, she circled his nipple with the tip of her tongue. She reveled in not only his flinch of surprise and pleasure, but also in the taste that hit her tongue: hot male skin, still slightly damp from his bath.

She flicked and nibbled the stiff nub, and he reared up, but he didn't take control, only skimmed his hands up her back, his fingers pushing into the ridges of her spine. At her neck, he buried his fingers into her hair, massaging her scalp, and she dropped her head, resting her forehead against a pec, moaning. It felt so good.

"You are full of surprises," he rumbled, but choked on a strangled oath when she again nipped and then blew cool air across his nipple.

"What? None of your other ladies paid any attention to this poor thing?" She gave his nipple another lick. As soon as the words left her mouth, the dark burn of jealousy flared in her again, and she shoved it away.

He gasped. "Nay."

"Shame on them," she muttered.

She darted her tongue down his torso until she reached his happy trail and glanced up. Both sides of her vision were filled by his powerful arms stretching to her head, the muscles bunching in his forearms and biceps. And her horizon was filled by the breathtaking stretch of pecs and the intense look in his eyes. In that instant, awareness of her intentions flashed through them, and he tossed his head back against the pillow and moaned.

Hmmm. That was promising. Very promising.

She dropped a kiss on his cute belly button—a very nice innie—and grabbed his waist. What she sought, though, lay past his belly button—his erection concealed under his damp kilt. She reached down and dragged an edge of the cloth up. And up.

Iain's body went very, very still.

Man, okay. Maybe kilts *were* sexy as all hell. Instant access?

His erection was long, thick, and hard, and lay pressed against his now kilt-covered belly. She inhaled his clean male scent, overlaid with damp wool and edged with the slight spice of his arousal.

She touched her lips to the tip, and it jerked. She gave a more open-mouthed kiss to the head, relishing his salty taste. His skin had that unique combo of coolness on the surface from a cold bath, with a distinct heat pulsing just beneath. She played her tongue along the crease and around the edge, and his whole body stiffened, while a long, low groan filled the room.

Oh God, there was nothing—*nothing*—like having a powerful man at her mercy like this. Her nipples tightened, and heat pooled in her sex as she gripped his base and took him fully into her mouth.

His hands jerked in her hair, and his hips arched up. His fingers didn't pull or direct—it was more as if the sensations she created made him desperate for an outlet. And oh, she understood. Restlessness and urgency were ratcheting higher and higher within herself, making her movements a bit shaky.

She pumped her hand and moved back up his length, playing the whole time with her tongue. She gave his head an extra suck. Heart pounding like mad now, she was about to pop free to ask him exactly how he liked it when her whole body was lifted into the air.

God, he made her feel as light as a down feather.

He settled her onto his hips, and she undulated back and forth along his hard length, relishing its pressure against her aching core even through her skirts.

"Enough, woman." But he was laughing as he said it. "This will be over soon enough as it is, I'm guessing."

He grabbed her skirts, and she lifted her hips so he could push the fabric out of the way. She eased back down, skin to delicious skin, though her skirts billowed around them and hid everything beneath their copious folds.

The sight, and what was hidden, shot another jolt of pleasure through her. She rubbed her core up his hard length, working herself against him, urgency coiling tighter.

"Ach, Jesus. You'll be the death of me, lass," he said, his voice hoarse with need.

His hungry gaze dropped to where her plump folds slid along his length. He shoved his hand under her skirt. She once again lifted upward, and when he tantalizingly nudged her core, she eased down, taking him all in, and oh, wow, he stretched her, inch by hot inch, a delicious ache that made her tremble.

When she was fully seated, she stopped. Their stuttered, heavy breaths filled the room, and he grasped her waist. But he didn't move her, he just shifted his hips slightly and stilled.

His heated gaze latched onto hers and, oh God, she didn't see the flirt she'd expected. His laughter and enjoyment still filled his gaze, but a strange rawness lurched outward and knocked against an element in herself she'd rather not examine. And rather not admit existed. A slow tremble started at her hips and cascaded up her body because it was clear he hadn't meant to reveal that vulnerability. A vulnerability he was desperately trying to extinguish from his eyes, from the space between them.

Her throat began to close up. To save them both, she slowly smiled and winked. Then she spread her hands across his muscled chest for leverage and eased back up his generous length, the molten slide inside her—the breathtaking fullness—making her tremble again. Afraid to go up too high and lose him, she eased back down, this time a little faster.

He grasped her shoulders and slid the sleeves down until her aching breasts tumbled free. She clenched around him as her nipples suddenly craved his calloused fingers, his calloused palm. He groaned and cupped them both in his strong hands and squeezed. Yes. She slammed down, each stroke getting more erratic. Desire tightened and tightened into a ball centered at her core. Where they were joined.

He started to flip her over, but she resisted, and despite possessing the strength to ignore her, he stopped. Instead, he angled her down until her thrusts stroked her clit against him, and the tips of her breasts brushed his chest with each drag across him.

But the position made her clumsy, so she reared back and continued to ride him. He massaged her breast with one hand, pinching and rolling its tip, his rough skin abrading her sensitive nipple. With his other hand, he slipped beneath her skirts again.

His fingers stroked a fiery path up her thigh until his thumb brushed her hard nub, just a playful pass. She gasped.

All vulnerability was gone from Iain's merciless gaze. Had she imagined it? All was frantic lust in a mutual pursuit of pleasure. Back on safer footing, she closed her eyes and surrendered to pure sensation.

"Harder," she moaned.

"Like this?" He pressed against her clit, stroking it, grinding it against her in small, tight circles.

"Yes. Oh damn." She slammed down one more time, and the tight, hot ball exploded, ripping through her, shaking her, convulsing her against him.

He gave a choked growl, his gaze spearing into hers. He grasped her hips and thrust—hard—into her. Again. Brutal, desperate strokes. Then he yanked her down on his next thrust, and his muscles tightened all over. He threw his head back and, on a strangled shout, his warmth shot inside her.

His hands fell away, and she collapsed on top of him, her heart beating so hard it felt as if it were in her throat. He tightened his arms around her and clasped her to his chest, his heart beating against her. Their breaths ragged.

He softened inside her, but she stayed in place, gripping him tighter, unwilling to feel him leave her, which was a new sensation. Usually, she moved off and collapsed beside a guy, the precursor to parting. The signal to say she knew what was expected and, no worries, she was on board.

But right now, she couldn't make herself move. She felt limp and fuzzy all over, so delicate and sated in the circle of his strong arms. His shoulders were so wide, she was able to lie across him with space on either side to spare.

He pressed his mouth to her temple, and she stiffened. She forced herself to relax. It was just a kiss. He didn't mean anything by it. It was *not* a tender gesture. And neither did the next one right by her ear, which sent a cascade of shivers all over her body. This was just his way of coming down from their high. That was all.

He stroked one hand up her back and cupped her head. A thumb hooked over her jaw, and he gently lifted her head. He kissed along her other jaw until he languidly kissed her mouth.

Nope, still didn't mean anything.

To be safe, she nipped his lip and gave a throaty laugh.

He chuckled. "Vixen," he rasped.

Impossibly, he began to stiffen inside her. She pulled away from his mouth enough to look in his eyes. She raised an eyebrow.

"Aye. I'd have ye again, if you're willing, *mo dhuslach rionnaige*."

A pounding on the door reverberated through the room, pulling them from their sensual cocoon.

"Time's up, Iain." Duncan's clear, strong voice came through the door. "We need to talk. Now."

Iain sighed, angled his head up, and gave her a quick kiss on her nose.

"Give us a minute, would ye? We'll be right down." He looked back at her and grinned.

Yes. She'd caved. This particular Highlander was a hottie in a kilt.

Chapter Twenty-One

$\mathcal{C}\mathcal{O}$

When Sol in shades of night was lost,
And all was fast asleep,
In glided murder'd Towly's ghost,
And stood at William's feet.
"Towly's Ghost," *Jacobite Reliques*

DUNCAN, IAIN, AND his minx of a wife gathered around the scarred wooden table at the inn. The rays of the dying sun poked through the grimy, diamond-paned window behind Duncan, bathing their area in a murky shaft of light. Iain supplied each of them with a flagon of ale, as it looked as if a weighty discussion loomed and he preferred his throat well-oiled for such an endeavor.

Besides, he'd come to enjoy this inn's homemade brew. Had a nice kick to it.

Traci snuggled against his left side, and her scent drove him mad. He adjusted his sporran to lay more fully against his still-hard cock. Far from taking the edge off, their bed sport had left him wanting her even more. She knew her mind and wasn't ashamed to take her own pleasure, God bless her. He ached to find satisfaction in her arms again. The sooner the better. But his desire was edged with a growing trepidation—had he succeeded in breaking through to her?

Yet he knew Duncan. The man would not rest until whatever was on the bastard's mind was aired. "What has your kilt tied in knots, Duncan?"

His cousin leaned back and crossed his arms. "We've attracted too much notice with our questions. We cannot stay here tonight. We need to leave."

Traci straightened beside him. "But my sister! She's in the castle. I told you."

The premonition Iain had had when he'd first seen her by the well slammed back into him. "Did you learn something new?"

"Yes. You'll think this is crazy. But I know Fiona is in there."

"How do you know?"

"She's the *gruagach*."

Iain jerked back. "Explain."

"Don't you see? She's pretending to be this creature. She dressed herself in rags, teased her hair, and is scaring the kitchen staff so she can get access to the food."

"How can you be sure of this?"

"You don't know my sister. That's totally something she'd do."

"If that's the case, why doesn't she just scare a guard from the gate and slip out? Or walk out at that, the same as she entered?"

She bit her lip. "I wondered about that. But she must be stockpiling food for a journey. This tells me she's safe and not being hurt because no one knows she's there. She must have been the one who entered on her own. The hauntings all started after the villagers said they saw her enter. And she's nuts about Scottish history and lore; she'd know about that kind of creature."

Iain gripped the handle on his flagon of ale. "But we can't act on this. There's no way to know if this is truly your sister, or just the superstitious imaginations of the kitchen staff. I can't risk action on such flimsy evidence."

"How's this for evidence? Earlier today, one of the villagers told us the creature has been known to moan the words, 'I am the ghost of Christmas past.'"

They stared at her blankly. 'Twas a strange thing to utter, but he couldn't see how that proved anything.

Her shoulders slumped. "You guys will just have to trust me. My sister is the only one who would say a line like that. It...it comes from something in our childhood."

"Explain," Duncan barked.

She turned pleading eyes to Iain, and he knew without her saying that it was specific to their future world. But he couldn't come right out and say that, and neither could she.

Under the cover of the table, he squeezed her thigh, letting her know he understood and would back her.

She turned to Duncan. "It's a...a line from a Christmas story that someone we know...back home wrote. It's not known outside of my family. So...don't you see? It's her. And she could be using that phrase in hopes the story of her haunting spread enough for me to hear about it. So that I'd know it was her!"

Duncan frowned. "I don't know…"

"Makes sense to me," Iain interjected. "It's a special signal her sister knew Traci would recognize. I don't think we could find a clearer one, if you ask me."

Duncan gave a gruff nod. "It still doesn't alter the fact that we cannot stay here tonight. Or in this village, for that matter."

"Aye. I agree."

Traci stiffened under his palm again, and from the corner of his eye, he saw her mouth part, ready to protest. Again, he squeezed her thigh. "We'll pack up and leave, but we'll hide in that glen to the west of here and plan our next steps." He turned to Traci. "We'll get your sister out of there. We just need to devise a plan. One that will not raise the ire of the Grant. This will take craft, not brawn."

Thankfully, she nodded. By degrees, Traci relaxed until he grew aware of her flesh, warm beneath his palm even through her skirts. He stroked his thumb in a tiny circle and was rewarded by her sharp intake of breath. He eased his hand up slightly, dragging her skirt up her skin. She clasped his wrist and, while answering a question of Duncan's, unceremoniously plopped his hand back into his own lap.

He chuckled, and she angled her face slightly to his and gave him one of her arch looks.

Oh, aye, he couldn't wait to again bed his little spitfire. But then he sobered. Christ, they'd have no chance, for they'd be camping out in the open with Duncan as company.

He lost his erection, which was probably a blessing, and his sporran lowered to rest at a more natural angle in his lap.

Certainly they'd have one more stolen moment together before she left. Wouldn't they? A moment where he could plead his case, ask her to stay.

He started to stand, but Traci grasped his arm. "Wait. Maybe we should scout out the castle grounds? See if there's a weakness we can exploit? Then we can regroup and plan."

"That sounds like a wise idea." Iain turned to his cousin. "Duncan?"

"You two go ahead. You'll be less conspicuous and can pose as love birds, if need be. I'll pay a visit to my new informant, see if he has any ideas and meet you at the ravine in the glen."

Iain grinned. Maybe he'd have a moment after all.

FORTY-FIVE MINUTES LATER, Traci and Iain leisurely rode on their ponies in the green swath of ground directly west of the walls to Urquhart Castle. When they'd settled their tab at the alehouse and saddled up their mounts, they'd made sure to leave no doubt that they were returning to Dungarbh keep, having given up their search for their missing clanswoman.

She tightened her fingers on Fiddich's reins as a thread of excitement coursed through her. She hoped they could not only get the lay of the land, but also spot a weakness they could exploit.

"What a gorgeous view," she whispered. The early evening sun illuminated a sprawling complex at the bottom of a hill overlooking the blue waters of Loch Ness. "But how the hell are we going to get past that?"

A double gate bisected the high curtain wall, which stretched an impressive distance from left to right. She stood in the stirrups. Not much was visible beyond the walls, though, except for a five-story building tucked into the extreme left corner.

"That's Grant Tower," Iain said, guessing where her attention rested.

A farmer crossed their path, his back bowed with his wicker burden, and disappeared into a maze of a dozen or so support buildings which littered the ground between them and a ditch protecting the castle's landward side. From the noise and smell, the motley complex housed a tannery, a blacksmith, and various woodworking trades.

Traci stroked Fiddich's neck. "Do you see any weaknesses?"

"Nay. Not yet."

They turned and rode parallel to the curtain wall, with Traci closest, so that Iain could observe the defenses while talking to her. Hopefully, to anyone watching, they gave the appearance of a couple simply conversing.

"A stone causeway traverses the ditch, with a drawbridge, which is closed up for the evening. The causeway on the other side of the drawbridge is protected by a smaller wall. I make out one...no, two sally ports in that smaller wall, as well as arrow slits. Access to the castle from there will have to be veiled in innocence, for we cannot assault or slip by their guards."

They meandered the length and back, and Iain repeated all the details. She recited them back. "What about the crumbled part?" On the right, the wall climbed up a small hill, which sported a ruined tower and the collapsed roof of another building.

Iain reined in his pony and shook his head. "The villagers say that the family and residents live and work in the northern section but that a separate wall protects it from the collapsed area on the hill."

She frowned. "So accessing the ruined area won't do us any good." There went that hope.

Iain confirmed her assessment with a shake of his head.

With darkness falling faster now, they turned their horses toward the setting sun and skirted around the hill directly before them.

Despite not finding an obvious weakness, the activity and focus had given her a sense of purpose she hadn't felt since she'd zapped back to this time. Now they just needed to get back to their rendezvous point, join their observations with Duncan's findings, and plan how to spring Fiona.

❧

As DARKNESS DESCENDED that evening, Iain led Traci westward to the hidden glen that had been handy since time immemorial to hide clansmen and their booty during cattle raids. It lay several miles west of Drumnadrochit, which itself was still several miles ahead. By degrees, Loch Ness disappeared behind them.

Iain nudged his pony closer to Traci's. He couldn't bear to have her farther than arm's length. Their interlude at the inn earlier today still shook him. How had this woman—in such a short time—cut through all his defenses and come to mean so much to him? It baffled him frankly. He'd ached to have her, he'd ached *while* he was having her, and now he ached with the knowledge that he'd never have her again.

But what shook him the most was his disappointment. A disappointment more profound than any in his past. He'd always fallen hard, aye. Had loved each one and hoped time and again the woman would see something in him worth holding onto. And each time, he'd experienced the pang of loss.

Why was this different? Why did the thought of her leaving his life make his future gape wide open? Surely he'd find another woman, and he'd try again, but the thought left him feeling…*barren*. What was the point? He needed to accept the truth: he had nothing to offer any woman, and since women were smart—at least those he was attracted to—they knew better than to choose him.

He drew alongside his latest love, and immediately that same sense of peace and comfort he always felt in her presence washed over him. Her thigh brushed against his as their ponies drew too close and stepped away.

He glanced down at her as they parted, and she gave him a sly smile. A smile that would have warmed him yesterday with its sensual teasing. A smile that would have evoked an answering quip. But today, that smile cut him as surely as the sharpest *sgian-dubh*, for that smile said that he meant as little to her as any other man.

He stilled. He'd seen that smile once before. When they'd made love.

There'd been a moment when he'd been overcome with the most profound feeling of wholeness and rightness, and something fleeting had crossed her face. And then that smile. It was one of concealment. The jealousy he'd fleetingly witnessed—had that *not* been his imagination?

A new and different ache grew within. An ache to *unpeel* her. Not the clothes from her body, but peel back this…this shell she clasped around her and discover who lay beneath. To know her secrets. To know what drove her. To know her secret fears and wishes so he could protect her from her fears and grant her greatest wishes. His heart swelled in an odd way, and he blinked at a suspicious hint of moisture in his eyes.

It hit him then. He'd never had this desire with any of the other women he'd supposedly loved and wanted to make a life with. But no matter how he prodded, he could not see a way to accomplish this. A new restlessness—good Lord, was that fear?—worked its way into him. For even if he *could* unpeel her, it would be for naught. He still had nothing to offer her beyond a good roll in the hay, and the pain would be more acute to unpeel her and still not be what she wanted. Unpeeling worked both ways, he suspected, and she'd find nothing to hold onto within him. No other had.

Her shell, her barriers, simultaneously spoke to him but also butted up against his own failings, making a mockery of him.

Plus, she'd been fiercely determined this evening in the scouting of the castle. So had their interlude meant nothing to her? She seemed renewed in her determination to rescue her sister and return to her time.

But what if he *did* have more to offer? For it was becoming increasingly clear that his uncle was failing his people. What if he… stepped up? The thought left him more than a little dizzy.

Perhaps he *could* risk unpeeling her.

"Can you tell me some of your life in the future?" His voice sounded natural, thank heavens.

She turned her face up to him, her dark red hair blending with the light of the setting sun. "Sure. What would you like to know?"

"What do you miss most about it?" He winced. Was he *trying* to stoke her determination to return?

She gave a wistful sigh. Curse it.

"Hot showers."

He cocked his head. "What are these hot showers?"

She groaned. Almost sexually, and he grew strangely jealous. "They are like closets where hot water comes out of the wall from a pipe. That's how we bathe."

Curse it, that did sound pleasant. "They have such devices for people to use in each town?"

"They have one in each house!"

Iain's eyes bugged at that. Her time did indeed have wonders. As she continued to talk, she spoke of machines that carried people through the air for great distances and of how she could use the portrait-making device she carried to talk to people wherever they were in the world.

His heart grew heavier and heavier with each new wonder. His goal of convincing her to stay now seemed naïve. Even if he somehow became chieftain, that would be no competition.

She must have sensed his shift in mood, for she trailed off, and they lapsed into silence. Which was fortunate, for it allowed him to hear voices up ahead. His mount's ears pricked forward, stiff.

His hand shot to the side, and he grasped Traci's arm to halt her as well. Their ponies pranced in place, frustration making them snort and rear their heads.

"What's wrong?"

"People ahead. In the glen."

Iain searched their surroundings. He pointed to an overhanging crag. "Let's make our way there." With a caution to be quiet, he led her up the slope. At the halfway mark, he had them dismount, and they crawled the rest of the way. His estimation of Traci rose by degrees as she not only didn't protest but kept up with him without loss of breath.

At the top, shielded by a boulder, they observed the party below.

"Who is it?" Traci whispered.

Iain could only stare in disbelief. "Well, that's just it. It's a party of our own men."

"What are they doing here?"

He rubbed his chin. "I know not. This isn't our land. We risk enough already being here." He took in as much as the moon's glow and the firelight allowed. "We must join them." He released Traci's arm, which surprisingly he'd been gripping the entire time.

"Should we be joining them? They might not be on board with our plans."

His mouth set in a grim line. "That remains to be seen. But we must know their purpose. Besides, it's too late, for I see Duncan."

She nodded. The simple trust she exhibited, this fierce woman from the future, did something funny to his insides, and he vowed that whatever happened, he'd not prove that trust misplaced. He'd not fail *her* at least.

He stroked his knuckles against her cheek, unable to resist that small touch. The sooner they figured out what to do next, the better. The emotions she stirred made him restless. Eager to act. Eager to express. Eager to do *something*.

Chapter Twenty-Two

ↄↄ

There's right in the cause, and might in the will,
To the bonny bonny lad that is valiant still.
"Be Valiant Still," *Jacobite Reliques*

NOW THAT TRACI had finally taken the first step in rescuing Fiona, the events of the day washed over her as they trotted down the ravine into this hidden cut through the vast Highland plain. Iain had called it the Great Glen.

Far from taking the edge off by sleeping with him, she felt more *raw*, more exposed than ever. Her ability to read him was gone. Was he the flirt? Or something more?

Now, she had no clue what to make of him. At times, she'd caught glimpses of a different man behind his flirtatious behavior. Had she imagined that he didn't like the role? But if so, then why did he keep it up?

None of these speculations mattered. She was not here to get involved with a guy. But now… Now all her assumptions were overturned. Now she seemed to skate across slippery moss and couldn't find purchase. Couldn't find the horizon she needed to focus. It made her feel *ill*, this uncertainty. And she hated it. She wanted to get back to their easy banter, when she *knew* what was happening and what was expected between them.

She hated… Yeah. Fuck.

She hated that she wondered if he wanted *more*.

This was *not* good.

A new thought trickled into this mess: Katy suspected the case brought the wielder to their love match. Could…could that be what—

No. Her wish had been in service of winning that bet, and then to find her sister. It had *not* been to find "twoo wuv."

She snorted, drew her plaid tighter, and followed Iain into the camp of his clansmen. But as she gripped the fabric, she felt as if she were using it to protect herself from the outside world. Protect herself from herself. As if the blanket could re-erect the shield she'd held so successfully around her heart up until now.

She had *no* shield now.

Yeah, she was raw.

And over a damn man who was nothing but a flirt. A flirt just like the guy she'd fallen for in college. And the joke had been on her that time too. She'd wanted a harmless hookup after Brad crushed her heart and her dreams. Who better than one of her gaming pals who was drop-dead gorgeous and a dedicated flirt? But the hookup had turned into another and another, and soon she'd discovered to her humiliation that she'd fallen for Johnny. Her rebound guy. He'd set her straight and given her a bit of advice: *Never let them see you pine.*

She sure as fuck didn't let Johnny see her pine.

At first, they'd stayed friends—platonic—and he'd even been the one to introduce her to her first employer designing computer games. He'd also helped to make sure she kept her relationships purely physical. But it wasn't long before he'd excused himself from her life.

Iain's voice startled her from her thoughts. He greeted his men in Gaelic and swung from his horse with ease. She remained on hers, unsure how to proceed, and she hated that too. Where was her fucking shield?

God, she'd been faking it all the other times she'd interacted with guys, pretending for so long that she was a hopeless flirt like them. And now she couldn't keep doing it?

Get a grip, girl.

Soon enough, Iain strode toward her. Frantic, she scrambled in her mind to piece herself back together. She threw him a strained, but saucy grin. "Hey there, big guy. So what's the fuss here?"

"The fuss is to be determined, *mo dhuslach rionnaige*. Now let's get you down from there, shall we?"

He clasped his strong hands at her waist and pulled her effortlessly from Fiddich as if she weren't some five-foot-eleven chick carrying about ten pounds too much on her big-boned frame.

Of course, he made sure to drag her down his body, keeping his laughing, teasing eyes latched onto hers the whole time. And with that, she found her old self and grasped it like a friggin' life preserver.

"If you're not careful," she said, giving her hip a little roll as she passed his already hard erection, "we'll end up making a fuss of a different kind. Not sure I'm up for any kind of public *display*. Are you?"

His eyes flared with heat, and he squeezed her butt as her feet touched ground. "Nay. I find I have no wish to have others witness the kind of *display* you like to exhibit. That is all for me."

"All for you, is it? Hmm…" She pinched his chin. "We'll see about that." She winked and was relieved to see he understood she was only teasing him. Their easy banter went a long way to settling her attack of nerves, but doubt still swirled within.

What was it about this man that stirred up all of her emotions? He was supposed to be a safe flirtation, and despite their stepping back onto familiar ground with their banter, part of her still wasn't sure of anything anymore.

And what did that say about herself? And what lay ahead?

∞

STILL UNSURE OF where he stood with Traci, but also unwilling to have her far from him, Iain settled her down by the fire. She claimed to be exhausted and, staring at her face, he saw the circles under her eyes and the worry for her sister in her gaze.

The men knew they were married, so it only felt natural to arrange her to lay with her head in his lap, but it was only when she complied without protest that he was struck by its ease and singularity. Perhaps he had a chance… He stroked her nose and her hair to urge her to sleep, while he discussed matters in low tones with his men.

Soon, her steady breaths signaled she'd succeeded in falling asleep. So far, he'd learned only one thing from the other party: they were keeping something from him, and he liked it not.

Ross sat across from him beside the fire, and Iain turned the full force of his attention to the man. He'd get to the bottom of this, by God.

Duncan passed him a flask of whisky, and Iain took a sip and passed it to Ross. "What is your true purpose here?"

"It's as I told you. We heard reports about a nest of cattle thieves who were planning to raid against our clan. Nothing for you to care about, I assure you." Ross laughed and tossed back a large gulp of whisky.

Unbidden, a surge of anger, so unlike him, rushed through him.

The man lied.

And he was treating Iain as everyone in his clan did—justified though it might be—as if he were a frivolous appendage. Before, he'd been content enough to play that role. Now, it chafed. Yes, he'd toyed with the idea of changing to win Traci, but this was a potent reminder. He *was* a bumbler. 'Twas safer for the clan for him to continue playing his role, was it not?

Nay, a part of him protested.

And that part was connected to his feelings for Traci. For he sensed what lay ahead, what was being kept from him, affected her too.

He leaned back, putting his weight on his hands behind him. "Ah. You know me. I *don't* care. 'Tis true. But you can tell me the truth precisely for that reason. You know I'd never hurt the clan. But my bumbling could. 'Twould be better for me to know what's truly happening, so I might steer clear."

Ross eyed him sharply, but the suspicion quickly disappeared and the usual dismissal replaced the shrewdness. He laughed. "Aye. Perhaps you have the right of it." He stretched his legs in front of him. "We are to keep an eye on you, if you must know."

Another burst of anger flashed through him, but he forced a careless laugh. "Me? Afraid I'll get in trouble? Not that I blame the chieftain."

Ross shook his head and softly chuckled. "In a way. The chieftain wishes to ensure you get to the bottom of this business with the sisters."

"Yeah. I haven't had much luck in that direction. She avers she's an innocent, but…"

"Exactly. I suppose it does no harm to let you know that I've been tasked with making sure you retrieve the other sister, or do it myself. Have you discovered where she went after she left Urquhart?"

Ah, so their story at Invergarry had worked. "Our information was wrong. She never left it."

"Well then, we must retrieve her."

Iain rubbed the back of his neck. "Why is he keen on that? Whatever secrets she gleaned from us—if she is a spy—have already been spilled. She poses no threat."

"The chieftain does not like being made into a fool. Especially by some Campbell *nighean*. He wants her back at Dungarbh. Therefore, keep doing what you're doing—keep this one distracted—and leave the rest in our competent hands."

Resentment, clear and strong, surged through him, and he realized with a shock that the resentment had always been present, ever since his uncle had become chieftain. He'd just been so determined to fit in, he'd not even recognized the feeling for what it was.

He caught Duncan's gaze across the fire. "That is no longer acceptable, it pains me to say."

After what Iain had learned from Duncan at Invergarry, he could very well believe that there was a deeper play here than simple mistrust. His uncle had sent these men precisely so he could take the opportunity to undermine Iain in Ross's eyes—pretend he needed looking after.

On the heels of this thought, he began replaying past situations with his uncle and saw that at every turn, he was purposely cast in this role.

And as he looked around the gathered men and witnessed the postures of Duncan, Gavin, Lochloinn, and the others, he realized something else he'd never noticed—it was only his uncle and his lackey Ross who treated him this way.

He'd been such a fool. Now knowing that all of his uncle's motives were no longer pure, Iain began to question some of his deepest assumptions—like had his mother really become unstable? Could she be in the nunnery against her will? Sure, she'd been high-spirited and suffered from depressed spirits from time to time, but wouldn't that be natural after losing a husband and a son?

Iain caught Ross's gaze and held it. "You will include me in your plans, or I will impede them."

Shock registered on the other man's face, and the low hum of conversation around the fire lessened.

Duncan leaned forward. "Aye. We are to be part of this, make no mistake."

"But the chieftain said—"

Iain cut him off with the wave of a hand. "What does the chieftain know about the situation here? Duncan and I have been questioning the locals and gathering the information we need to successfully retrieve the sister."

"Her name is Fiona, by the way," added Duncan, glaring at Ross.

Ross looked back and forth between the two of them and at some of the other men. His lips thinned. "Very well. What have you learned?"

Iain related what he and Traci had seen of the castle's defenses, and Duncan related what he'd learned. They left out their suspicions of Fiona impersonating a *gruagach*.

"By my reckoning, we have two avenues, one more risky than the other," Duncan finished. "We can take a boat to the castle's postern gate at first light when they're expecting deliveries of that morning's fishing haul. My informant tells me we can join a man named Callum. He regularly makes deliveries and is confident we can bribe the guard at that gate to gain entrance—he's got a weakness for the whisky."

Duncan stretched his legs out and crossed his arms. "Or the safer bet is head to a local farmer I know of, who has Jacobite sympathies. They make deliveries to the castle semi-regularly, and we can devise a strategy to gain entrance that way. Or send Traci in with the wife."

Ross clapped his hands together, startling Traci awake. "We will do the first. I do not like relying on the wench. But no need to bribe the man at the gate. We have enough men to overpower him and the fisherman if need be."

Iain sat up straighter. "Are you mad? Why take such a path when there are other, more practical ones?"

"We have not the time. And I have no whisky to spare. Do you? We'd have to procure that, which could delay us for days. We have six days at most before we must leave to rendezvous with Dundee. I want to be done with this business."

"I like this not," Iain stated.

"I'm in charge of this party. You're either a part of it, or you can stay here as I first advised."

Iain narrowed his eyes and glanced at Duncan, who did not appear pleased either by this turn of events. "We will take my wife." Including her might temper the violence intended by Ross. Besides, he had no intention leaving her behind with whomever Ross chose.

"Nay. She will remain behind with some of my men."

Iain worked to keep his growing temper in check. "Nay, she will not."

Ross's lip curled. "Don't trust our own men with your wench?"

"She is my wife," Iain said, barely able to push the words out through his stiffened jaw. "What will you do when you get inside? You dinnae know where the sister is, but she does. And what if you do find her? Will you take her forcibly? That would be the only way you'd succeed since you are strangers to her. If she's anything like my wife, she will kick up a fuss, and then you'll have the entire garrison on us. If you take Traci, though, she can aid us, and her sister will come along willingly, for she'd see it as a rescue, not an abduction."

He spared a glance at Traci, whose eyes were questioning. He leaned down to her ear. "I will explain later," he whispered in English.

Ross bunched his fists, clearly not liking to be countered. He didn't bother looking at Duncan, but he did take in the rest of the men.

"I agree with Iain," spoke up one of the more powerful tacksmen. "We need to do this quickly, aye, but we also do not wish to become embroiled in a clan dispute, which fighting with the garrison at Urquhart would surely engender."

The others grumbled agreement, and Ross succumbed to the way the mood had turned. "Then, Duncan, tell me of this Callum, and let us prepare to depart. Daybreak is not far off."

✌

THE AIR WAS cool and crisp as Iain, Duncan, Traci, and Ross slipped into the fishing boat steered by Callum the fisherman. Mist blanketed the hushed waters of Loch Ness, making visibility difficult. Uneasiness itched across Iain's skin as he settled next to Traci. Earlier, he'd filled her in on their plan, and while she was eager to be retrieving her sister, she was as wary as he was of Ross and his plan.

She wrapped her plaid around her head, shielding her features, so as to be more easily mistaken for Callum's sister who sometimes accompanied him. The rest of the men had procured a boat and were to meet them by the postern gate at dawn.

They shoved out into Loch Ness, its waters lapping against the hull. A touch of superstitious fear rose within him, conjured by the lake and its denizen. The morning was too quiet.

Duncan and Callum rowed, and they made quick time down the shore. The first rays of dawn peeked over the mountains to the east and illuminated the castle fortress nestled on the shelf of land below the hill. The shelf lay above a small rise, but steps rose at the water's edge to the water gate cut into the back of the fortress. However, their destination was the postern gate at the bottom of Grant Tower.

The other boat emerged, cutting through the swirling mist from the south side of the castle. Iain stole a glance at Callum. Duncan had negotiated terms with him prior to Ross's arrival. Callum stilled his movements, and the boat stalled.

"Keep rowing, old man," Ross growled. "Those are our men."

Callum cast a nervous glance to Duncan, clearly not pleased with the turn of events.

Traci reached across the small space between them and grasped Iain's hand. He placed his other hand over hers and squeezed. Had he miscalculated in bringing her? He'd never forgive himself if something happened to her.

Soon they reached the postern gate and slipped alongside the other fishing boat. Ross nodded to a man on board, who leaped onto the dock and took position near the iron-banded oaken door.

Callum paused in securing the boat with a rope. "Hey now, this isna how we agreed."

Ross gripped the hilt of his sword. "Plans have changed. Keep quiet, and follow your normal routine."

Callum grumbled under his breath and secured his boat. He swung onto the wooden platform and leaned down to help Traci. Iain aided her ascent, for the tide was low and the dock's edge was chest-high. He expected her to balk, or to shake with nerves, but she gazed back steadily and gave a curt nod. With Ross and his men dogging her steps, she and her sister couldn't disappear once reunited, so she'd be returning. Och, he was a selfish bastard, for he was glad their parting would be delayed.

He swallowed a thickening lump in his throat and shoved aside thoughts of her departure. That would come soon enough.

"Do as you're told, lassie," Ross said in English, his voice low but harsh. "Once my man has overpowered the guard, you will wait until we join ye, and then we go inside."

Traci nodded, cast an unreadable look Iain's way, and turned to the gate. Callum lifted his catch from the boat and joined her. He yanked twice on a string near the door and waited.

eᴖ

BLOOD POUNDING IN her ears, Traci gripped her skirts and waited next to the fisherman. She didn't trust these men, but what choice did she have? Despite the chill morning air, sweat trickled down her back.

Distantly, she made out the sound of steps behind the huge oaken door, and she willed herself to remain calm.

The door swung outward. Instead of one guard emerging as they'd expected, three burst forth, their swords raised.

Chapter Twenty-Three

Ah ! cruel bloody fate,
What canst thou now do more?
"Dagon's Fall," *Jacobite Reliques*

TRACI WAS SHOVED from behind and landed with a *thud* onto the rough wooden planks. Her palms stung as they scraped its surface.

What the hell? The heavy weight of a body covered her. Trying not to panic, she angled her head around. It was the fisherman shielding her. Somehow, he'd warned the garrison inside.

From her position, she witnessed snatches of the action, but one image she wished she'd missed—the clansman by the door dropping to his knees with a slit across his throat. Then Callum was rolling her across the dock, and all was jumbled.

The fisherman shouted to her in Gaelic and scrambled into his boat. The other boat's occupants swarmed the dock and attacked the guards.

"Traci!"

Iain's voice cut through the clamor, and his face appeared near her knee just below the dock's edge. "Grab my hand and get on the boat!"

He'd get no argument from her.

She reached down, and he pulled her on board, his grip and his movements steady and purposeful and welcome. So, so welcome. She fell onto her knees, rocking the boat slightly, and scrabbled to the far end. She plopped onto her butt and took in the scene. Ross stood at the bow, yelling at Iain and Duncan and waving them onto the deck, but they ignored him. Iain barked harsh words to the other men on the dock, and the tone of the battle shifted. Instead of going for killing thrusts, they disarmed each of the guardsmen, one by one, until each was held back by a sword pointed at their necks.

Holy shit. Traci gripped the edge of her seat.

The rest of the men knocked out the guardsmen from behind, and they retreated to their boats. Ross's face turned a mottled red, and his voice rose. Iain and Duncan shouted him down and dipped their oars into the loch. If the alacrity with which Iain was obeyed didn't convince him he was a natural leader, she didn't know what would.

The dock receded, and disappointment swept through her. *Fiona!*

But Iain was right to retreat. The alarm was raised now. No way could they enter and find her without bloodshed. As it was, they were lucky they'd had only one killed.

Just then, arrows flew from slits in the wall above, and everyone ducked. The mist still hugging the boat provided some obscurity. Iain's arms wrapped around her at the same time she tried to shield him. They pressed each other into the safety of the hull.

But Ross was facing the occupants of the boat, still on a tear. Two arrows *thunked* in quick succession into his back, and he listed sideways into the loch, slipping below the water.

Iain lurched forward, hand outstretched. He glanced at the ramparts, clearly calculating if they should risk stopping.

Traci took a shuddering breath. "Iain. Leave him." She pointed at the body now floating face down. "It's too late."

His lips rolled inward, and he nodded grimly. They rowed swiftly out of range.

What had just happened?

∾

IAIN CLENCHED AND unclenched his fists, vibrating with anger and pent-up frustration. *Damn Ross.* The men aboard both boats were subdued as they rowed to safety, and the fisherman cast uneasy glances at Iain, unsure probably, at how he'd be punished.

They pulled up at the fisherman's hut, which hugged the shore north of the castle. "Callum, Traci, and Duncan, with me. The rest of ye, form up on the rise. We must be gone from this vicinity. If trouble overtakes us, break up and meet back at the ravine. It should be far enough away from potential patrols."

The others quickly stashed the boat, and Iain turned to Callum. "Fear not. I'm sorry we didn't alert you to the change of plans, and I do not blame you for acting how you saw fit."

163

The fisherman slumped in obvious relief. "Too many depend on the goods I receive in exchange for my catch. You did not ask, but we have a prearranged signal. If all is normal, I pull the string that rings the bell once. Caution, I pull twice."

Iain gripped his shoulder. "I understand, my friend. Now we must depart." He stepped away and finally did what he'd been aching to do since those men had burst out of the postern gate. He yanked Traci to him and clutched her against his body. "Are ye well, lass?" he whispered. He inhaled her sweet scent.

"Yes." Her voice was strong and clear, and the last of his fear and anger eased away. "Thank God you're okay."

He massaged his fingers through her hair, needing to feel their silk brush past his skin. "Sometime soon you're going to tell me what 'o-kai' means."

She chuckled. "Okay."

"Wench." He pulled away and gripped her chin, moving her face side to side. "Ye are truly well, then?"

Duncan cleared his throat. "We need to depart."

Iain clenched his jaw and grabbed her hand. "You have our thanks, Callum." He nodded to the fisherman, and Traci thanked him as well. He led her up the hill, Duncan following behind.

❧

TRACI WAS STILL shaking from this morning's failed attempt to retrieve her sister.

She'd seen two men die. And she could personally attest to all the critics of computer games, that its violence did *not* inure one to it.

Every time she closed her eyes, the sword sliced across the man's neck, and he fell to his knees. She clasped her hands to her stomach and dropped onto a nearby rock. They'd finally reached their rendezvous spot over an hour away, and the men were starting a fire.

Iain knelt before her, concern clear on his face. "Ye all right, lass?"

She bit her lip. "Is there a place where I can bathe? I'd like to be alone, if it's possible."

He dragged a knuckle across her cheek. "I dinnae think that is wise."

"You and Duncan can be within shouting distance, but I want to feel I'm alone, even if I'm not truly."

He searched her eyes and, God help her, she drew strength from his concerned, but steady, gaze. He helped her to stand. "Duncan, can you accompany us? We will guard her while she washes in the stream."

They followed the ravine until it curved and narrowed, bringing the stream that meandered through closer to the center. Iain stopped at the curve. "We shall wait here. No one can get to ye without passing through us. You will be safe. Ahead is only a waterfall."

She rubbed his arm and smiled. "Thank you." She only realized she still had her hand on his arm when his eyes darkened and Duncan cleared his throat.

"Right." She squeezed his arm and stepped away. Could there be more? Her emotions were all over the place, but the violence earlier had made one thing clear—she didn't want *anything* to happen to him.

Shaking still from the spent adrenaline, she hiked another hundred yards and knelt on the rough bank of the stream. She plunged her hands into the cool water and let it flow over her fingers. She splashed water on her face and relished the cold bite against her skin. It wouldn't be as easy to wash away the fear and the sight of that man losing his life, but she wanted to feel something normal against her skin.

She glanced back down the ravine. Iain and Duncan still had their backs to her. She quickly stripped and bathed in the cool water. Finishing as fast as she could, she sloshed onto a nearby rock and settled back to let the morning sun dry her skin.

She was beginning to nod off when a curious sound came from behind her—a *womp-whirr* sound and a slight *pop*.

She startled and began to turn around, when a cultured British voice said in a low, distressed voice, "Oh, dear. Oh my, oh my, oh my. My most humble apologies—"

Traci froze, and she stretched her fingers down and grabbed a rock.

She turned her head and... What the hell? A man stood with his back to her dressed in very proper attire—well, proper if he lived in Regency England—complete with tails and top hat.

She lowered the rock, for clearly he intended no harm. "Who are you?"

He cleared his throat. "I am Mr. Podbury, and I regret that I caught you at this most unfortunate time. I humbly beg your forgiveness."

Her heart popped into her throat, and she brought the rock back up, ready to bash him if he so much as moved. For she knew who he was. "You're the man Isabelle met back in 1834. The one researching time travel. Katy told me about you...and that you'd tried to take the calling card case from her once."

She darted her gaze to Iain and Duncan, but they remained still, far enough away apparently to not hear them.

He removed his hat and dug his fingers into his black hair. "Yes, well. I was acting on orders from my superiors. I was sent to retrieve it, you see. We needed to figure out what happened. The case should not have those abilities. It must have picked up temporal properties when I dropped it in the middle of a transport."

"But time travel *is* possible. You're here, and I take it not because of the case." *Since I have it here.*

He looked down and rotated his hat round and round. "Can you, er, don your clothes? I would wish to be able to converse more agreeably."

What a funny man. She leaned forward to stand, but sat back. "No. Apparently you're a gentleman, and my nakedness is keeping you at bay. I think I'll remain undressed."

He sighed. "Very well. I suppose I cannot blame you." He flicked his coat tails away and sat down on a rock, his back still to her. "Where to start…"

"How about with why you're here?"

"I don't suppose you will hand over the case."

Her heart skipped a beat, and she darted a glance to her clothes, where the case lay stitched into the pouch. "I don't have it."

He shook his head. "You do, or I'd not be here. My employers have created a device able to trace its temporal signature in the aether waves that comprise the time continuum. It's not precise, mind you, which is why I haven't had better luck in the past, but I know it's within a hundred feet and within an hour or so."

"I can't let you have it." She bit her lip. "I didn't mean to stay this long in 1689, but I can't give it back just yet. My sister also came back with me, and I need to get her first. I've been trying to reach her. Once I do, we'll return back to the present where we belong." She crossed her fingers at what she was beginning to think was a lie.

Because *what if—what-if—what if* had been twining through her all day.

"Will you hand over the case then?"

"Yes."

"Excellent. Excellent. To make this easier for me, because, as I said, our instruments are not fine-tuned, what year do you live in normally?"

She saw no harm in telling him, so she did.

"And have you observed that time runs the same once you've engaged the silver calling card case as a transportation device?"

"Yes."

"So very interesting…" He pulled something from his inner coat pocket, if she interpreted his movements correctly, and she prepared herself to duck or chuck the rock in case it were a weapon. But he bent his head, and his hand moved. Ah, he was taking notes.

"And if you may be so kind, what is your direction?"

She frowned. "My direction?"

"Yes. In your time, where do you live? I shall find you there once you return."

She gave him the address to her London flat. "Can I…Can I ask you something?" Traci tapped the rock against another.

"You may."

She took a shaky breath, for his answer affected whether she *could* even contemplate thinking past What If. "What theory of time travel applies? Am I messing up the timeline? Can I accidentally blink myself out of existence, or someone important?"

He heaved a sigh, and her heart stuttered. "We're still working things out. But here's what we believe so far—yes, you can change the timeline, but whatever you do has already been done by you by the time you are born. So for you, in this timeline, you cannot change it."

Huh? "I thought you said I could?"

He shook his head. "It's not as simple as that."

"I had a feeling you were going to say that," she grumbled and rubbed the top of her head.

"You see, changes made spawn new worlds where that possibility or decision has been made, and *that's* the world you're born into. You live in a closed loop comprising all the decisions everyone, including yourself, has made up until your birth."

She pursed her lips. "What happens to the other world?"

"It continues on. In fact, we believe your friend Isabelle created the new world she was born into, as well as yourself."

She sat straighter. "Wait, what? We didn't notice our history change after she went back."

"You haven't been listening. Since her living in 1834 comes before your birth, you were *already* part of the new world her 1834-self spawned."

Er… She'd have to take his word on that, because her head was seriously starting to bend now. "How did she change it?"

"Her decision to fund Charles Babbage's Analytical Engine. My superiors haven't perfected world jumping, but they can observe, and in the ones where she doesn't find the case or different decisions are made, it's fully another hundred years before computers are invented, and technology is somewhat different."

Oh wow. "But what—"

"Traci, are you finished yet?" Iain's voice echoed down the ravine.

She whipped around, but they were still facing away. "In a moment," she yelled.

Mr. Podbury stood. "I must go. I do not wish to be seen by the others as I am not in period appropriate attire. I shall see you anon. Good luck with your sister."

And with that, he pulled something from his vest, and his hand twisted. The air around him swirled and then pinched inward.

Pop.

He was gone.

ᛕ

"*MO DHUSLACH RIONNAIGE*, let me assist you. If you're not careful, you can hurt yourself."

Traci was holding the musket the men had loaned her and thought she had it propped correctly against her shoulder. She shifted again in a desperate attempt to get it right. The damn thing weighed at least ten pounds.

"Ach. That's even worse. You're hopeless."

"I'll have you know, I'm perfectly capable of shooting a Beretta."

"A Beretta?" Duncan asked, an eyebrow raised.

"Er, yes."

It was later that morning, and Iain had told the men he'd promised to teach her how to defend herself. Not wanting to argue, because dammit, she did want to know how to shoot one of these things, she'd agreed. Especially after the failed rescue this morning. How were they going to get in now that the castle had been alerted to trouble?

Iain stepped behind her, took her hand that was holding the stock, and repositioned it. He stood closer than necessary, and his heat spilled over her. Just like that, her hormones went all nuts again. And her emotions. Her hands almost shook with the enormity of what she was even contemplating—she might just dare to put a voice to her question. *What if I stayed?* Push it into the space between them and see what he said. The next time they were alone…

Iain twined an arm around her waist and snugged her tight against his chest. Then he basically used his body as a mold to put her in the proper position to shoot a musket and sustain the kick back as best as she could. Having him in contact with her whole backside was making it really hard to think, the enormity of her question like another entity beside them demanding attention. She jutted out her chin. Then his words registered—he was telling her something other than how to shoot a gun.

"Listen. Those men still believe you and your sister to be spies for the Williamite government."

She stiffened. "But—"

"Shhh. I brought you out here so that you, Duncan, and I can devise a plan. This will be tough, as they cannot know we're aiding you. They're without their leader, which helps."

Duncan now approached and stood on her other side.

"You're in on this, too?" she whispered.

Duncan only nodded.

Her knees almost buckled at the enormity of what this meant. They were defying their clan to help *her*. The knowledge bolstered her resolve. For if he was willing to defy his clan for her, it could mean he had feelings for her. And that her idea to remain after she found her sister wasn't as crazy as she initially thought.

"That's it, lass. Good form." Iain spoke louder and stepped back. "Now shoot the target."

The target was a patch of heather on a stump about a hundred yards away. She checked her position and squeezed the trigger.

The recoil was harsher than she anticipated, and she reared back. She almost fell on her butt, except she careened into Iain's warm body instead. He righted her. Okay, she was enjoying this too. A giddy sense of anticipation filled her. One she hadn't felt since college, when she'd gone all gushy over Brad, her first serious boyfriend. Or so she'd thought. Fear chased the giddy anticipation. A fear that once again, she'd bare herself to someone only to be made into a fool.

"Excellent. Guns are the perfect weapon for the weaker sex. A true warrior fights with their blade."

"How come they're letting you do this? Wouldn't the last thing they'd want would be for a spy to learn how to shoot?"

"I assured them I'd teach you poorly, that you'd been pestering me so much I couldn't stand it, and to not do so would be suspicious."

She frowned. "And that worked?"

"Aye. They underestimate women. And think me a simpleton, so…"

She lowered the gun and stared at him. "They think you're a simpleton? You're joking."

He laughed, clearly enjoying her outrage on his behalf. "I assure you, I'm not. Simpleton might be too strong a word. But 'tis true no one takes me too seriously. An advantage for the first time in my life."

Duncan cleared his throat. "I do not think you have the right of it, Iain. Not after this morning. They followed Ross reluctantly. You witnessed how quickly they listened to you order them to subdue and retreat. If not for you, we could have had a bloodbath on our hands. They know this. You have their respect."

Iain glanced away, clearly discomfited by this assessment.

She spoke up to distract him. "Okay, then show me how to do this right, and I'll make sure to be horrible."

"Your biggest challenge, besides the recoil, is the loading. Duncan, block their view, will you?"

Iain ran through all the steps involved in loading the ball and powder, and she rehearsed it with him until she had it memorized. "From here on out, I'll load so they will think you haven't learned this necessary step. We'll work on your stance while we discuss how to retrieve your sister."

Duncan crossed his arms. "This will not be easy. We cannot involve any of the other men. It is too dangerous."

She cocked her head. "Why are *you* willing?"

He stared off into the distance, a muscle ticking in his jaw, and answered in a flat voice. "Besides the fact that I believe your plight and feel honor bound to aid you, let's just say it tickles me to defy the chieftain in this small way, even though he'll never learn of it. Iain told me that once you retrieve your sister, you will be *disappearing*, I think was his word. Serves the chieftain right for his underhandedness. Increasingly, he's not acting as a chieftain should. He hoards the clan's wealth. Manipulates his followers." He looked to Iain. "Plus, I owe Iain a debt."

"You already paid it with your warning at Invergarry."

She figured it was time for another pitiful shot, and so she nodded solemnly and raised her musket into position. She made sure to feel the correct way to hold her body, aided by Iain, and once ready, moved her foot an inch back to put herself off-balance. She squeezed the trigger, and once again flew into Iain's waiting hold.

"You're enjoying this, aren't you?" She mock glowered at him.

"I'll not deny it pleases me to have you continuously falling into my arms."

Duncan rolled his eyes.

Iain helped her back into position. In the lower voice they used to discuss their plans, he said, "I think in order for this to work, we must pretend you've escaped. I'll order a search party, but if we play this right, the others can be made to go in the wrong direction, and Duncan and I can pursue you. Thusly, we can aid you in getting inside and fetching your sister."

"There's a farmer nearby who has Jacobite sympathies," Duncan said. " 'Twas the plan Iain and I favored at the outset. We head there and persuade him that we need to enter the castle."

"We could sneak in on a wagon he drives, perhaps," she added.

"That might work." Iain adjusted her stance again. As before, she memorized how she stood and then purposely shot the musket off-balance.

They fine-tuned their plan, making sure she could recite the exact path to the farm, while over and over she shot off-balance and fell back into his arms. He chuckled each time, adding in a butt squeeze here and there, which she pretended to be outraged about.

They'd just decided on the diversion she'd need to escape tonight when shouts at the camp drifted over to them.

Iain and Duncan were instantly alert and drew their weapons. Motioning her to stay quiet and behind them, they nimbly navigated the ravine and ducked behind the last rock shielding them from camp. Duncan scouted ahead.

Her heart beat, beat, beat because now they were alone, his solid strength and presence beside her, and she could now voice her *what if*, but she couldn't because it wasn't the right time—something could be wrong in the camp.

Shortly, Duncan returned. "Nothing amiss, but a messenger has arrived. We should join them."

Chapter Twenty-Four

For our brave Scots are all on foot,
Proclaiming loud, wheree'er they go,
With sound of trumpet, pipe, and drum,
'The clans are coming, o-ho ! oh-ho !...'
"The Clans Are Coming," *Jacobite Reliques*

GRIPPING TRACI'S HAND in his, Iain strode into camp, Duncan at the rear. Soon he saw what Duncan had reported—James, a member of their clan, dismounted from a horse shaking and sweating from a hard ride. James didn't appear to have fared much better.

Iain, Duncan, and Traci merged with the others as they formed a circle to hear the news James surely brought.

James took a long draught of whisky and wiped his chin. "Dundee's on the move."

Shouts and murmurs rose, and Iain dropped onto a nearby rock. "I thought we were to rendezvous with his men on the twenty-ninth."

"Aye. But word arrived that Mackay's forces are threatening to arrive at Blair Castle earlier than we'd supposed. The chieftain orders all his tacksmen to ride there posthaste so we can augment our clan's army. He's promised two hundred from our sept alone, including himself."

More cursing followed, for Blair Castle was a good two days' ride. That was all his men were concerned about, but Iain was frozen in place as Duncan gave him a weighted stare and shook his head slightly. For the first time in his life, Iain couldn't understand Duncan's intentions.

Inside, he was at a loss as well. Defying this small group to aid Traci was one matter, but to defy his uncle and chieftain so openly?

Before he could analyze his own feelings, he must know Duncan's. He lurched to his feet, ignoring Traci's confused stare. She couldn't understand what was being said, but he couldn't translate for her in front of everyone. "I'm taking a piss."

He pushed through the men, making sure to bump Duncan's shoulder, and stomped away for fifty yards. Keeping up appearances, he emptied his bladder.

On the return trip, as he'd hoped, Duncan was making for the same spot with the same excuse. As they drew closer, he said loudly enough for the others, "Couldn't resist emulating me, cousin?" Under his breath he said, "Where do you stand?"

Duncan clapped him on his shoulder. "I'm sorry. I cannot do aught but follow my chieftain now. Be careful, whatever you decide."

Iain swallowed hard but laughed as if they'd shared some joke. He ambled back to camp as if he had not a care in the world, but his emotions and thoughts were a jumbled mess. He couldn't blame Duncan, but at the same time, his quick decision threw Iain into even more turmoil. To Duncan, there was no doubt. And there shouldn't be for Iain either. His duty was to his clan and chieftain.

What was he to do?

∽

TRACI BEGAN TO shake. Something serious was happening, and never before had she felt as helpless as she did now, surrounded by all these rough warriors babbling in a language she had no hope of understanding.

She tried to read Iain, but he'd joked with everyone and went to pee, if she interpreted his posture in the distance correctly.

Whatever had happened had galvanized everyone in the group but him; he appeared unconcerned.

Everyone else began packing their belongings and saddling their horses.

And she just sat there feeling completely helpless.

Iain finally strolled into camp and said something with a smile on his face to the new arrival. If she wasn't mistaken, they were making lewd jokes, for the others stared back and forth between her and Iain.

Then he sauntered up to her, a grin on his face. He held out his hand. "Up with you," he said in English. "I wish to exercise my marital rights." He winked at her.

"What!" She pushed to her feet, ignoring his hand, while everyone chuckled and ribbed Iain.

He leaned back on his heels, mock affront on his face. "Ah, *mo ghràidh*, you know you want it. You were practically begging me this morn." But he darted his gaze off to the right, and his eyes held a different message.

Now she faked offense but followed his lead to take the opportunity to be alone. Finally, she'd learn what was happening.

He looped an arm around her shoulders and steered her down the ravine, thankfully in the opposite direction from where he and Duncan had peed.

As soon as they rounded the sharp corner in the ravine, she drew away and faced him. "What's going on, Iain?"

All pretense at lightheartedness disappeared, and he began to pace, though he kept out of sight of the camp. "Nothing good." And he filled her in on the messenger's news.

As he finished his story, her sense of dread grew. And only increased when he told her Duncan would no longer participate in their scheme. When he finished, she shoved off the rock. "What about you?"

He threw up his hands. "Ach. I don't know. I'm torn in two. This is a direct order from the chieftain. If I disobey, I'll be a broken man, don't you understand?"

At first, she thought he meant he'd be upset about it, but he'd said it as if it had an extra meaning. "Broken man?"

"Aye. What we call a man who has no clan to claim. If I helped you, I'd be cast out. Broken men are considered as nothing better than outlaws, forced to steal from others to live. They usually meet their fate at the end of a rope. 'Tis not without reason that we have the old proverb, *Cha duine, duine 'na aonar: A person by himself is not a person.*"

She opened her mouth to say, *We could move somewhere and start over,* because she was finally alone with him and her What If question still burned to come out, but she snapped her mouth shut in horror when his words caught up to her—*if I helped you.*

Good God.

She'd…she'd…she'd fucking done it again!

If I helped you.

Not one word about them as a couple.

Not one word about a future for them after her sister was recovered.

She'd let her stupid, giddy, squishy, goddamn heart believe a whole hell of a lot more was going on than it really was. Again.

All the old humiliation crashed into her, filling her, making her doubt herself, Iain, everything.

Tears choked up her throat as she watched him struggle about whether to *help* her or not. Playboy or not, he *was* an honorable man, and so *would* be torn about keeping his promise.

And then she pictured what he described for Broken Men. To live apart from his clan was unthinkable to him.

She swallowed hard, willing the hot tears threatening to burst forth, to just go away already.

Never let them see you pine.

She could do this alone. His help wasn't needed. He'd be spared worrying about which path his honor demanded, and she would never let him see that she thought their interaction had ever been more than an extended bit of harmless fun.

☙

IAIN PACED IN front of Traci. Restless and groundless, as if the world had been knocked askew, and he had no idea how to click it back into place. Events were slipping past him, and he couldn't take control of any of it. The unfairness of it all roiled through him, tightening his muscles, making his strides jerky as he paced across the rocky ground.

He'd barely had enough time with her, and he'd known it was limited. He wanted more time, damn it.

Plus, he'd promised to help Traci, and now he either kept that promise—and forever gave up his clan—or broke that promise to prove himself to his clan in battle. And never saw her again.

For if he left now, he'd have no more chances to convince her to stay before she'd find her sister and return to her own time.

Clan or Traci, repeated over and over in his mind, and it worked him into a frantic state. This right here, this was exactly why he couldn't be depended on, for a huge part of him clamored to do the impulsive thing and aid her no matter what. But he must think of the long term—even if he did aid her and they were successful, then what? She'd still be lost to him, because she planned to leave, and he'd have even less to offer her as an inducement to remain. He'd be a man with no clan. A Broken Man.

He stopped and stared at Traci. She stared back at him, seemingly calm. A hot wash of shame spread through him. There wasn't a single sign that she even cared about his dilemma. He'd been building agitated castles in the air, while she merely wished to do what she'd always said:

rescue her sister.

She no longer wanted his help. She clearly didn't think he was dependable.

If he had any room for doubt, she destroyed it with her next words.

"Well, Iain. This is goodbye then." She smiled brightly, which cut right through him, as sure as any blade. "We both knew it would come to this eventually, and I want you to know how much I appreciate all of your help. I couldn't have gotten this far without you, that's for damn sure." And then she winked. Winked! "And we had fun along the way, didn't we?"

She strode forward and clasped his arm. "One last kiss?"

Anger and lust slammed through him in equal measure. He grabbed her by the hips and yanked her against him. She yelped, but he captured her mouth in a searing kiss.

So. He could now add her to the ranks of all the others who thought him only a good fuck. She wanted a last kiss? He'd give it to her. That and more.

He crowded her against the rock, cupped her face, punished her with his mouth. God. Her taste. This was it. He wanted to take and take and take until he had her taste, her scent, her everything seared into every part of his being.

She probed and sucked and bit right along with him, her hands frantic as they clutched and scratched up and down his back while her hips ground against him.

He tore his mouth from hers and, avoiding her eyes, lifted her by the waist. Pushed her against the rock. Raised her skirts and fisted them in one hand. With his other, he yanked on the belt holding his plaid.

She scraped her fingers into his hair and tightened, and he relished the slight sting. Her breaths fanned across his ear. "Yes," she breathed.

Cock now free, and not even waiting to see if she was ready, he probed her sex and plunged into her. Deep and hard. Oh, Jesus, fuck.

"Iain!"

Aye, he'd make her scream his name. Again and again. If this was goodbye, he'd damn well make it a good one. Ruin her for any other man.

Her mouth slammed into his, a fractured moan escaping around the edges of their desperate kisses. She hiked her legs around his waist, taking him even deeper. He used the motion to thrust his arms around her, one hand gripping the nape of her neck, the other wound tight around her waist. He drove into her, his forearms scraping against the rock, pulled out, and thrust again, over and over, with aggressive, greedy strokes. Each fevered slide into her hot, tight channel spiraled his lust into a compact, furious ball in his lower back.

Each stroke an attempt to shatter past her defenses, shatter past her calm dismissal of him. If he was only good for fucking, well... He'd fuck her. Good and hard.

His climax, it was barreling down on him. "Not yet..." he gritted out. He stopped inside her. Body shaking, her sumptuous breasts crushed against his chest, he eased out, then surged into her, hard. Slow, delicious drag-out, her warmth clutching him the whole way. Slam. Drag out. Slam.

But the change in pace only delayed the inevitable. He'd never been much of a talker during sex, but desperate times...

He pressed his temple to hers, his mouth by her ear, the sweet-salty taste of her damp skin kissing his lips. "Is that how you like it, Traci?"

"Yes," she gasped on his next thrust. Those gasps, timed with each hard drive into her, they scrambled his mind, his defenses. His desperation.

"You like a good fuck? A Good." Thrust. "Hard." Thrust. "Fuck?" Thrust.

"Jesus, I do now. Give it to me. Harder."

"As you wish." Again, anger seared through him that she still only saw him in this way.

She cinched her knees lower on his hips, changing the angle of his penetration. God, he couldn't hold out... She bit his shoulder and cried out, violent shudders wracking her body, her sex milking his shaft as he pumped into her. His control shattered. He pounded into her furiously until the hot ball of his lust seized him fully, and he bucked and exploded inside her, his mind going blank and white, his body shaking.

He was only dimly aware of their bodies plastered in sweat, their breaths coming in deep lungfuls and his knees about to buckle.

He pulled her away from the boulder and collapsed onto the ground with her in his lap and his rod—only partially soft—still fully embedded.

Under the pretense of needing to regain his breath, he clutched her to his chest and memorized every spot where they touched, how her body felt molded to his, how it felt to be inside her. How she smelled. Like well-fucked woman, but *his* well-fucked woman.

His heart beat frantically against hers, and he squeezed his eyes shut. He took no small gratification in noting that she held onto him just as tightly.

God. So this was it.

Goodbye.

When his breathing could no longer be an excuse, he began to ease away. But when his mouth neared her temple, he paused. She stilled in his arms, her breath now more even as well.

He ached to move his mouth, just a fraction, to kiss that sweet skin, still damp with perspiration. To taste her one last time. To edge down to the corner of her mouth.

The ache was intense, as if he were being torn in two.

Her breathing stuttered as he shifted his head to bring his mouth that much closer. *No.* He squeezed his eyes shut and fisted his hands, bunching up the fabric of her dress he still gripped in his hands.

And he began to harden.

Fuck.

He changed his motion into a quick peck and edged back to look in her face, making damn sure he had the brightest, most disarming smile plastered on his own.

"Aye. That was fun. Good idea about the goodbye kiss." His voice was the proper mix of jovial and carefree. To spare himself any more torture by gazing on her lovely, dear face, he bussed the tip of her nose. "But we'd better return."

He levered to his feet, still holding her clasped around his waist. And looked down to where they were joined so she couldn't see his face as he clenched his jaw and eased out of her. He set her aside, dove for his plaid, and went about the business of wrapping himself back up.

Chapter Twenty-Five

My love he stood for his true king
"My Love He Was a Highland Lad," *Jacobite Reliques*

WHAT THE HELL had just happened? Traci scrambled to not only straighten her skirts but also to wrangle her emotions. And tried not to feel hurt at his dismissal. And how right she'd been.

But as she re-braided her hair, the humiliating wave crested and her familiar self eased back in. Who needed guys? He was doing her a *favor*.

When she tied off the end of her braid, she raked him up and down with her eyes, making sure he saw her. "Yep. Men in kilts are hot, all right."

She smiled at his stunned face, gave her skirts another tug, and began walking back to camp.

"Wait."

Her stupid heart leapt. Maybe…she'd been wrong about him.

She turned.

"Your sister. This is the perfect chance. You need to leave. Now. They plan to take you back to Invergarry castle on the way to Dundee."

She swallowed her disappointment. Of course. Fiona.

"Will they just let me leave?"

"I'm betting they're too focused on getting to the rendezvous point now to care, or to take the time to hunt after you. But to be safe…"

To her astonishment, he grabbed a good-sized rock and bashed it against his forehead. He barely staggered, but blood was running fast down his face. He threw the rock down and jabbed his thumb behind him. "Go. Quickly. To the farmer like we planned. He'll help you. Tell him you're my wife. He speaks English."

She stumbled forward a few steps, searching his face for any sign. Any sign at all. Of what?

She was an idiot. But as she passed by him, her gaze locked with his.

Was it only her stupid hard-to-kill romantic heart that saw his tight jaw muscles and the emotion flaring in his eyes and interpreted it as something more?

"Bye," she whispered. And blindly tore down the ravine, her tears obscuring and refracting the way forward into swaths of green, gray, purple.

♥

Iain rubbed his forehead as he stomped back into the camp. He'd been a little too enthusiastic in the bashing of his own head.

He smiled, though it was a pained smile, stiff and edged with all the sharpness at her departure. In truth, he had been so angry at himself, her, and his clan that he'd near caused himself to pass out. As it was, his vision had blurred, and he'd had to lock his knees and blink to see her clearly as she'd jogged past him.

He'd given her a few moments to get away, and now it was time. He clenched his jaw. Time to do his duty to his clan.

The questions peppered him as soon as he entered the camp. Several jumped to their feet. "We must go after her," one growled.

Iain glared and barked out, "Ah, leave off, will ye? You're all a bunch of kale-eaters, all worked up over one wee lass. What can she do now, even if she were a spy? Tell someone we're on our way to Dundee? So what! We'll be there before they can be." He chopped his hand down. "Let's go. We have a king to put back on the throne." The rest of them could go to hell for all he cared.

His rare show of temper, and their need for haste, stayed the men.

But anger was all he had left after watching her run away like that. Run away from him.

Women. He'd never understand them. Maybe he should take a break from them. He snatched up his belongings and saddled his mount, his whole body vibrating with the hurt and anger coursing through him. He caught sight of Glenfiddich, who neighed. Iain closed his eyes and swallowed before stomping over and securing her to his saddle.

♥

Later that day, as Iain followed the others in their frantic ride through Lochaber to reach the rest of the clan at Blair Castle, Duncan drew alongside.

"You made the right decision."

Iain's anger was muted now, though it still kept his body taut in his saddle. All afternoon, he'd relived their parting. "Then why does it feel like the wrong one?"

"Sometimes that's how it feels. Especially when you wish to follow both paths."

Iain grunted and stared ahead. "This is why I'm not fit to lead."

"You could have fooled me."

"Don't toy with me, Duncan. I'm not in the mood. Remember, I'm the frivolous one."

"Because you let others view you that way."

"What's the difference?"

Duncan reined in his horse and turned it toward him, blocking his way. "The difference, damn it all, is that you're the rightful chieftain."

"That may be. But it does not mean I *should*. You know the truth."

"Is this about that fool nonsense your father uttered when he died?"

Anger, hotter than before, blurred the edges of his vision red. "Died. Aye. At my hand, let us not forget."

"How can I when you won't let anyone else forget? It was wrong of your father to say that."

"It was true nonetheless."

"How old were you?"

"Old enough."

"Perhaps, but you talk about decisions and how you're incapable of them. Did you know it was a poor decision of your father's that put us there to begin with?"

Iain's gaze sharpened.

Duncan held up a hand. "Your father was a great chieftain, don't mistake me. No one would deny that. One of the best in the Highlands, many have said. But it doesn't mean he always made the *right* decisions. That excursion to aid the Macleans against the Campbells was only to be that. A show of strength to encourage Argyll to rethink his plans to invade Mull. But on the way home, your father decided to have a wee bit of fun with a cattle raid. You'd been serious enough in the fight against the Campbells, but the spontaneity of the raid affected you. Your father should have known better than to push and pull you through such swings of emotions after your first battle. We should have gone straight home. Instead, you were almost giddy in the release of tension.

No one blamed you. Except for yourself."

Iain nudged his mount to push past Duncan, but his cousin gripped his arm, staying him. "We all make mistakes." And then he broke into a grin. "Even old Glengarry couldn't keep ahold of one wee lass."

Iain's eyes narrowed a bit at the way Duncan seemed to say the last two words, with a touch of softness. But he yanked his arm from Duncan's grasp, unwilling to listen to more. There was only one thing he wanted to focus on right now, and that was the upcoming battle looming over the horizon. He wished to lose himself in that battle and forget all of his troubles. Forget how he was responsible for his father's death. Forget how Traci left him with nary a regret crossing her pretty features.

Chapter Twenty-Six

๛

Let us never depart
From the faith of an honest true blue, true blue,
From the faith of an honest true blue.
"True Blue," *Jacobite Reliques*

*T*HE LATE AFTERNOON sun warmed the back of Traci's neck as she shuffled across the wooden planks of the low-ered drawbridge to Urquhart Castle. She kept her face down and si-dled closer to the farmer's wife. A blacksmith's hammer clanged be-hind her, over and over—*TANG-ding-ding, TANG-ding-ding*.

Gah. The sound jerked against her brain. She pictured various ways the industrious blacksmith could lose his stupid hammer.

"Dinnae fash," Mrs. MacKiaran said in a low voice. "Nothing wrong or unusual about what we're doing." Other villagers were ahead and behind, all wishing to enter before the gates closed for the evening.

The wicker basket of cheese Traci carried bounced against her thigh, and she tightened her grip. God, had it been only several hours since she'd barged in on this family? Iain's and Duncan's directions had been flawless, which was a good thing because she'd been stumbling along, only half aware of her surroundings. They'd welcomed her, and their five kids bunched around her legs and chattered away in Gaelic while she told them her plight.

Now they were delivering cheese to the castle's kitchen. She was so close to her goal, and yet… She felt scooped out, hollow.

Rescuing her sister was something she was doing by rote.

Their steps changed in tone as they left the wooden drawbridge and strode onto the stone causeway. A high wall with arrow slits rose above her head on either side, and up ahead loomed the rounded twin towers comprising the gatehouse. Two bulky warriors guarded the entrance, their shadows stretching out behind them and blending into the shad-owed coolness of the gatehouse's interior.

Mrs. MacKiaran greeted the guards in Gaelic, but they held up their hands and crossed their halberds, the metal of the wicked-looking axes at the top *shhhreeching* as they passed each other, the sharp edges glinting in the sun. And like that, Traci's knees morphed into shaky goo, and her heart thumped in her throat. She might not understand Gaelic, but it was clear the guards weren't letting them enter.

Finally, Mrs. MacKiaran tutted, grabbed the basket from Traci's grip, and placed it at the guard's feet. She pulled Traci out of the line of folks waiting to enter. A woman with a wicker basket strapped to her back bumped into Traci as she surged forward to take her place. Once out of ear shot, Mrs. MacKiaran said, "He won't allow strangers through. Something about needing to keep out of any of the troubles, what with the rebels meeting up with Dundee. Apparently, they had a spot of trouble in the wee hours of the morn. I tried to shame them— what could they fear from a mere lass—but there was a woman involved in the attack."

Her chest tightened. That ill-advised raid *still* caused her trouble. "But my sister—"

"We'll get ye in. Leave the means to me."

Traci stared back at the crenelated ramparts as pent-up frustration and impotence swelled up her throat. She swallowed hard.

Don't barge in. Don't barge in. Don't barge in.

She had to repeat that over and over because her muscles and instincts itched to push past the guard and holler for her sister. She was so close. She could feel it, under her skin, that Fiona was on the other side of those imposing, impenetrable walls. Somewhere inside. Alone. Scared.

Running around as a Dickens ghost.

Traci took a deep breath. *I'm almost there, Fiona. Hang on.*

ᥱᥱ

"A BARREL? YOU'RE going to smuggle me into the castle in a barrel?"

That was Mrs. MacKiaran's solution? But…she didn't have a better one.

Traci blinked the morning sleepies from her eyes and sipped the hot herbal drink the MacKiarans had brewed for her the next morning. The refreshing tang of mint and other herbs hit her tongue, and she sighed. Not half bad…

"Aye," said Mr. MacKiaran, his voice rough and no nonsense in the cozy confines of the common room of their farmhouse. A peat fire was gaining strength in their fireplace, and the sweet-smoky scent filled the room.

His kind wife winced and nodded. "It's the only way, dearie. You'll have plenty of room. Husband only delivers his oats once a week, and that's this morn. So in with ye." She clapped her hands twice and shooed them toward Traci as if she were a misbehaving child on a playground.

"And where will you put me once inside?"

The terrier that was curled up by the fire whimpered in his sleep and dug an imaginary hole.

"In the storage room one floor below the kitchens. You'll need to wait out the day and only come out at nightfall. I've packed ye some food and a flask of water."

Traci shuddered. "And…and will there be rats?"

"Rats. Och, I'm sure. 'Tis where they store grain after all."

Her blood *wooshed* straight from her head to pool in her toes.

Mrs. MacKiaran peered closer at Traci. "You've a fear of the rats, do you?"

"A little," she whispered. And by *a little*, she meant *heaps*.

Mr. MacKiaran shook his head, and Mrs. MacKiaran put her hands on her ample hips. "They can't get to ye in a barrel, now can they? You'll be as safe as rain. Just bide your time, and come out when ye hear the bells strike thirty minutes past the eleventh hour."

But what about when she got *out* of the barrel?

ಌ

THAT NIGHT, TRACI huddled in the barely-large-enough barrel. Overriding the oaty smell of the interior was the smell of yeast and the storage room's cool, damp stone. A shifty, scurrying noise came from the left. *It's not rats.*

Okay. Maybe it was. But she was larger, dammit, and for now, she was tucked up inside her barrel. It had been a tight fit, and she'd lost the feeling in her butt and calves ages ago, but she was safe.

And inside the castle.

Now came the tricky part—finding Fiona.

"Oh, please. Please be right," she whispered. Her sister just *had* to be the *gruagach*. All the stories agreed on one point: the creature appeared when the chapel bells chimed midnight.

To take her mind off the no-doubt humongous, Scottish-sized rats, she focused on other sounds. There—the soft lapping of the waters of Loch Ness against the rocks on the other side of the castle wall. The slight keening of the wind around the stone ramparts.

The bells began to chime, and the tempo of her heartbeats quickened as if racing the clanging notes. When the last tone faded, declaring it was thirty minutes past the eleventh hour, she listened to the pregnant silence.

"Show time."

She shoved the heels of her hands against the lid of the barrel, and it clattered to the floor. She stilled, listening. But her blood pounded more from picturing the rats closing in on her with their horribly beady eyes, twitching snouts, and big, pointy teeth than from humans who might have heard. She scrambled up and perched on the rim, her calf muscles stinging from the sudden flow of blood. *Ow. Ow. Ow.* She massaged them, though maybe it'd help her disguise to lurch around as if she had stumps for legs. She fumbled inside the barrel for the candle, lit it with the tinder they'd given her, and thrust the light in front of her.

A pair of eyes glinted in the far corner, and her heart lurched. "I see you," she said defiantly.

She shifted the candle left and right, pushing back the shadows to make out the shape of the room. No bigger than her dining room in her London flat, it was roughly lined with fist-sized stone and had a barrel-shaped ceiling. Not a lot of places to hide.

She dragged out the white sheet she'd gotten from Mrs. MacKiaran. By the light of the flickering candle, and while darting her gaze again and again to the rat's corner, she smeared the sheet through all the spider webs she could find. She'd frayed its edges back at the MacKiaran's, making it as ratty as she could.

Jesus. This felt stupid as hell. Would this really fool anyone?

She whipped it over her head and poked her head through the hole she'd made. She fluffed her already teased-out hair.

Adrenaline now twitching her fingers, she looked up to the vaulted ceiling. "Please work." She patted her hip—case still there.

She blew out the candle and placed it and the tinder just inside the storeroom door. The rest of the way she'd have to go by feel and Mrs. MacKiaran's directions.

At the door, she listened. All clear. She eased it open and slipped out. According to Mrs. MacKiaran, the larder was one floor up, beside the kitchen. Okay. If anyone appeared, she'd raise her arms and moan. Convincingly.

She slid her hand along the cool stone blocks on her left and carefully followed with her feet. Her toe bumped against the first step. Fifteen in all, Mrs. MacKiaran had told her, wound tightly in a spiral. With no handrails and the steps narrow in depth, but high, she felt forward until her hands touched the step above. She gripped it for balance and guidance and stepped up. She repeated this again and again, but stopped every few seconds and listened for any other noise.

So far, so good.

Her breaths felt overly loud bouncing around the close confines of the dark tower, but she reached the top without incident. She pressed against the rough, wooden door and listened.

All was quiet.

With as much care as she could manage, she eased the large door open, its creaky hinges adding a drawn-out atmospheric touch. She held her breath, ready to accompany that noise with as much macabre flutterings and moanings as she could muster.

A fire burned low in the fireplace, providing just enough light to see. An oaken table and chairs occupied the center of a room slightly larger than the storage room. Ghostly shadows cast by the flames jerked and skittered across the plaster walls painted with heraldic crests. But this wasn't her final destination. Another flight of stairs led up and, hearing no one, she crept across the room to the outside door and eased it open.

She didn't slip out. Not yet. Outside, a lone torch sputtered in a wall socket and revealed a stone-cobbled courtyard with a squat, thatched-roof building opposite. The kitchen. And next to it, the larder. Nearby, the chapel bells began their long chiming for the midnight hour.

This was it.

A refreshing breeze off the loch whistled past and ruffled her hair. The courtyard was deserted, which made sense—at this hour, the *gru-agach* haunted.

Then she heard it. A slight clank and shuffling steps beyond the skittering glow of the single torch.

Cold sweat chilled her skin. This was her sister—she *knew* that—but her body was creeped-the-hell-out. Especially when the torch light revealed her first glimpse of the creature. The hunched figure lurched with each step and emitted a keening wail. Wispy gray cloth and highly teased hair fluttered with each jerky movement, aided by the winds swirling off Loch Ness.

Shivers skirted right up Traci's spine. Yeah. It was scary as hell.

The wail morphed into a low moan, and a voice emerged. "I aaaam the ghooost of Christmaaaaaas paaaaast."

Traci straightened and covered her mouth to stifle a snort. Oh, yes, that was Fiona all right. She recognized her attempt to sound male and menacing.

The relief bobbed her knees for a sec, and a stupid-wide grin escaped. Traci edged through the door, knowing she could only be partially seen in the murky light. She raised her arms. "I aaaaam the ghooost of Christmaaaaas futurrrre," she moaned.

Fiona shrieked, and the nails-on-chalkboard sound reverberated along the stone walls. Ha. Now the residents would be even more terrified of coming here at this time.

Unfortunately, her sister accompanied the shriek with a full pivot away from her and sprinted down the cobble-stoned courtyard and up a narrow stone incline.

Shit.

"Fiona!" she said in a loud, harsh whisper. But her sister couldn't hear her over her own screeching. How could she *not* know it was her? She must be strung out with nerves.

Damn it.

Traci tore down the courtyard, the sheet fluttering behind. Thank God, she'd cut the sheet to reach only past her knees. Not so with her much shorter sister. She snagged on the sheet's edge and sprawled onto the stone surface.

Traci put on an extra burst of speed, leaped, and landed on top of Fiona.

She was all frantic elbows and screams, and Traci clamped a hand over Fiona's mouth. "It's me, you idiot. Now hush, and let's get out of here."

Her sister stilled, then slumped. To Traci's complete surprise, she quietly sobbed. "I can't believe you're here. I can't believe you found me." She repeated "you're here" over and over, gulping down breaths, until she managed to calm down.

Traci crawled off her, grabbed her hand, and helped her stand. And was knocked backward by the force of Fiona's hug.

Traci stroked her sister's gnarled hair and softly cooed. Both of them trembling. She pulled away and soaked in the sight of Fiona. Skinnier than she'd seen her last, and dark circles bruising the pale skin under her eyes. But otherwise, she looked whole.

She'd done it. She'd found her sister. "Are you okay?"

"Yes. Oh God. Are you?"

Traci nodded.

Her sister began to shake. "Do you…do you have the calling card case?"

Traci patted the pouch on her belt. "I do. But what happened to you?"

"Never mind that now. I just want to get back home. Where it's safe. And clean. And I can take a showeeeerrrr." The last word was a drawn-out sob.

"Okay, okay. We'll leave now." Traci fished under the sheet and pulled open the pouch. She felt inside until her fingers closed around the cool contours of the silver case. "Come over here and hug me, okay? We don't want to take any chances."

"Thank you. God. I was so scared. But I knew you'd find me."

"You did?" Pride made her voice wobble.

"Yeah," Fiona whispered. "I did."

Heart full with her sister's faith in her, but also aching at leaving Iain, Traci whispered, "Hold on." And she rubbed the case and made her wish.

Chapter Twenty-Seven

~

For all thy bold conspiracies.
Thy head must pay the score ;
Thy cheats and lies, thy box and dice.
Will serve thy turn no more.
"Lament for the Apprehending of Sir Thomas Arm-
strong," *Jacobite Reliques*

Two days later

AFTER SEVERAL DAYS of hard riding, Iain and his party arrived at Dundee's camp in Struan. Early morning mist still clung to the ground and swirled about his feet as he wended his way through the encampment, intent on finding his uncle.

For a reckoning was long past due.

He'd lost Traci, but he for damn sure wasn't going to lose himself again. A figure stepped out of a nearby tent and grasped his arm. Duncan and Gavin spread out to either side, backs stiff, but there was no cause for alarm.

"Alasdair. Are ye well? I'd heard you'd come here." Glengarry had hedged their clan's bets in the dynastic fight by staying home and sending his son to represent the clan. Whichever way the rebellion went—win or lose—one of them would be on the winning side and so maintain the security of their clan and the people who depended on them.

Alasdair raised a brow and glanced at the three of them in turn. "Aye. I was just informed of your arrival and of your late night flight from my father's castle. You knew we intended for your wife to remain with the chief."

"Nay." He paused to marshal his thoughts, and he kept his eyes and voice steady. "You and your father were part of a deception meant to discredit me in the eyes of your father, our chief." He quickly filled him in on his uncle's machinations, as well as his failings as chieftain.

Especially the most damning for a chieftain—his stinginess.

"He is *not* what your father was."

Duncan and Gavin grunted their assent, and Iain shook his head. "That, he is not. If you'll excuse me, I'm on my way now to confront him."

Alasdair's eyes gleamed. "This I must see."

Iain grunted and strode to his uncle's tent, pent-up resentment and the promise of confrontation fueling his strides. His uncle's tent came into view at the next turn. Most of the men slept in the open—only the chiefs and the minor chieftains like his uncle had such shelter.

"I'd have a word with you, uncle," he said loud enough to penetrate within and to carry to those nearby.

A rustle of cloth came from within, and shortly his uncle threw back the flap of his tent and straightened. His eyes shifted to take in those gathered around, but they never landed on his. "Well, if it isn't my incompetent nephew. Where's that wife of yours?"

"She was never a threat, and you know it." He kept his stance loose but ready.

"How can a lackwit such as yourself determine such a matter?"

He refused to take the bait. "Know this, mine uncle. After this rebellion, when we have time to speak without the distraction of war, we will come to an understanding. Your aspersions and manipulations, I will no longer tolerate. Your actions show you to be weak-willed if you need to lower me in the eyes of others in order to raise yourself."

His uncle's eyes narrowed, and again they darted around, but he only rolled his lips inward and raised his chin. It wasn't lost on his uncle that Alasdair, Duncan, and Gavin stood nearby, witnesses.

Alasdair crossed his arms. "My father—your *chief*—will not be pleased to hear that he was not dealt with honestly. If you have an issue with your men, you deal with it. Do not use him to do your dirty work."

Iain began to turn. By turning his back, yet keeping his senses heightened, he'd allow his uncle to prove his assessment wrong. Prove his uncle would not take the coward's route and stab him in the back.

From the corner of his eye, Iain caught the quick movement as his uncle lunged forward with his dirk. His uncle was a weak man.

Iain spun and knocked the deadly knife from his grip with a quick, sharp blow. He grabbed his uncle's wrist and whirled him around until his uncle's arm pressed high against his back. At the same instant, his own dirk was at his uncle's neck.

"Do *not* test me again." He shoved his uncle away, who landed on his knees with a grunt.

Iain curled his lip and turned his back on his uncle in a show of strength. He marched through the parting crowd, and Duncan and Gavin closed ranks beside him.

The crowd stopped parting, and before him loomed an imposing man. By the wealth of his clothes and its Lowlander styling, combined with the air of authority he exuded, it could be only one man: Dundee.

As a true sprig of the noble trees of both Bruce and Stuart, Dundee was well-formed and formidable. He stood now, erect and tall, like a venerable oak, commanding the attention and respect of all the men he sheltered.

"My thanks to you for avoiding bloodshed," he said in tolerable *Gàidhlig*. In some ironic twist fate enjoys betimes, the Highlanders were led by a Lowlander—Dundee—while the government forces were led by a Highlander—Mackay. "You have just arrived, I've been informed. Will you and your leading men join me? For I wish to apprise you of how our situation currently stands and my expectations of your men."

Iain bowed his head. "Of course, my lord."

ℰℛ

Traci shoved her design sketchbook and pens into her leather satchel and ducked out of her office on the top floor of a modest-looking stone building in the heart of the hip, tech district of London.

Her ploy to avoid introspection? A big, fat fail. She'd come back only to face another week left of her vacation. So she'd begged to return to work, and her boss had snatched at the chance to have her help in the final round of testing Team B's game.

Which had ended just now.

"Take the rest of your holiday," her boss had ordered.

Now she had six days to rattle around in.

Frustration clipped her steps as she marched down the gray marble hallway. She hadn't felt fully seated in her body since she'd returned. Sure, she'd buried herself with work. But that no longer…satisfied. Had it ever? She mashed the elevator button and gripped her satchel. Glared at the slowly churning floor numbers above the door. It ticked to another floor. Annnnd stopped. She mashed the button again. "Come on, damn you."

She eyed the stair exit, her normal route—a way to keep her weight off—but perversely, she refused. She'd come back to technology, and that technology should *deliver*, dammit. She jabbed her thumb on the button in quick succession. She switched to her other thumb. Then both thumbs, one after the other, her satchel thumping against the wall as it dangled from her other fingers.

She'd given up and turned for the stairs when the door *dinged*. "Stupid elevator." She hurried inside and hit the ground floor button.

A chipper electronic beat tweeted from the elevator's speakers, interrupted by the low-pitched *dong* of each passing floor. Had she been kidding herself the entire time she'd been working here in London? She'd moved here to escape her family and to forge her own life, her own identity. And had found it. She thought. But really all she'd done was to fill her life with work. And more work. And empty victories.

Two days ago, when she'd gripped Fiona on the cobblestones of Urquhart Castle, her heart beating a no-no-no rhythm, she'd hoped that returning would purge her mind of Iain.

Iain.

Her throat closed up, and she swallowed.

That hadn't worked, had it?

No.

She craved him. Craved his voice. Craved his laughter. Craved the ease she felt around him. Geez, it had gotten so bad, that each night before bed, she pulled up their photograph, touched his cheek, and kissed him.

She barked a laugh. God, she was pathetic. She covered her mouth and glanced at the security camera. The on-duty guy must think her crazy. She waved her fingers. The elevator *dinged* open, and she threaded her way through the lobby and out onto the clogged street.

No, she hadn't purged Iain from her thoughts. Even worse, she'd reverted to her old high school and college habit of analyzing every-friggin'-thing. Every interaction they'd shared, hoping to glean from it every shred of meaning.

Yes. This was worse, worse than her craving, because the last time she'd analyzed like this was the last time she'd ever daydreamed about finding love.

She stopped, and Londoners swirled past her.

Well, shit. Now she knew what she'd do with the six days gaping before her. Time to hole up in her apartment and figure her life out. Finally.

೧

STACKS OF HISTORY books lay sprawled around Traci in the living room of her London apartment. Day One of her Figure Shit Out Week, and she'd caved to curiosity. Near as she could tell, the rendez-vous with Dundee that Iain and his clan had rushed off to led straight into a battle. The Battle of Killiecrankie.

Iain's clan had been on—she picked up her notes—the right flank, but not a single one of these books mentioned his name. Or Duncan's. And that lack of info worked deeper and deeper into her, coiling into a nameless, helpless sense of foreboding. Apparently his sept wasn't significant enough for their chieftains to make any listings. Did Iain ever become the chieftain?

She threw down the last history book, which slithered across the precarious pile. She'd never been good at history or the research involved. But the more she read about the battle, the more her foreboding grew into a weird sense that she needed to do something. But what? Tomorrow, three hundred and something years ago, Iain and his clan had fought in that battle. Did he survive?

When she'd first come back, she'd looked forward to Mr. Podbury arriving and taking the case away, and she'd wished she knew exactly when that'd be. But now, as the unease grew, she wasn't so sure…

Her apartment's buzzer rang, and she lurched over and thumbed the speaker button. "Yes?"

"It's me," came Fiona's clear tones. "I have sushi. Can I come up?"

Finally. Since their return, all she'd gotten out of her sister was that nothing bad had happened to her—she hadn't been raped or beaten. But she'd been scared, and it had shaken her. She'd checked into a nearby hotel for the rest of her vacation. Traci had told her she could crash with her, but Fiona had mumbled something about needing alone time, and Traci hadn't pressed.

"Since you have sushi…." Traci teased and punched the button to unlock the street door.

Her sister soon sprang into her apartment, her face more alive than Traci had seen it since they'd returned. Fiona set the to-go bags on the hall table. "You look like crap."

"Well, gee, thanks."

"Have you not been sleeping well?"

Traci stomped into her galley kitchen and pulled down two plates rather than reply. She tossed the utensils onto the dining table. "All I have is water. Want some?"

"What? No bubbly? Not even vitamin water?"

Traci shrugged. "Haven't had a chance to shop much since we got back. Work's been keeping me busy." She settled at the table, and Fiona joined her. They divvied up the sushi rolls and chowed down in silence.

Fiona wiped her mouth after polishing off a third roll. "Work's been keeping you busy, or you've been letting it keep you busy?"

Traci glared. "Same thing."

"No. It's not." Fiona tossed her napkin down. "Come on. You've been this way ever since we got back. I'm not an idiot. It's Iain, isn't it?"

She stiffened. "I haven't told you anything about Iain."

A cat-caught-the-cream grin broke across Fiona's face, and she bounced once in her seat. "Ha. I knew it. Outside of mentioning that you'd run across him, and that he'd helped you, no, you haven't. But it was the way you skirted around that topic…"

Traci set down her chopsticks and shoved away her plate, a half-eaten tiger roll listing pathetically. She couldn't…she couldn't talk about this. Not with Fiona. They'd never been *that* close.

Ready to tell her to mind her own business, she lifted her gaze. Caught a note of vulnerability there. And just a touch of daring. As if it was not only important for Traci to share, but also that Fiona was nervous about pushing, knowing it was new bonding territory as not-so-close sisters. Traci's heart ached a bit at that.

"Okay. Yes. We…we got a little involved."

Excitement and relief animated Fiona's face. "Spill, sister. That was one hunky highlander in a kilt."

Traci laughed. "You're still convinced of all that, are you?"

"Yes." She held out her hand, palm open. "And you owe me a hundred bucks."

The worry she'd held inside loosened. "So you really *are* okay? You weren't just telling me that?"

Fiona sighed and looked at a point over Traci's shoulder. "Yes. The men who took me were rough-looking, I won't lie, and I really thought this was it—I'm going to be raped and left for dead." She pulled her hand back and returned her gaze to Traci's. "But they didn't hurt me. Their Gaelic was rougher than what I'd learned. And the chief they brought me to made me nervous, so, as soon as I could escape, I did." She waved her hand.

"What happened after that?"

Fiona looked to the side. "Not much. I was scared to death and really, really hungry by the time I reached Urquhart Castle. But I didn't want to run into trouble inside, so I stayed hidden in their old hall, which had a collapsed roof, and took up the *gruagach* business. Didn't think they'd appreciate a free loader. I stockpiled food and stole some silver, which I'd planned to sell at the next village on my way back to the inn. Always go back to the beginning, right?"

Traci chuckled. "Right."

Fiona popped another bite of sushi into her mouth and chewed, keeping her gaze fixed on Traci. She swallowed. "Anyway, enough about me." She pointed her chopsticks at Traci. "Spill."

So Traci did. And, in doing so, found a strange catharsis.

❧

ABOUT AN HOUR later, Traci and Fiona settled on plushy cushions around Traci's glass coffee table, eating the chocolate torte Fiona had brought for dessert. Early afternoon sun streaked through the lone window in her flat.

"So, yeah. Iain…" Fiona licked chocolate frosting off her finger and pointed it at Traci. "What are you going to do about that?"

Traci eased her fork into her slice. "What do you mean?"

Fiona's spoon clattered onto the table, and she glared at her. Hard.

"What?" Traci adjusted her cushion, not looking at her sister.

"Are you serious? That's it? You're not going back?" Her voice rose with each question.

A strange mixture of horror and elation crashed through Traci, and she inhaled deeply. The new sensation mingled with the restlessness and foreboding that had set up shop ever since she learned the battle would be tomorrow in his time. All she could manage was a strangled, "Go back?"

"Yes. Go back. You're not normally this dense."

"Gee, thanks, sis."

Fiona edged closer to the table and leaned in. "Do you love him?"

"I…I'm not sure." It was too soon for that. Wasn't it?

"Well, I think it's safe to say you have the hots for him."

She shrugged. "So what? There are men here, where there are showers…" She lifted a bite. "And chocolate…"

"And you've experienced that same level of connection with other men you've dated?"

Traci slumped against the couch, the edge digging into her back. "No," she mumbled.

"Aha!"

"There's nothing to 'aha' about, you goof." She tossed her wadded up napkin, which hit her sister's forehead and bounced to the floor.

Fiona narrowed her eyes. "Yes, there is. You should go back. See how it goes. You can always zap back if it doesn't work out, right?"

Panic clawed up at the idea of popping back into Iain's life, as if she expected that she meant something more to him than a good lay. "I can't," she choked out.

"This doesn't seem like you." Fiona cocked her head. "Granted, we haven't hung out all that much since you went off to college, but we had fun getting reacquainted in Scotland. And you always seem so strong and sure about everything. It makes me ridiculously jealous. So, yeah, this…*meekness*—dare I say, wussiness?—doesn't seem like you."

Traci curled her lip. *God*. She *was* being a wimp, wasn't she?

Fiona folded her arms and rested them against the table. "You know what's also different?" She leaned forward. "I remember you being such a romantic sap when we were kids. You'd sneak into my room, crawl under the covers with me, and we'd speculate about our future husbands. You'd say, *wistfully* I might add, 'Just think, Fiona. Out there somewhere right now, growing up just like us, are our husbands.'"

She'd been such an idiot back then. A naïve fool. She vaguely remembered those conversations and wanted to say to that little girl, *Bless your heart*. "Yeah, well. Reality and all that. I grew up."

Fiona leaned back onto her hands. "But what if…what if our future husbands weren't growing up somewhere out there?"

"That's what I'm trying to tell you."

"No." She shook her head. "I mean—what if they're back there? You know, back in 1689?"

Again, a formless panic fluttered in her chest. "Fiona. Yes, I was attracted to Iain. We had great sex, but…"

"But what?"

Fuck it. She was sick of lying to herself. Sick of pretending. "What if that was all it was to him, okay?" She crossed her arms and curled forward, horrified to hear the hurt in her voice and that it was almost panicky-loud. "That'd be really embarrassing to show up and say, 'Here I am!' and he's all like, 'Wait-what?' Especially because he'd know how much I was sacrificing to come back to him."

Fiona's gaze seemed to take her all in. "Did he make you feel like you were nothing more to him? Did he say that exactly? Or was he saving face when you pushed him away?"

Traci's heart gave a what-if stutter as she sifted through the charged memories of their last encounter. There'd been a hesitation, a moment when she'd wondered if he'd leave his clan. Then panic and hurt and humiliation when she realized he was only debating about whether to help her or not.

Then that hotter-than-sin sex. She flushed all over just thinking about it. But as she replayed it in light of her sister's words? Oh, wow, yes. He'd been *angry.* And he'd almost too cheerfully taken up the role of love-'em-and-leave-'em. She'd assumed it was because he was relieved. But combined with the anger? Could he have been pissed thinking that was all she'd seen in him and played the role to the hilt to deflect? Like *she* always did?

A choking sob lurched out of her throat. "Oh God. Did I make a mistake?"

"Only one way to find out," her sister said so cheerfully that Traci almost considered sororicide.

"It's not that easy," she said, enunciating each word.

"Yes, it is. Come on. Life is short, and love is hard enough to find as it is. Take a chance. What's the worst that can happen?"

Her stomach curdled. "I go there, and he laughs."

Fiona looked shocked. "Are you serious? Is that what this is about? Woman up, sister. If he does, then you know he wasn't the guy and can move on."

Easy for her to say. "But I'd still look like a fool for thinking there was potential with him when there wasn't." She didn't think she could again face that pain. For a third time.

Fiona covered her hand. Squeezed it. "It doesn't make you a fool to have believed someone better than they end up being."

The truth of her sister's words punched her in the stomach. Ever since senior year in college three years ago, when she'd had the double-whammy of falling for Brad *and* Johnny, she'd allowed the experience and the overwhelming emotions to rule her relationships with men. She'd engineered her life so she'd never play the fool again. All this time, she'd seen it as a practical way to scratch her itches and avoid drama. But...

But what had that gotten her? Except for the occasional, unsatisfying bed gymnastics.

In a last ditch effort of self-preservation, she trotted out the line she always used with her friends. "I'd rather be single and happy than in a relationship and miserable."

Her sister frowned and placed another hand over hers. "But what if you could be *happy* and in a relationship? Are you willing to risk missing that?"

Traci pulled in a shaky breath.

Could she do this?

Overriding all was the bigger question: What if she *didn't?*

Both she and Iain used flirtation as a tool. As a mask. One of them had to risk taking it off. To...to see if there was something *more.* She'd been almost ready to do that before he'd had to join Dundee.

"Fiona. What does 'mo gooslak rinekuh' mean?"

" '*Mo dhuslach rionnaige?*'" She cocked her head. "It means 'my dust of a star.' Why?"

"My dust of..." She frowned. And then her whole body jerked and she choked on a sob. *Stardust.*

Heart pounding, she swallowed hard and looked at her sister. "Okay. I'll do it."

Fiona clapped. "Oh, good." She jumped up and hurried to her honkin'-big purse. She dragged out a cloth sack and held it up, eyes gleaming. "I'm coming with you."

Chapter Twenty-Eight

Short the consultation made by the King's people,
Up the side of the hill they went ;
Copiously poured the sweat from each brow,
As thro' the north side of the pass they climbed.
"King James' Army Marching to the Battle of Killie-
crankie," by Iain Lom MacDonald

CHRIST, THE SUSPENSE was killing him. In the wee dark hours of the morn, Iain conversed with Donald Glas MacGregor of Glengyle near one end of the great hall at Blair Castle. Though the room was filled with officers and fellow Highlanders milling about and exchanging clan news, tension defined their movements and their speech. All awaited word from the scouts sent forth sometime before midnight. Their aim: discover the position of the government forces led by General Hugh Mackay.

Yesterday, they'd marched to the castle, beating Mackay's men to the strategic location.

MacGregor's eighteen-year-old son, Rob, pushed past Highland warriors twice his bulk and reached his father's side, his face alight with excitement. His crop of curly red hair, which gave him his nickname Rob Ruadh, or Rob Roy as the English were already calling him, could be discerned even in the murky light of the hall. "The scouts are back. Dundee is calling a council."

At last. Iain searched the crowd for Alasdair, Glengarry's son. He stood near the fireplace conversing with the MacNiall of Barra. Iain nodded and made his way to join him. Since Iain's confrontation with his uncle, he'd forged a new bond with the future chief of the Mac-Donells. Now Iain and Duncan were more often than not at Alasdair's side rather than their uncle's.

Iain could no longer stomach being near his uncle. 'Twas now clear how he had manipulated Iain. And like the weak leader he was, his uncle sensed the shift in the demeanor of their fellow clansmen and kept his distance.

Alasdair fell in beside Iain, and they followed the others as they converged around Dundee. He sat at the great table with Cameron of Lochiel and other leading chiefs. Alasdair clapped Iain on the back. "Are you ready to fight this day? I can feel it in me blood. Today's the day, I tell you."

Duncan joined them as Iain said, "Aye. Let us be done with this."

Alasdair chuckled, and the trio nudged through the gathering until they reached Lochiel's right side and could hear the talk.

Dundee stood, lifted his empty pistol, and banged the butt twice on the heavy plank table. The wax candles on the ornate silver candelabra before him sputtered and flickered. The men instantly grew silent.

There was not a Highlander here who would not follow him wherever he led.

"The hour is at hand, my loyal followers." His voice rang with the educated accent of the Lowlanders that Iain had encountered at university, its timbre strong and clear and filling the depths of the room. "We have three choices before us, and I solicit your advice. Mackay is encamped at Dunkeld and will march here at dawn's light.

"Do we wait to attack until the bulk of the clans can join us on the twenty-ninth as planned and harass him until then? The scouts have returned and estimate his force at four thousand, while we barely command two thousand. Or do we attack at the narrow pass of Killie-crankie? Our other option is to allow his passage and engage him on open ground. What say you?"

Shouts erupted all around as various chiefs and officers sought to make their opinions heard, but Iain cared not—as long as he'd be soon lifting his sword. One of Dundee's officers advocated waiting for reinforcements. This opinion was bolstered by many of the Lowlanders, for they were still upset that King James had sent but three hundred Irish instead of the several thousand promised.

Alasdair stepped forward and spoke. "I say we engage. We are not like these paid soldiers. We may be with hunger, we may be fatigued, but we still relish a good fight."

Dundee nodded and angled toward Lochiel. "What say you, my friend?"

Though sixty years of age, Lochiel was a fierce warrior. Iain had heard tell that back during the fight against the Covenanters, an English soldier had wrestled Lochiel to the ground, trapping his arms beneath him. But before the soldier could deliver the killing blow, Lochiel had raised his head and bitten out the man's throat. Looking at the still fearsome man now, Iain could well believe it.

The old Highlander straightened his broad shoulders and pounded his fist once on the table. He looked each major chief in the eye, one by one, until he had impressed them with the gravity of what he was about to say. "Fight at once. Fight, even if you have only one to three. Let the Saxons fairly through the pass, and let us press home." He stood then. "And I do not fear the result. Once we are fairly engaged, then we will lose our army or gain a complete victory. We should dare to attack the enemy at odds of nearly two to one."

A great roar from the other Highland chiefs met this speech. Iain closed his eyes, lifted his head to the ceiling, and merged his shout with theirs, his blood roaring in anticipation.

Dundee placed a hand on the table, his face both grave and pleased. "I agree. We will engage."

Dundee's officers protested, but the Highlanders outnumbered them and were with Dundee.

Lochiel wasn't finished. He turned to his friend. "You must command. But you must not fight. On you rests the fate of our small army and the plight of King James. Not one of us will lift a sword unless you agree."

Again the Highlanders shouted in agreement. Dundee raised his hand for silence. The candlelight glinted off the silver embroidery on his kid gloves.

"No. I will refrain in the future, but give me this day to fight at least, and I will be content. What leader would I be to all of you if I did not endanger my life the same as you?"

Many grumbled, for Dundee had the rare talent of uniting the oft-feuding clans. He had their respect, which was no small feat.

Yet Dundee made it clear that he meant to lead the charge, and he gave the final instructions for their march. They would leave at dawn's break. And engage a force twice their size. If they lost, the survivors would be treated as traitors.

Oh Mary Mother, help them all.

ဆ

TRACI CROSSED THE gravel lot to their rental car outside the Killie-crankie Visitor Center, Fiona quick-stepping beside her. They again wore *earasaids*, but this time they had strapped knives to their calves, and Traci had a reproduction doglock musket and ammo. Thankfully, they didn't look too out of place. Costumed reenactors were already arriving for events leading up to Saturday's battle reenactment. Too bad it was being held on the closest Saturday to the battle instead of on the actual anniversary, today, or their task of getting onto the battle-field would have been much easier.

"Can you believe Mom and Dad?"

"Nuts," Fiona answered. "But not surprising."

Last night, they'd called their folks from a hotel on the north end of Manchester where they'd stopped for the night. They'd tried to tell them they were going on a remote camping trip, but when their parents insisted they take satellite phones, they'd had to fess up. Plus, what if Fiona decided not to return?

Of course, her parents hadn't believed them at first. *That* had taken lots of explaining. But when they'd finally been convinced, they'd insist-ed on retiring with them in 1689.

Given how obsessed her parents were, it wasn't surprising.

Nor was it surprising that they hadn't even realized how out of char-acter it was for Traci. It was all, "Of course you have to go back" and "Of course you love Scotland."

Traci shook her head. She'd never understand her parents, and they'd never understand her.

Fiona had taken over the call and assured their parents they'd return in a few weeks to say goodbye and plan their parents' retirement in five years' time in Ye Olde Scotland.

Traci's mind couldn't go that far into the future. This was all assum-ing everything worked out with Iain.

First, she had to get there. And find him. Make sure he was safe. And lay herself friggin' bare.

The more difficult call had been with Katy. Katy who, despite having found her own love, had been frantic about talking Traci out of it. Finally, Fiona had grabbed the phone, said, "We're going," and hung up.

Traci settled behind the wheel. When Fiona entered on the other side, she eased the car out of the lot and drove toward the quaint village of Killiecrankie.

Fiona unfolded the rough, pencil-drawn map they'd received from the tour guide at the visitor center. "You sure this is when you want to find him? In the middle of a battle?"

Chapter Twenty-Nine

❧

On the crest of the hill,
Above the dark of the thicket,
Stood the men who could rout the evil-doers.
"Killiecrankie," by Iain Lom MacDonald

IN THE MIDDLE of a battle.

Traci gripped the steering wheel tighter at her sister's words. "Yes. It's too late to meet him beforehand—he's already with his clan at the battle site. But afterward? No way. I'm worried as hell he might die." She'd finally identified the restlessness and foreboding. Yesterday, when she'd committed to go back, the restlessness had clicked into a conviction that she had to get there in time for the battle. In time to save Iain. Nothing else mattered.

"If he dies, it doesn't have to be then. He could have had an accident on the way to the battle."

She flexed her wrists forward and back on the wheel and glared at her sister. "Not helping."

Fiona picked at the edge of the paper map. "By the way, was Duncan going to this battle too?" Oh, she said it casually enough, but Traci wasn't fooled.

She chuckled. "So…Duncan, is it? I should've known you were coming with me for more than sisterly affection and seventeenth-century scenery."

Fiona shrugged and looked out the window. "They really do have funny looking cows up here. So shaggy."

"Whatever. But, yes. Duncan was with him."

Out of the corner of her eye, she noticed Fiona's fingers tighten around the cloth sack in her lap, the paper map fluttering forgotten to the floor. What *had* happened between them that one night?

Traci looked out the passenger window. "Here's the Claverhouse Stone the guide mentioned." On their right stretched a sheep field enclosed by a barbed-wire fence. In the middle lay a standing stone. With no room to pull over, Traci continued for a couple hundred yards to the first driveway. She pulled the car up to the house's gate, an ornate affectation that seemed out of place. She set the brake and snagged the rough map where it had fallen on the floor.

"According to the map, the government forces left their baggage train on this field." She peered out of the windshield and pointed to the tree-covered ridge behind the sheep. "Somehow we need to get up there. That's where the government forces met the Jacobites." The land rose in a series of ledges, to the summit of Creag Eallaich, and it was the first ledge they needed to reach. She wanted to get as close to the Jacobites right flank as she could before they zapped back.

She had no do-overs here. *That*, she was keenly aware of. Time flowed at the same pace for both of them now, and she had only one chance to get there in time.

Fiona studied the two-lane road they'd come down. "I saw a paved road back there that led up that way. It was right after we passed through the village but before the sheep field. Maybe that will get us where we want?"

Traci fished out the OS Explorer map of the Pitlochry region from the center console and found the road. "No. That only heads straight up for a short bit." She scanned the map. "This is the gate for the private drive that leads up to Urrard House, which is where we need to be. The center of the battle ends up there. If we go a little farther up the road behind us, it looks like there's a lane that will bring us mostly there."

The battle started several hours from now at sundown. Her plan—zap back well before the battle so they could safely sneak into Urrard House, one portion of which was original. According to the map, Iain's men would be with the MacDonells of Glengarry, who were right next to the center line. The house was in the center, so that was where they'd hide and watch, be ready to act.

Traci backed out onto the road, and they found the lane. They traveled as far as they could until it became a private drive. They had no time to get permission from its owners. "This is it. We'll have to zap back here." She exited the car and strapped her reproduction doglock musket to her back. It was the most accurate she could find and the lightest, weighing nine pounds. She'd bought it yesterday from a dealer in Manchester. Next, she retrieved her own cloth sack and slipped the strap over her head so it lay crosswise across her body.

Fiona did the same.

She took a deep breath and met Fiona's eyes. "You ready?" A last gasp of self-protection bubbled up within her, telling her to grab that damn steering wheel, turn right back around, and *leave*. But she was tired of hiding from herself. Hiding from love's potential. And there was that *pull*—not only to return to Iain, but to return there *today*.

"Yes." Her sister's gaze held steady, her voice full of conviction. Conviction that Traci felt now at a bone-deep level.

"Let's do this."

Together they gazed across the stretch of ground that would bring them to the center line of the Jacobites. And to their men. Maybe.

ᴄ⁄ɔ

CHRIST, BUT IAIN was exhausted. They'd been marching since dawn, but as Iain studied the ground below and the placement of Mackay's forces, he had to admit: Dundee's brilliance was indeed evident.

Earlier, Dundee had dispatched a small force of Camerons to act as a decoy, while Iain and the rest of their army had crossed the River Tilt and turned left to march sunwise around the back of the hills, thus keeping their movements invisible to Mackay's men in the valley below. When they'd emerged, the government forces were lined up below, facing the castle. Facing the wrong way. The decoy had worked. Mackay had to execute a turn of his entire line to face them.

Their strategic position couldn't be more favorable. Mackay's men had the River Garry to their backs—their only line of retreat the tortuous narrow pass—while the Jacobites had the high ground. Their downhill charge would give them momentum and speed, and the series of ledges would render them intermittently invisible to the enemy below.

A lesser commander would have been satisfied with such a strategic position, but Dundee was not such a one. With their inferior numbers, he took no chances and wrung out every advantage. He'd next ordered a continuous march around the hill to give the appearance that their numbers were greater than the reality. And, since the enemy could not advance up the hill, they could only defend. Which meant they had to wait.

So Dundee made them wait. And sweat. For several hours. There was a power in being able to name the timing of a battle. Iain could well imagine that the government soldiers were jumpy now from spent adrenaline, wondering when the Highlanders would execute their infamous charge. They were probably fair quaking in their boots.

They waited for nightfall, for the setting sun was in the Highlanders' eyes and a Highlander could fight at night as well as the day. Iain poured powder down the barrel of his musket, following it with a ball and wadding. He extracted the rammer and shoved it down the barrel. The others nearby did the same. Since he and the leading men of his clan were better-armed, they comprised the front line—the farther back in the formation, the more humble their weapons until reaching those armed with naught but perhaps a dirk or hay fork.

Duncan and Gavin and his uncle were arrayed on his left, while Alasdair MacDonell was on his right. The canny bastard had found an old tattered coat while encamped at Blair Castle, and he wore it now so that the enemy could not distinguish him as the chief from a distance. He did, however, sport three eagle feathers in his bonnet to signal his status. Iain's uncle wore two as a minor chieftain, and Iain and Duncan only the one.

Iain fingered his feather and touched the patch of heath he'd pinned to his bonnet earlier this morn. The memory of telling Traci about their plant badge rekindled his anger and frustration.

Dundee strode the length of the line, his stirring speech working everyone up to a pitch, but Iain barely listened. He only awaited the word to charge. The sooner that happened, the sooner he could lose himself in the violence of battle.

When Dundee finished, the men howled, their voices echoing to great effect off the hills. Goose bumps broke out across Iain's skin, and his blood stirred with anticipation.

Below, the enemy responded, but their war cries were feeble and pathetic in comparison. Iain grinned. Upper ground they had, and now they'd won the intimidation game. Despite their inferior numbers, confidence suffused Iain. Aye, fear was also present. It was inescapable before a battle, but Iain relished the fear. Any emotion was better than the hurt he felt at losing Traci.

Shortly after sunset, the order rolled down the line. With an ear-splitting howl, he and his fellow Highlanders yanked off their plaids and shoes and charged down the hill in tight formation, wearing only their weapons and their shirts. He bent low, with his targe strapped to his forearm out in front, and careened down the hill. The scene before him jounced and skittered. He screamed so fiercely, his throat grew hoarse.

And then the enemy was only yards ahead. Without stopping, as one, he and the others with him raised their muskets and fired into the thin, enemy ranks. Iain's bullet flew true, striking his target in the chest. Iain threw his musket to the ground and drew his broadsword from his baldric, as well as his dirk. The enemy was now close. Close enough for him to witness the panic in their eyes as they frantically tried to fix their bayonets in time to meet the Highlanders' charge. But they weren't fast enough. With another howl, Iain swung his broadsword at the closest man.

ↂ

IAIN WHIPPED AROUND and surveyed the battlefield. The light from the three-quarter moon mixing with the white gunpowder smoke cast the scene in an otherworldly glow. He'd been among the first down the hill, and while it had felt like forever, only moments had passed since he first brought his sword to bear against the enemy.

Already, many of the Williamites had turned tail and fled. Cowards. The battle still raged along the central and left flank, though. The Jacobites' work was not done.

Iain dragged his forearm across his face and wiped off the sweat with the sleeve of his shirt. Dundee charged by on his horse at the head of a column of cavalry and straight into the thickest and heaviest fighting in the center, the Earl of Dunfermline close on his heels.

Sir William Wallace's cavalry protected Dundee's left flank, but as they reached the flat ground, to Iain's horror, the cavalry veered off, leaving Dundee dangerously exposed.

Iain charged forward. "To Dundee!"

"Forget Dundee!" His uncle waved and pointed down the next hill with his broadsword. "The *Sasannaich* left their baggage train. Ripe for picking!" Without waiting to see how his words were received, his uncle bounded down the hill.

His fellow clansmen hesitated and looked to Iain, who shouted, "What does their frippery mean compared to such as Dundee? He needs our help. Any Lowlander can rob an undefended baggage train. Follow me!"

He hastened to the left, where last he'd seen Dundee, and was gratified when Duncan, Gavin, and the others followed. However, the remnants of Leven's forces spilled forth and blocked their way. Despite sweat and blood stinging his eyes, Iain spotted Dundee still upright and swinging his broadsword with an economy of movements. His momentum carried him toward a stone house encircled by a stand of yew trees.

Leven's men stood between them.

Then Iain heard the strangest sound.

He whipped around—he'd swear to God in Heaven a woman screamed his name—and turned in time to see a sword bearing down on him. *Sweet Mother Mary.* Had the scream been one of the magical *sìthiche*, sent to warn him? He blocked the vicious strike with his targe and pushed.

The smoke and tangle of bodies briefly parted, revealing a woman leaning out of an upper window in the house, musket in hand. His heart clenched. Traci? The fickle moon surely deceived him. He sidestepped a thrust and brought his sword around in a full-body pivot. Traci's musket was aimed at his attacker, and he saw it buck.

Dear God, those weren't accurate at that distance. His assailant ducked Iain's swing, which left the man vulnerable enough but saved him from Traci's bullet. Iain finished him off, only to see a look of horror cross Traci's face. He spun around. Dundee was no longer on his horse. And he'd been in the line of her fire.

Nay.

Duncan shouted and bolted toward the abandoned horse but whipped unnaturally to the side as if struck. Another female screamed, and the fear Iain had channeled so successfully up till now surfaced. Adrenaline pumped through him, and he shoved through the rest of Leven's men, who were fleeing—the battle, for them, lost.

Instead of running to his cousin or to Dundee's aid, Iain's feet carried him to the house and Traci. He halted, and disbelief paralyzed his muscles at the sight. Traci and wee Fiona, framed by the window, looking like the fiercest warriors, but by God, they were shaking. Traci's eyes were huge, her gaze locked with his, while Fiona, her eyes equally large, stared where Duncan had fallen. They disappeared from the window.

Iain darted around the corner, and the lasses shot out the back door. Iain stumbled across the last few feet, grasped Traci's precious face in his hands, and gave her the fiercest, most frustrated kiss of his sorry life.

"Are you daft, woman?" he shouted as soon as he lifted his face.

The field was clear of the enemy, and Fiona sprinted across the rocky terrain.

On a curse, he grabbed Traci's hand, and they raced after Fiona.

Chapter Thirty

cx

Lang hae we parted been, Lassie, my dearie;
Now we are met again, Lassie, lie near me.
"Lassie, Lie Near Me," *Jacobite Reliques*

*I*AIN AND TRACI chased Fiona, who chased after Duncan, who
now stumbled to Dundee's side, and all Iain could think while
he held Traci's hand in his tight grip was, "Dear God, what is happening?" Would events ever slow enough for him to figure it out?

They converged on Dundee, where another Highlander was helping
him to stand.

Duncan clutched his shoulder, his face gravely pale. "My lord!"

Dundee rasped, "How did the day go?"

The one helping him replied, "Well for the king. What happened
to you? Are you wounded?"

"Only my pride. A bullet spooked my horse."

Iain could only whisper, "Thank you, Mary Mother."

Duncan swayed, and one knee buckled. Fiona leaped forward and
gentled his fall to the ground.

Iain glanced at Traci, who had an odd expression on her face and
rubbed the crown of her head. She caught his gaze, and her face flooded
with color. "I think that was my fault. I was trying to save *you*."

cx

Later that night

WITH THE HIGHLAND army scattered and chasing the enemy, Iain
managed to carry Duncan to safety back up the hill they'd charged
down, Traci and Fiona tight on either side. On the way, they grabbed
a few abandoned plaids and settled into a hollow.

Duncan was alive, thank Christ. But his wound wasn't superficial.

The bullet had lodged against a bone in his shoulder. With the lasses holding him down, Iain dug out the slug with his *sgian-dubh*. They gathered around the fire he kindled, Duncan stretched before it, and Fiona cleaned his wound with items Iain had never seen.

Duncan's eyes fluttered open, and Fiona pulled back on a gasp. His eyes were too fogged with pain for him to register much of his surroundings, Iain could see. But he managed to catch Iain's gaze. "I hope…" He cleared his raspy throat. "I hope you're ready to be chieftain, my cousin."

Iain's chest tightened, and he surveyed the hill, as if it held the interpretation to Duncan's words. "Uncle is chieftain."

Duncan barely moved his head. "Nay. I saw him fall. 'Twas a mortal wound." With that, he closed his eyes and pulled in another shaky breath.

A mottled stew of emotions bubbled forth—fear, grief, frustration—and Iain reared back.

His uncle. Dead.

His throat tightened, and he rubbed his hands briskly up and down his face, tightening his jaw.

Please, Lord, let that be our clan's only loss.

He glanced over and caught Traci turning her gaze away from him. The flickering firelight limned her lovely features, and an intense rush of emotions swept through him, pushing out all thoughts of loss and grief and worry.

She was here.

She'd chosen *him*. Ach, aye, he knew he could be fanciful, but that had to be the reason the lass was here. He was almost afraid to ask, for how could such a one as he have enough to hold onto?

But as he beheld the two women who'd risked much to be here, as well as Duncan's prostrate form with his life in question—for infection still loomed—everything crystallized. He'd been living life with a lot of noise, and now all was quiet. Quiet enough for him to realize one truth.

All his life, he'd played the frivolous role, using it as a shield.

All his life, he'd lived a lie so as not to make his father a liar.

All his life, he'd used this to protect himself from further guilt, excusing it as part of his nature.

Good God.

"Traci," he whispered, not wishing to disturb Duncan's troubled sleep.

Her head whipped up, and she bit her lip.

In that instant, another truth hit him—she was just as unsure.

He patted the ground next to him, too exhausted to move much more than that, and not trusting his voice at the moment. But one truth he'd seen earlier: having her near made him comfortable in his own skin, allowed him to be…himself.

She settled beside him. And everything within him relaxed.

She picked up a small pebble in front of her and rolled it around in her hand.

"So…" he said.

"So…" she whispered, her face turned to his. God, she looked so vulnerable.

"So." He nudged her arm. "You couldn't resist me after all."

She stiffened and moved to stand. He clasped her arm, preventing her from leaving his side. He screwed his eyes shut. Aye, he now knew himself, but abandoning his shield, his easy role, had left him like a harpist with all thumbs. He leaned over and whispered in her ear, his emotions roughening his words, "I jest."

"Iain. I don't want to joke anymore."

"Ever?"

She huffed. "Iain."

He couldn't wait. If she could risk coming back, he could risk assuming it was for him. He gently lifted her and settled her across his lap, cradling her so that her face was inches from his. Her eyes were wary.

"Where's your plaid?"

He shrugged. "Somewhere. 'Twas too hot and cumbersome to wear." He touched his forehead to hers, closed his eyes, and swallowed. "Stay."

"In your lap?"

"Now who's teasing, wench?" he whispered, chuckling. And dear God in heaven, had that been tears thickening his chuckle? Her soft, sweet breath skated across his cheeks, but anything more they wished to say was forestalled by Duncan's moan. Iain met her eyes and saw that she understood—with dead and dying men scattered below, with Duncan wounded beside them, and Fiona fussing over him—that now was not the time for their heart talk. "Later, I promise. We'll talk later."

⁂

Dawn the next day

TRACI CROUCHED DOWN at the stream to dip strips of cloth into the water. Her wild shot at Iain's attacker had spooked Dundee's horse and thrown him, but it looked like he'd suffered only a bruised shoulder.

Duncan was another matter, and worry weighted her limbs. She wrung out the cloths, hoping the temperature would help keep him cool. She stood and then stepped back at the sight of a man lounging against a nearby tree in a burgundy swallow-tail coat, buff-colored pants, and a top hat.

"Mr. Podbury. I, uh…" Damn, was he going to take the case back? Was he going to make *her* go back?

"Hello, Miss Campbell. I don't have much time, so I must be quick. Tell me. When you were at Urrard House, did you feel anything… unusual right before Dundee fell from his horse?"

She cocked her head. "Unusual?"

He pushed away from the tree and picked his way toward her. "Yes. The symptoms are different for each person when they're near a paradox event. The problem is, I am no longer sensitive to the nuances—neither are my cohorts. We're numb to it now, so we couldn't verify. Therefore, I'd like to know if you felt any kind of…sensation. My employers have worked hard to close off this world into a stable loop, and we need to know if we were successful."

She stood with her mouth open.

"I don't have time to explain more. Your Mr. MacCowan will be here soon. I came back to verify that events are happening as they should in this loop. In this timeline that Isabelle created, Dundee lives. I needed to make sure we'd been successful in closing the loop, and we were. You saved him. Duncan took his bullet. In the other timeline, Dundee dies. If the loop continues to be stable, we will not require the case's return. But for my studies, I'd love to record your symptoms."

She still just stood there. She'd saved Dundee? He wasn't supposed to have lived? She rubbed the top of her head. "I did feel a tingling in the top of my head."

His eyes lit up, and he pulled out his notebook. "Tingling. Fascinating. Simply fascinating. Thank you."

A chiming sound emerged from his vest pocket. He pulled out an overlarge pocket watch, fitted with dials and an antenna. "Time to go." He flicked a switch on the contraption, pushed a button, and *whomp*, he was gone.

What just…? Okay… Traci shook herself. This was going to take time to process. She rubbed the crown of her head again.

"Traci? Are you all right?" Iain's urgent tone carried down the incline. "You've been gone longer than a moment." He appeared over the crest of the hill, and he hustled down the slope. When he neared, he stopped, his eyes searching hers.

"You're still here," he whispered. He glanced back over his shoulder, and then cradled her face. "Seeing you here, in dawn's light, makes my heart ache. We won't have much time to talk. It will take us several days to return to Dungarbh, and we'll have to camp in the open with the men. But I couldn't wait any longer to tell you it makes my heart glad that you returned, and to do this."

He crushed her mouth with his, and she returned his kiss eagerly. She grasped the back of his head and nearly whimpered at how *right* it felt to be here with him.

❧

Several days later, Dungarbh

Despite Iain's promise that they'd talk later, events had overtaken them. They had arrived only this morning from the battle site, having camped along the way. There had been no chance to be alone. She had been pleased more than she'd expected at the sight of Fiddich back at their camp.

Traci clasped Fiona's hand, while around them milled the Mac-Cowan clanswomen in their finery. She shivered. The haunting cries of the keening women who'd followed the procession of the old chieftain's body as it was laid to rest still shadowed the air around them.

Iain's kind aunt approached, her face stoic in her grief. "It's done."

Traci and the other women had waited in an anteroom off the hall while the council met to elect their new chieftain. Iain had wanted to delay and give his uncle a proper grieving period, but the clan had insisted. With the fate of the rebellion still up in the air, they had no wish to be leaderless.

Marjorie's strong hands gripped hers. "Iain is our new chieftain. Come, the ceremony will commence soon by the sacred tree."

Pride on Iain's behalf bloomed inside her.

Traci laced her arm through Fiona's, and together they followed the other women heading to the courtyard. They ducked through the main doors and out into the sun and strolled across the wooden bridge to the courtyard island, enclosed by a wall. There grew a stout, but majestic, yew tree, bent and twisted from wind and age.

Below its arching branches, several clansmen stacked rocks into a pyramid. Murmurs arose, and the crowd parted, revealing Iain, fresh-washed and resplendent in a brightly colored kilt and tartan pants they called trews.

No bagpipes echoed across the courtyard, but damned if Traci didn't supply them in her head as Iain strode toward her, his shoulders squared, his smile and demeanor putting everyone at ease. As he passed by, he winked.

At the base of the makeshift pyramid, he paused. A priest stood nearby, intoning words in Gaelic, and Iain placed his right foot into a depression in a rock. Once the priest stopped speaking, Iain climbed the several steps to the top of the makeshift stone mound.

Another man paraded forward, his Gaelic chant-like. Marjorie leaned over. "That is our clan *seanachaidh*—poet—and he's reciting Iain's ancestry, as well as its heroic deeds, in order to inspire him in his new role."

Traci saw what the others saw—a leader—but whenever Iain's gaze locked with hers throughout the ceremony, he telegraphed to her his unease, his doubts. And each time, she projected back her belief in him.

They still needed to discuss their future, but in this, she had no doubt: Iain was destined to be a fine leader of his clan. The afternoon light filtered through the yew leaves and branches, speckling him in dappled light. When the poet ceased and stepped back, Iain lifted his head, and their eyes met. Everything around her—the myriad multi-colored plaids, Fiona's hand hotly clasped in her own, the imaginary bagpipes—arrowed into her and carved out this moment. A moment suffused with promise. A promise of belonging. And for once, the alien, unintelligible sounds of Gaelic around her no longer made her feel separate. Instead, they too held promise.

Because no matter what happened when she and Iain were finally alone, she'd dared.

Dared to ask, to hope—in the most unlikely of places—for love.
Dared to believe the little silver case *had* brought her to her soul mate.

Chapter Thirty-One

೧

Then let us be merry and gay,
Since none are so happy as we.
"There's None So Happy As We," *Jacobite Reliques*

IAIN HELD TRACI'S gaze as the poet backed away. Her belief in him—shining from her eyes—made him feel simultaneously light and able to do anything.

Gavin stepped forward and presented the sword of Iain's father, hilt first, one of the last traditions in their clan's ceremony. When the hilt graced and warmed his palm, the moment's true significance swamped him.

In his hands lay the welfare of all these people, as well as the tenants on their land. Like his father. And his father before him. For the first time, the prospect didn't fill him with a nameless fear.

Only one thing marred the ceremony—Duncan, as the man closest to him, should have been the one to present the sword. But he lay in the family apartments, still resting from his wounds. This event was the first time Iain had seen Fiona leave his side.

Iain placed the sword's tip at the mouth of his scabbard and paused, taking in the sight of his fist wrapped around the hilt of the sword that had seen his father through many a battle. Another was missing from this ceremony: his mother.

As soon as the ceremonies finished, he'd write to the convent and know her wishes.

Iain slid his father's sword into the scabbard at his waist, surprised at the satisfaction the action—and his decision—gave him. Gavin next handed him a white rod—the *slat tighearnais*, the rod of sovereignty— and a yellowed-with-age ivory drinking horn. Edged with hammered silver and carved with symbols, it had been in his family farther back than anyone could remember. Legend told of an ancestor who brought it back from the Holy Lands while on crusade. Whatever its true origins, it had been used for generations to install new chieftains. Iain took a deep breath, let it out, and drank the warm claret in one long pull.

When he finished, his people cheered, and he again caught Traci's gaze. This time, the belief shining from her eyes wasn't *giving* him confidence in his new role, but showing what was already present in him.

He lifted his head and addressed the assembled crowd. "I am honored by the trust you have placed in me. I will *not* fail you. My uncle was a good man and met the best end any warrior could wish for, fighting for the rightful king and our way of life. That fight is not over, but it can abide for today."

He held out the ceremonial horn, and Gavin refilled it. "To mine uncle!" He raised the horn and took a healthy swig. Those around him cheered.

He raised it again. "And to Dundee!"

Cheers broke out again. He handed the horn to Gavin for him to pass around to the assembled gathering. "To the keep. We will enjoy a feast worthy of mine uncle's memory." He descended the ceremonial mound and slapped Gavin on the back. The man nodded, and Iain stepped away.

His first duty as new chieftain was to demonstrate his generosity to all under his care. Every tenant would soon be arriving to partake in the feast, and he'd need to preside and make merry.

But he had a sliver of time before that obligation. And he'd take that time to be with his wife.

His wife who'd come back. For him.

৶

TRACI STRODE THROUGH the cozy hall in the keep, squeezing past the growing crowd of clansmen and their tenants. Already folks were singing and playing instruments, and the cheerful notes dipped and swirled through the animated conversations around her.

The ceremony had affected her on a level she hadn't expected—*this* was her Scottish heritage. As she witnessed the rituals, it was clear each aspect had roots deep, deep in the past. Roots which no longer existed in her day. But for the first time in her life, she felt at one with her heritage. She *was* Scottish. The conviction locked into place, and she felt part of a bigger whole.

But now that the ceremony was over, she hummed with the need to find Iain, to be alone with him. She didn't *think* she'd made the wrong choice in staying, but she wanted to finally have their discussion. Where the hell was he?

She stood on her tiptoes and craned her head over a knot of villagers. No Iain.

"Will you be all right on your own?" Fiona pitched her voice to be heard over the general noise of the crowd. Lord, she'd forgotten her sister had been next to her, so intent she was on finding Iain.

Traci smiled a smile that came fully from within her. *This*, she had to do on her own. "Yes. Plus, isn't there a certain someone whose side you'd rather be next to?"

Fiona laughed, but Traci frowned, for it contained a fragile note. Fiona hugged her. "Good luck," she whispered. She backed away, winked, and scampered through the crowd to the tower stairs.

Giddiness swept through Traci at the audacity of her decision. She'd come back in time. For a *man*. And instead of scaring the freckles right off her, the possibilities and the promise made her mind and body feel free. Finally, she was reconnected to her younger self who had believed in love. Who had believed in finding her soul mate.

And if the risk didn't work out? That was *okay*.

She would no longer be scared of ever finding it. Of exposing herself to the possibility.

She wedged herself through another clump, grinning stupidly. Still no Iain. She backed up and stumbled.

Strong, warm hands gripped her waist. "Whoa, there, lass. I have ye." Iain's melodic voice tickled her ear and elicited a cascade of shivers down her body.

She'd found him.

☙

WITH FIONA BACK by Duncan's side and his clan momentarily left to their own devices before the feast began, Iain was finally alone with his wife. As they stepped off the high wooden bridge that led from the keep and into the hallway at the top floor of their family apartments, Traci's body brushed his. Her presence beside him was so weighted with meaning, he felt as if the whole space they traversed was thick with promise and awareness.

Iain darted a glance toward her and caught her gaze. She grinned, her eyes twinkling, and they sprinted the rest of the way down the hallway, the decorative tapestries lining one wall fluttering in their wake.

They burst into their room, out of breath and laughing.

He grabbed her hand and tugged until her hips bumped deliciously against his.

Everything he wished to say since she reappeared crowded his tongue, and his breathing hitched.

But instead, he blurted, "I'm chieftain."

The smile that lit her face was one that spoke of an inner knowledge of each other, and his heart turned over.

Her hand tightened on his. "I know."

Throughout the chieftain ceremony, her trust and belief in him had shone in her gaze. It had bolstered his confidence, helped see him through it. Helped him pretend.

"I don't know what I'm doing."

She cradled his face in her wee palms, her soft skin a cool and welcome caress on his cheeks. "Yes, you do."

He clasped her hands and covered his heart with them. She'd returned. For him. "I'm sorry."

She cocked her head and frowned.

He cleared his throat. "For breaking my promise and not aiding ye."

"Iain, you did what you had to do." She uncurled her fingers and spread her hands over his heart. "That's why you'll make a great leader. Your duty was to your clan."

"But it was also with ye."

She grimaced, and his heart clenched. "Well, I didn't give you much of a chance, did I? I know you were angry with me when we parted, and you had every right to be." She took a shaky breath, as if steeling herself. "Iain, the truth is, I was a big fat wuss."

"Wuss?"

"Weakling. Scaredy cat. I didn't dare probe further into what we could mean to each other. I...I...didn't trust my instincts where guys were concerned, and I think...I think because my feelings are deeper than they've ever been, I mistrusted them even more. I was so afraid..." She trailed off.

To be sure, Iain wanted to shake her and say, *You? Afraid?* But he held the moment delicately. "What did you fear?" he whispered.

"I feared looking like a fool if you rejected me." Her voice had started out a touch tentative, but she finished strong. Aye, but her confession cut through him, because he understood, didn't he?

He touched his forehead to hers. "Ach, lassie. In truth, I'd believed that I'd felt love's bite a number of times over the years. But I hadn't. Not truly. Always, it was about me. I looked to fall in love because I desired it so badly. The acceptance of another. But that's not it, is it?" He cupped her cheek and rubbed his thumb across her bottom lip. She shuddered in his arms. "When I look at ye, it's not about me and what I need. It's you. And I'd do anything for ye."

She choked on a sob. "Oh, Iain. Is that your convoluted way of saying you...you love me?"

He swallowed around the lump in his throat. "Aye," he whispered.

Her breath expelled and brushed against his lips. "Thank God, because I love you too, you big flirt."

This time, those words didn't wound. This time, the wielder knew he was more. She saw him. The whole him. And loved him.

"But what about your life? The one ye left in the future?" It near killed him to remind her of all she'd forsaken, but he wished to make sure she had no hesitation—for he had none, and if she did, it would bode ill.

She drew back slightly and clasped his shoulders. "You said you'd do anything for me, right?"

"Aye..."

She gave him a slight shake. "Can't you see it's the same for me? None of that matters. It's all material, superficial trappings. Love is so hard to find. I realized I couldn't throw ours away for modern luxuries."

"Even the hot shower?"

She pinched his nose and kissed it. "Yes." Her smile lit up her face, but it held no trace of regret. The last of his worry evaporated. She was here. Truly and fully. For him.

"You'll have to create this miraculous closet."

She laughed. "I'm not sure I have the skill, but as they say, 'Where there's a will, there's a way.'" Her face sobered. "We're still married, right?"

He hugged her with all his strength. "Aye, we are. Though, I'd like to formalize it before the priest leaves." He reached into his sporran with a shaking hand. "This belonged to my mother, and I know ye had to give up your valuable ring. Will you take this and promise to be mine past a year and a day?"

Her eyes glistened. "Yes."

Ach, Jesus, his own eyes were threatening to overfill. "That's…" He cleared his throat. "That's wonderful." Then the next word he said, though he'd been using it before to tease, was imbued with new meaning. With promise. With acceptance. With love.

"Wife," he whispered and slipped the ring onto her finger.

ev

TRACI'S INSIDES GLOWED with happiness. And fulfillment.

And then something else entirely. She backed up and gave him a wicked smile. "Stay right where you are. No, wait. Move over to the hearth." She grabbed his upper arms and shuffle-walked him into position. She stepped back, then angled him just so.

She scrambled onto the huge four poster bed and curled up by the gap in the curtains. She eased back a fold and took in his puzzled expression as he stood obediently by the fireplace, three-quarters of him facing her.

Perfect.

"Now, strip," she cooed.

Instantly, his eyes darkened, and his lids drooped. He formed a seductive grin as he placed his hands on the brooch pin holding up the kilt at his left shoulder.

This time, she'd be able to do what she couldn't do those other nights he'd teased her with his strip show—invite him into her bed. Their bed. And have it not be a stupid move.

Now. Now, it would be the start of something. Something wonderful, heady, that would last a lifetime. She thumbed the ring he'd given her. He hadn't known what the other symbolized, but she chose to see this as a promise of their future, instead of looking into the past.

The kilt dropped, and he dispensed with the rest of his clothes and stalked toward her, gloriously naked, his gaze never leaving hers. Her insides fluttered. This was Iain. The man she'd come back for, but he was so much more than that. He pulled back the curtain, and his hungry gaze took all of her in as if she were bare before him. And she was, in a way. Bare to him like she'd never been before with a man. He knew her faults. He knew how deeply she felt about him to have given up so much. As he'd see it. But she didn't see it as a sacrifice at all. More like a trade—a half-life for a full one of love.

He placed his knee on the edge of the bed, which dipped with his weight. He leaned toward her, one hand landing beside her head. With his other, he gently cupped her face, the rough calluses of his palms a bare whisper against her cheek.

"*Mo dhuslach rionnaige*," he murmured. Her heart turned to sappy goo at that. He'd been calling her "my stardust" this whole time. He gently captured her lips, and the rush of contact, the taste of him after so long, shuddered through her.

She stretched out and smoothed her hands up his muscled chest and gripped his shoulders, her blood heating and racing with anticipation. Being here, with him…it felt as if all the parts of her were here, in sync, with him. And she wanted to join with him to complete that new bond.

They scooted farther onto the bed, and Iain pressed his body against hers. The weight—his weight—felt delicious, increasing her anticipation. She squeezed his gorgeous ass, and he groaned into her mouth.

He levered up, his eyes a dark blue and hooded. "You are wearing entirely too many clothes." His voice was low and rough.

"Yes." They reached for the same button on her *earasaid,* and their hands bumped each other as if it was their first time.

He chuckled and reached down to her skirt's hem, pulling it up, the soft linen sliding across her sensitized calf and thigh. Goosebumps prickled across her skin.

When he reached her core, he stroked a strong, blunt finger along her cleft. "You are already prepared."

Desire shot from her chest downward, and she writhed against his hand. Her hands shook, and she fumbled with her second button. "Dammit." She gripped his face. "Never mind my dress. I want you, Iain. Now."

His eyes flared with heat, and he fell onto his elbows, bracketing her in his wonderful, sexy self. He locked his gaze with hers and surged inside her in one, sure stroke.

Oh, yes. The feel of him, hot and hard, stretching her and filling her so fully, felt like a completion, an answer. And a start of their new commitment. Together. She wrapped her arms tightly around him and raised her knees to cradle his hips. He remained still and touched his forehead to hers. "You're mine. I'm yours."

Her heart swelled, and she swallowed against her suddenly thick throat. She *was* his, fully and completely. And he hers.

As he slowly made love to her, and she shattered gently around him, she finally felt what she'd searched for for so long—belonging.

Epilogue

$\mathcal{A}$ s SOON AS Iain had swept Traci away, Fiona allowed herself a moment to be still and just…breathe in. And out.

Cuz, yeah, holy crap. She was here in seventeenth-century Scotland. Surrounded by everything she'd ever fantasized about.

She slipped up the tower stairs from the keep and headed to the top where a wooden bridge led to the living quarters on the next island over. Now that she was no longer needed to lend moral support to her sister, she was compelled to go where she wasn't at all sure she was wanted.

Duncan's sick room.

The stairs were steep and winding, and she could feel the burn in her calves by the time she reached the top. She pushed open the heavy oak door and stepped out onto the bridge. In just the time it took for her to make her way through the keep and up the stairs, the weather had shifted. Dark, gray clouds muffled the sky, and the wind blew sharply through the space between the two buildings, buffeting her. Wisps of hair snaked and tickled across her face, and she tucked them behind her ear.

Halfway across the bridge, she paused and drank in the view. Before her was the northern shore of Loch Garry, with the stretch of water interrupted only by a small, rocky island. On the far side, the bank rose sharply almost to a level with the bridge, and draped behind was the peak of Meall Dubh.

Here she was. In a historic castle at a time when Highlanders still had a hold on their traditions. When the coming horror of the Battle of Culloden in 1746 had not yet depressed the confidence and spirit of the people in these lands. Here she was, as she'd always dreamed.

She should have been ecstatic.

But as all dreams end up, it wasn't quite what she'd imagined. She took a shuddering breath.

Oh God. Did I make a mistake?

She bit her lip and sucked up the conviction she'd found earlier, when she'd resolved on finding her sister at her flat and talking her into coming back, or at least giving Fiona the calling card case. For the family legend her granpappy had told her every time she saw him, the one that was her absolute favorite, was about *her*.

She was the mysterious Fiona Campbell who had saved her ancestor from certain death. Sometime this year, she needed to be at Urquhart Castle when it was under siege. She'd stupidly thought it had already been happening, and so had hightailed it up there from Invergarry, only to find out how wrong she'd been.

According to her research, it wouldn't be until the fall.

She turned and faced the door into the living quarters. Inside was the other reason she'd come back. She'd felt honor-bound to do so, for she owed Duncan not only an apology, but something more. A chance.

However, she also faced the very real possibility that this Campbell ancestor was an enemy of her sister's new clan.

She swallowed her doubts and fears and straightened, pulling her plaid tighter around her shoulders. She strode down the rest of the bridge and made her way through its corridors to the sick room. The oak door gave way with ease, and she crept to his bedside.

Duncan had been in and out of consciousness for most of the trip. Fiona had kept him sedated with the medicines she'd brought back, desperate to give him the chance to heal and fight the probable infection from his wound. Unsurprisingly, he hadn't noticed her on the battlefield, having been wounded and all. She dreaded what he might say when he did wake up and realize she was here.

As if sensing her turmoil, Duncan groaned, and his eyes flickered open. At first, they were fogged from pain and unfocused.

Then they cleared, and he frowned in confusion. "So you've returned. The woman who one moment handfasted with me, and the next turned me out of bed in disgust."

Historical Note

Ⓔⓞ

I STRIVED TO be as authentic as possible in the constraints of the story, but there were some liberties I took with the historical record. The biggest is that Dundee, who later became known as Bonnie Dundee, died at the Battle of Killiecrankie, dooming the Jacobite cause for another generation.

Also, due to the destruction of villages and records during the Highland Clearances—an awful, awful time in the history of the Scottish Highlands that the region hasn't fully recovered from—it's impossible to know whether there was an inn in 1689 where the current Cluanie Inn currently stands.

I hope that sticklers will also forgive me for the liberties I took with the custom of handfasting. Handfasting was actually a Lowland Scots tradition, not Highland, though the Highlanders had a similar tradition called a Trial Marriage. However, since that only happens once a year, and it was later than the events of the Battle of Killiecrankie, I took the liberty of borrowing the Lowland Scots tradition. And as far as that tradition goes, accounts vary, but I found multiple sources that said that witnesses were not needed, though it did make it easier to prove.

While the MacCowans were a sept of the MacDonells of Glengarry, the persons in this story are fiction, as is Dungarbh, which I set on the cluster of islands visible from the shores of Loch Garry. This island cluster is called Garbh Eilean, meaning "rough isle," so that's how I came up with the name for the MacCowan's keep Dungarbh, meaning "rough fort."

The MacDonell chief and his son Alasdair are historical personages, and the chief did send his son in his stead to the Battle of Killiecrankie to hedge his bets. Also, Cameron of Lochiel was a historical person, and the story of him biting out the throat of a British soldier can be found in several places, though it might be apocryphal. And there was a little cameo of the famous Rob Roy, who fought at the Battle of Killiecrankie. Some sources I found said his father was still alive and at the battle too, so I placed him there.

I've read many Scottish history books, but I found the books *Warriors of the Word*, by Michael Newton, and *Scottish Customs: From the Cradle to the Grave*, by Margaret Bennet especially helpful. It was during this reading that I discovered that Highlanders have long used the term kale-eaters to disparage Lowlanders, where eating kale was popular.

About the Author

Photo by Keyhole Photography

WINNER OF THE prestigious national book award, the RITA®, Angela Quarles is a *USA Today* bestselling author of time travel and steampunk romance. *Library Journal* named her steampunk, *Steam Me Up, Rawley*, Best Self-Published Romance of 2015. Her time travel romance *Must Love Chainmail* won the Romance Writer's of America's RITA® in 2016, becoming the first self-published author to win in the paranormal category. Her debut novel *Must Love Breeches* made the *USA Today* bestseller list in 2015. She has published four books and one novelette. Angela loves history, folklore, and family history. She decided to take this love of history and her active imagination and write stories of romance and adventure for others to enjoy. When not writing, she's either working at the local indie bookstore or enjoying the usual stuff like gardening, reading, hanging out, eating, drinking, chasing squirrels out of the walls, and creating the occasional knitted scarf.

She has a B.A. in Anthropology and International Studies with a minor in German from Emory University, and a Masters in Heritage Preservation from Georgia State University. She was an exchange student to Finland in high school and studied abroad in Vienna one summer in college.

Find Angela Quarles Online:
www.angelaquarles.com
@angelaquarles
Facebook.com/authorangelaquarles
Mailing list: www.angelaquarles.com/join-my-mailing-list

Acknowledgments

❧

WRITING A HISTORICAL novel cannot be done solo, at least for me! I'm hugely indebted to a number of people who helped me out with the historical aspects of the plot, description, and characters. I'd like to specifically thank the following for helping me; any mistakes or inaccuracies, however, are my own.

I'd like to thank the folks who helped me when I scouted the locations for this novel in Scotland. To my hosts Isobel and Ian Mackinlay who provided a great cottage for me to stay in that week and were so helpful during my stay. And to Stewart MacGlashan who was so kind and generous to show me around for a day around the battle site of Killiecrankie and providing me with the disposition of the troops and also local anecdotes about the battle that I hadn't found in any history books. His knowledge was invaluable not only with the facts, but also in helping me visualize how Iain and his clansmen would have seen that day unfold. He also provided a nice map of troop placements and the script he and the reenactors use for the public when they give tours on the anniversary weekend of the battle. To Rulzion Rattray who also gave me information on the battle via email, especially the detail that they marched sunrise around the mountain before the battle. As he related in his email, "In the battle we see some great examples of their unique and superstitious outlook and way of thinking, starting with the importance of the direction and route of their march to the battle site, which took a sunwise (deiseal) the old Gaels had a saying 'deiseal air gach ni', the sunward course with everything — south course, right direction."

To Monique and Andy, the proprietors of Cluanie Inn, and the bartender Andy, who answered my many questions about the region, thank you! And may their two cute, friendly dogs—Kye and Sweep—who keep the patrons company in the public spaces always have great doggie dreams and endless supplies of treats.

I'd like to thank the Alpha readers of the full manuscript who gave me helpful feedback, my best Beta buddy Jami Gold, as well as Buffy Armstrong—you helped me see where I was on track, or wasn't.

I had two Beta rounds, and I'd like to thank Shaila Patel who read it both times as well as Jami (again!), Zoe York, Megan Finnegan Grimes, Meggan Haller, Courtney Case, Barbara Coffman, Karysa Faire, Tauline Rutherford, and Lenore English. Every one of you gave me invaluable feedback that made this book better than it would have been on its own. Special thanks goes to Jami, Buffy, and Shaila for always being available via Facebook chat when I needed encouragement or yanking back from some fruitless rabbit hole of research detail or for helping me brainstorm some tricky plot problem. Shout out also to the Divas on RomanceDivas forum for their help and encouragement.

To my editors who helped me get this into final shape! Jessa Slade for reading a pretty rough draft and helping me firm up the plot and characterization; Sharron Gunn for the Gaelic and Highland history and culture fact checking; Erynn Newman and Julie Glover for the word-smithing—you understood my voice and helped me make it shine; and finally to my proofreader Judi Lauren.

I also want to thank the members of my facebook fan group—Angela's Time-Traveling Steampunk Regency Assassins—for their help and support! And to Megan who won the contest for naming Traci's pony Glenfiddich :) It was the perfect name, and right when she suggested it, I was like 'of course!' And to Alex McLeod, my multiverse consultant, for his help with the mind-bendy time travel stuff.

To Pam, Diane, and the rest of the crew at the Government Street location of Starbucks who keep me supplied in food and decaf when I camp out there to write/revise; I get so much work done there and it helps me stay off the social media. I revised this book there numerous times.

To the members of the old forum Longbourn Loungers who first got me started writing fiction. The scene where Iain washes by the well is for you—sorry I couldn't make it a water pump, but that would've been anachronistic :)

I'd also like to thank my facebook and twitter friends who are always willing to answer questions I pose, whether it's about writing, or character ideas, or an opinion sought.

And finally to my family, who have always believed in me and make it possible for me to pursue writing.

A devoted history buff finds the re-enactment of a pre-Victorian ball in London a bit boring…until a mysterious artifact sweeps her back in time to the real event, and into the arms of a compelling British lord.

Isabelle Rochon can't believe it when she finds herself in the reality of 1830's London high society. She's thrilled to witness events and people she's studied. But she may also have to survive without modern tools or career–unless she can find a way to return to her time. And then there's Viscount Lord Montagu, a man whose embrace curls her toes, but who has a dangerous agenda of his own.

Lord Phineas Montagu is on a mission to avenge his sister, and he'll stop at nothing, including convincing an alluring stranger to pose as his respectable fiancé. He's happy to repay her by helping her search for her stolen calling card case that brought her back in time. But he doesn't bargain for the lady being his intellectual match–or for the irresistible attraction that flames between them.

They're both certain they know what they want, but as passion flares, Phineas must keep both himself and Isabella safe from unseen opponents, and she must choose when and where her heart belongs. Can they ever be together for good?